# AFTER
## WE WERE
# STOLEN

# AFTER
## WE WERE
# STOLEN

### A NOVEL

## BROOKE BEYFUSS

Published by Sourcebooks Landmark, an imprint of Sourcebooks
P.O. Box 4410, Naperville, Illinois 60567-4410
(630) 961-3900
sourcebooks.com

Library of Congress Cataloging-in-Publication Data

Names: Beyfuss, Brooke, author.
Title: After we were stolen : a novel / Brooke Beyfuss.
Description: Naperville, Illinois : Sourcebooks Landmark, [2022]
Identifiers: LCCN 2021042273 (print) | LCCN 2021042274
   (ebook) | (trade paperback) | (epub)
Subjects: LCSH: Cults--Fiction. | Kidnapping victims--Fiction. | LCGFT:
   Bildungsromans. | Novels.
Classification: LCC PS3602.E945 A38 2022  (print) | LCC PS3602.E945
   (ebook) | DDC 813/.6--dc23/eng/20211201
LC record available at https://lccn.loc.gov/2021042273
LC ebook record available at https://lccn.loc.gov/2021042274

Printed and bound in Canada.
MBP 10 9 8 7 6 5 4 3 2 1

*For my brother, Daniel*

# AUTHOR'S NOTE

Dear Reader,

First and foremost, I would like to thank you for picking up *After We Were Stolen*; I am so grateful for the opportunity to share this story with you. In writing this novel, it was my goal to celebrate the strength of the human spirit and the fortitude needed to break the cycle of abuse and emerge triumphant.

In order to do that, the characters had to suffer many hardships. I can tell you honestly, portions of this book were difficult to write, and I understand they may be difficult to read as well. We are all dealing with our own personal struggles, and it is not my intention to cause anyone undue pain or discomfort. That's why I would like to be fully transparent about potentially triggering aspects of this novel.

*After We Were Stolen* is the story of a survivalist cult made up of adults and children. The narrative contains instances of child abuse (both physical and emotional), references to sexual assault, stillbirth, realistic depictions of animals raised on a farm (including husbandry), suicide, kidnapping, police interaction, and traumatic death.

Everyone has their own demons to bear, and your comfort level is paramount to me. I want you to experience this story without fear or trepidation in your heart, and I hope this information will help you prepare for the journey.

With love and best wishes,
Brooke

# PART ONE

# ONE

---

He was the only baby I ever saw born, and he died ten minutes later. We were all there, all the kids, shoulder to shoulder in the smallest room in the compound. Mother told us the birth would take hours, and it did: hours spent standing and sweating in the heavy air just so we could be there the moment the baby emerged in a slick of watery blood and blue cord. But he didn't cry—not when he came out and not when we took turns pounding his tiny back to try and make him. When it was over, none of us cried either—we just stood there looking around at the walls and each other. I guess we were all hoping one of us knew how we were supposed to feel.

My brothers and sisters and I had all tipped half-cooked baby chicks out of broken shells and watched runty piglets get crushed under bigger hooves, so it wasn't like we didn't know it could happen.

The baby was born okay, but he didn't get pink like he was supposed to. He stayed purple and limp, his toes all spread out and poking through the blanket. To my eyes it looked like living was terrible, so the minute his painful gasps stopped, the minute his toes quit bulging, I decided to be a little bit happy for him and a little bit sad for us.

My father remained the most solid presence in the room, even when the silence became absolute. Even so, none of us, not even the little kids, ran to him—not to comfort or be comforted. We knew better. As the other girls moved to help Mother, he placed the baby in my arms and told me to take care of it.

I washed him first, dipping his tiny body into the tub of water we'd been keeping warm. I wiped his face, trying to keep the water away from his nose and mouth, even though it didn't matter now. He was covered in blood and something white and waxy that was hard to rub away.

When he was clean, I brought the baby to the table we'd padded with clean towels and wrapped him in a white blanket, tucking his arms and legs tightly in the cotton. Once he was bundled up, it was easy to pretend it had all gone okay.

I carried him to the barn next to the garden. Cole went with me. The baby felt good in my arms, so I held him while Cole grabbed a hammer and fixed up a box to bury him in. He was smart about it too—he used the little bed we'd already made for the baby to sleep in, and all it needed was a top. My job was harder—I forgot to put gloves on before I started digging and the shovel rubbed my hands raw, my palms bubbling with blisters.

The shovel refused to sink more than an inch or two into the sunbaked earth, but I dug until the hole was waist deep. By then it was nearly dusk. Cole had arranged the baby in the box, and from my position, they were nothing but black shapes against the setting sun. I shaded my eyes so I could see them. I asked, "That deep enough, you think?"

"Yeah. Is anyone else coming?"

"No. You weren't even supposed to come. Dad told me to do it."

Cole shrugged and grabbed my hand as my feet scrambled against the dirt walls. He kept the lid off the box until I was out. "You want to look at him again?"

I didn't, but I looked anyway. The baby's skin was bluish and mottled, and his nose was dotted with tiny white spots that looked like pimples. But he already had hair, beautiful dark hair with matching lashes that rested like feathers on his cheeks—he could have been sleeping. I kissed the tip of my finger and pressed it to the baby's lips before Cole hammered the lid into place.

There were no clocks or calendars at the compound. We kept track of time by the seasons. It was spring; my nineteenth year, I think, though I can't be sure when I started to count. When Mother had gone into labor, it was still early morning cool, but by the time I was finished digging, the sun sat low on the horizon. My chest and shoulders were damp as I stretched out in the dirt next to the hole. Cole handed me the box, and as I placed it at the bottom, I felt happy for the baby again. We'd chosen a spot near the vegetable patch, right next to the path we took to pick corn and lima beans. It would be a nice place to sleep.

"I wish we had something to mark it with," Cole said as I patted the last of the dirt into place.

"We don't need anything. We'll remember." I tucked the shovel under my arm and examined my palm. Blisters bloomed across my hands. Our tiny brother was the eleventh baby to come out of that small, dark room, but he was the first we'd had to bury. We'd all been born there—I was the second and Cole was the fifth. Cole had been born *en caul*, and that's lucky. He emerged like an egg, fully cocooned in the watery sac that held him for nine months. My grandfather was still alive then, and he named him Nicholas because a caul-bearer meant victory, a sign we were moving in the right direction. The caul had been dried and buried somewhere in the middle of our land, like a blessing. A tiny piece of Cole tasked with protecting all of us.

I thought about that as I looked at my hands; thin, shiny membranes had bubbled up to shield the wounded skin underneath.

"Don't break those," said Cole. He grabbed my wrist to keep me from working a grimy fingernail into one of the blisters. "You'll get an infection. You have to wash them out and put a bandage on."

"I'll rinse them before I go to bed."

"Do you have soap?"

"No."

"So do it inside."

"They won't let me back inside."

He looked at me for a beat without blinking. "I'll bring you soap," he said, dropping my wrist.

I nodded. If I thought he'd get caught, I'd have said no, but I knew he wouldn't. Cole was like water—he could slide around no matter where you put him.

The light was turning gold as we walked back to the barn, and the setting sun found every auburn streak in his dark hair. He was quiet. Normally he never shut up. The silence was nice after such a loud day, and he seemed so lost in thought that I left him there. It was a long time before he spoke. "What are you going to do now?"

"I might work in the vegetable rows for a while. The beets are just about ready to pull. My hands'll be worse tomorrow."

"You need to wash them with soap and—"

"You said that already."

"Oh." Cole rubbed his eyes. He got headaches often, sharp, stabbing pains that arrived without warning and settled into a dull throb that lasted for hours. He opened and closed his mouth a few times. "Avery?"

"Yeah?"

"Did you know? That the baby was coming today?"

"No, but I knew it would be soon."

He stopped walking and got in front of me so I had to stop too. I used to be able to tackle Cole to the ground with one arm, but he was nearly a full head taller than me now, the skin on his cheeks just starting to roughen. Over his shoulder, the barn was a splash of red paint against the sky. "Were you scared?" he asked.

"No way, kiddo, that's not allowed—"

"No, really," he said. His eyes locked on mine, tired and dusty like everything else. "Were you?"

I was going to disappoint him. Really, I wasn't scared at all, but Cole wasn't like me. I'd spent my whole life being hacked and gouged into a workable chunk while he was carefully sanded into something much softer. His edges weren't as rough. "It's nothing to be scared of," I told him.

"It scared me."

"When he came out?"

"No," he said, flailing his arms at everything at once and nothing at all. "It was just—it was just *happening*, and then he—he died, Avery. We were all there, and we couldn't stop it."

"We tried."

"But we couldn't. And we're supposed to be able to do anything. We're supposed to be prepared."

When he said that, I got it. And I was surprised at the pain that rose in my throat. I didn't know who it was for. "But Cole…he—the baby—it isn't important," I told him. "We need to be ready for what is. This only feels important because it's happening now, but when the real time comes, we'll know what to do. He…" My voice wavered, and for a moment, my next words were true of all three of us. "He was weak."

We walked the rest of the way to the barn in silence, and by the time we got there, some of the worry had left Cole's forehead. I hooked the shovel onto a peg while he laid the hammer in the toolbox. In the corner of the barn, the heifer, heavy with her first calf, stood in the hay, looking at me hopefully. I pulled out the banana I'd hidden in the bib of my dress and fed it to her in two chunks, patting the top of her head.

"When do you think the calf'll come?" Cole asked me.

"She's dry," I said, smiling into her sad brown eyes. "It'll be soon."

"Are you sure?" His forehead wrinkled again. "It'd be awful to lose a calf."

"She'll let me know when it's time."

"But you've never delivered a baby before."

I lost my smile and turned so Cole wouldn't see. I'd never buried one either. But that was our lives, filled with never-haves. "I'll figure it out. I'm going to ask Dad if I can move into the hayloft so I can keep an eye on her."

"Okay. I'll get you some stuff for those blisters. Don't break them!" His feet made tracks through the sawdust. I followed them out. He wouldn't be back—not with the whole family inside, and I could rinse my hands off under the pump just as easy. I ran through the barn doors and back up the path. I could have brought the vegetable basket with me, but I didn't because what I said to Cole wasn't true—not really. Even if the baby wasn't a big thing, burying him was still important—important enough to be my only job for a little while.

The early spring sky had brightened to pink, shining strange light over the western edge of the woods. To the east it was already dark.

My hands were stiff, caked with dried mud. It was nearing dusk, still light enough to pull, but I was exhausted, and it hardly mattered anyway. Harvest season had barely warmed, and the crops were just moving into their prime. I had months of pulling ahead of me.

I weaved my way slowly through the rows. There were beets poking out of the ground, their purple skins vying for my attention, but I didn't bother with them. I went for carrots instead, working my fingers into the loose soil at the edge of the field. They were still on the scrawny side, and the potatoes were worse—the handful I dug up were barely walnut sized, but I tucked them into my apron anyway.

The gush from the water pump was a bigger reward. I opened my mouth to the first freezing wave that tumbled from the lip. It sent a spike of pain through my forehead, but I didn't move, letting the water rinse the sweat and dirt off my face. I primed the pump again to wash my hands, wincing a little at the sting. The blisters were deep. I cleaned them out as best I could before I unhooked the bucket and filled it to the brim.

I walked to the edge of the trees under the dying light until I reached my tent: sheets of canvas stretched taut across aluminum poles hammered into the earth. The structure was vaguely house shaped, with a pitched roof that shooed away falling rain and funneled it into the buckets set up in each corner. I checked the buckets out of habit, even though it hadn't rained in a while. The weather was traitorous and changeable; you could run through every season in a single day. By noon the sun was hot enough to burn, hot enough to erase every trace of winter. But the air was still thin, and when night fell, spring stood further away. It was always cold.

When I got to the tent, I set the water on top of a flat rock beside the canvas door, then I reached inside, groping for my fire-plow: a long piece of rough-hewn wood with a groove down the middle. My father and I carved it years ago, gouging our way through a heavy chunk of bur oak as he preached the benefits of quality tools. My skin was pebbled with goose bumps, but just trying for a fire would warm me up, even if the board didn't work. Fire-plowing was brutal, and I hated doing it. I *could* do it—I'd plowed embers into flames in the pouring rain, but it wasn't ideal. What was ideal was getting back to the tent before the sun went down. With sun, all it took was a magnifying glass and a bundle of dry weeds. Fire-plowing took forever. It made your hands hurt, and mine already did.

I scooped a panful of water from the bucket and dropped my carrots and potatoes inside the pan. It was an optimistic gesture. A few strips of muslin tied around my hands made a decent bandage, and I kneeled in front of the board and set the spindle in the groove. Then I pushed. Again and again, long firm strokes, searching for a spark, a curl of smoke…anything. The sting in my hands turned into an ache that spread to my wrists and then my arms, stretching toward my shoulder blades until every muscle froze in refusal to cooperate. I propped the board against the flat of my legs and pushed until I felt my skin tear and split. Poppies of blood bloomed on the makeshift bandages. The spindle fell to the ground.

I pulled the dripping vegetables from the pan and dropped them into my apron before using the water to rinse the blood off my hands.

The spindle looked feeble and spent lying in the dirt. I tossed it back into the tent. No fire. That meant no cooking and no light—no warning if something wanted to eat me, and there were plenty of things that lived in the dark. It meant I couldn't warm my bedding, or read, even though my books had been read so many times, the words would come if I needed them. And it wasn't that cold. I could see my breath where it met the air, but the trees were still.

I crawled into the tent, tied the door flaps shut, and stripped off my damp clothes, hanging my dress and shirt from the pitch to dry. I took off my boots, pulled on my thermals, and wiggled into my sleeping bag.

The roof of the tent had a plastic window, something I'd put in myself for the bad nights, nights when the fire didn't come. I stared at that tiny patch of sky full of pinprick stars—other suns warming other places. It was enough to see them. I chewed my way through the raw carrots, which were pretty good, and then the potatoes, which were not.

Two hundred yards away, near the footpath to the garden where the baby slept, stood the compound: three old warehouses that cut black squares into the horizon. Empty boxes long dismissed by the people on the outside who didn't know they held secrets—hidden rooms and underground tunnels and enough space to keep all the chosen safe, no matter how the earth stopped spinning.

There weren't that many of us. Not anymore.

Giant letters loomed above the brick and mortar, their long, skinny shadows stretching like fingers, the blackened reflection of a single word: CLOVELITE. I watched the shadows crawl toward me, covering my tent like a blanket. My parents had kept me out here for months.

But when the end came, I'd thank them for it. That's what they told me. Right before they shoved me outside and locked the door.

# TWO

———————

AFTER THE BABY WAS BURIED, NO ONE TALKED ABOUT HIM. MOTHER
rested, but everyone else seemed to be walking around with the entire
incident bleached from their minds. Even I woke the next morning
with no immediate memory, his tiny face washed away by sleep. The
first reminder came when I sat up in my dew-drenched tent—there
was a tightness to my hands that kept the sting of the blisters at bay.
The door flaps were still tied, but my hands had been wrapped in
layers of white. When I sat up, a roll of gauze, a bar of soap, and a
flash of silver tumbled into my lap.

I reached for the shine, pinching a foil-wrapped granola bar
between my fingers. Contraband. It was a foolish risk for Cole to
take, but I crammed the bar into my mouth anyway, tasting chocolate
and peanut butter.

The brightness of the day got me moving. I stripped and washed with the leftover water in my bucket, soaping myself as best I could, and then I considered my hands. A few strips of blood-splattered muslin did a good job of hiding the glare of the gauze. I buttoned my shirt, pulled on my dress, and pushed through the canvas flaps. The compound rose in the distance as I ran, steel-colored walls melting into the early morning sky.

My family lived on a commune, three buildings laid out like a face with two square eyes and a long, narrow mouth. There were twelve of us running the land—besides my parents, I had nine brothers and sisters—and we used every inch of space we had. The smaller buildings were connected by a glassed-in tube reinforced with sheets of aluminum so you couldn't see inside. The long building, the biggest one, was where we kept our stockpile—food and clothes, all kinds of stuff. We had an armory too. My father brought supplies back whenever he made trips to the outside. I'd never been off the compound, but Cole went once, and he said it was dirty and loud and he liked it here better.

It didn't matter. Nothing on the outside was going to last. We would last. Just like me, most of my brothers and sisters had never been off the grounds, but we could all hunt, build shelter, and dig water out of the ground, and everyone knew which leaves made the best toilet paper.

My parents had been running the compound ever since my

grandfather died. My grandfather, my father's father, was the first of the chosen, the one who saw the signs the world was dying. Not the earth but the people. And he knew that the only way to survive was to know how to live once everyone else was dead. The earth was full of gifts, he told us, but only if you knew where to look. Those were the lessons he taught his followers—how to find the right provisions, how to use them, how to survive. The land he bought to save his family was the land we'd lived on ever since. Forty acres that used to be part of a factory—no one wanted it on account of the warehouses. He wanted it because of them. There were other people listening to him by then, other people who wanted to be chosen. He didn't have a lot of followers, barely more than the twelve of us, but they thought big, and fear made them efficient. They tore out the insides of the buildings until they were nothing but empty shells, put up walls, installed generators and solar panels, and got the wells pumping again. Within a year they had a place big enough for all of them ten times over.

But that was a long time ago. After my grandfather passed, it seemed like everyone was afraid. He'd died suddenly in his sleep, leaving behind grown men and women who were aimless without him, panicked and desperate to leave the world before it left them.

Cole and I watched two of them go.

I don't know how old I was, but I remember I had a loose tooth that had been bugging me for days. I was in my room. Back then my prized possession, my only possession, was a tiny pair of ballet slippers. I would put them on and dance around my room to the melodies that lived in my head. I had no idea where I got the songs or the shoes, but I remember the feel of those pink slippers hugging my toes, the soft thud of my feet pounding the floor as I jumped and twirled.

That morning, I was dancing before the sun came up when Cole toddled in. He was too small to talk, but when he saw me, he rocked back and forth on bare feet and grinned, his tiny white teeth still tight in his mouth. When I moved to take his hands so we could dance together, I heard whispering through the walls—grown-up whispering. Cole laughed when I put my finger over my lips, and he followed me as I went slip-sliding down the hall on my leather soles.

We peered around the door. A man and a woman were sitting on the couch in the common room. I remember their faces and the way they were holding hands. I thought they looked happy. The man was holding something in his hand, and he touched it to the woman's chin. She smiled. Twin streams of tears trickled down her cheeks.

Then the wall behind her exploded in a cannon blast of red and black.

I didn't hear the shot; I only heard Cole screaming, felt him clawing at my skin, begging to be lifted. The man's hand moved again, and I screamed too. The second shot sent a shower of blood over us, and I fell on top of Cole, who was clutching me with his tiny, red-stained hands. We were on the floor in a tangled heap when our father ran in and grabbed us, one under each arm. When I peeked through my fingers, the man and the woman were still there, but I couldn't see their faces anymore. I could only see their feet, bent and twisted on the floor.

I still see their feet sometimes.

That night the bonfire mourned them. I sat with Cole on my lap, whispering mantras under the puffs of oily black smoke that leaked through the windows of my room. There was fear in that smoke, the release of pure terror escaping as its capsule melted away. Cole was asleep in my lap. He'd cried for hours, raw, terrifying shrieks that didn't let up until his throat sounded bloody. My mother had deposited the two of us in here and locked the door behind her.

There had been fires before, but that was the first one I understood—the first time I knew what made the smoke rise so sickly sweet. Cole's head was heavy on my chest as the flames choked the air with dirty clouds that traveled on the breeze, burning blacker than any wood.

Afterward, he didn't remember any of it. I was glad.

———————————

My grandfather's followers, the original Clovelite twenty, were dead by the time I buried the baby; they had been for years. Once my father stepped in, everything changed. He didn't see things the way my grandfather had, he didn't trust people from the outside, and in his eyes, if you hadn't been chosen by my father, you weren't chosen at all.

My father didn't dare banish them to the outside—we were well hidden, so it was too much of a risk. They were no less bound by the perimeter than we were. But the adults who remained on the compound had far more rules to live by, firmer boundaries to mind. And if they crossed those lines, there were no second chances. They killed themselves or my father took care of them, one at a time until, as he told us, his house was clean.

Even without being privy to the details, we all knew from an early age that it was best to know how to take care of yourself. Maybe that's why we never complained, never asked questions. There were only five of us when my grandfather died. Five kids who spent every single day learning how to find food and water and coax fire from wood so no one would ever have to take care of us.

Now, except for my parents, everyone on the compound had been born there. That meant running the land was up to us. And even though all the kids were old enough to chip in, being so few meant our days were always hard and always long.

But that was all we knew.

The sun was barely up when I got to the field the morning after the baby died. Peter and Candace were already by the barn, feeding the pigs. Benjamin was trudging out of the woods, a rifle slung over his shoulder.

"Benji!" I called.

He stopped, but he didn't turn. "What?"

"You want to help me pull?"

"Seth's taking me hunting," he said, picking up his feet again.

"You're going the wrong way."

"Dad wants to see me," he said. "Pulling's your job anyway."

My hands ached as I watched him go. The beets wouldn't wait—they were poking out of the earth under red-veined stalks. I moved from row to row with the basket on my hip, my bandaged hands filthy with dirt and smears of juice.

I dumped each basketful into the wheelbarrow, and when it was full, I picked it up and ran. If I hit my quota early, I could help can the beets, I thought as my feet kicked up dust. Cover them in hot water and salt, and it would get me inside, for just a little while. I could—

"Avery!"

I was almost to the fence. The shout threw a brick wall in front of me, and I stopped so short that a wave of beets tumbled to the dirt. My back stiffened and twitched. I raised my head slowly, praying the jump hadn't shown.

My father stood at the fence, one hand resting on the gate. He wore no expression at all, and that scared me so badly, my voice barely made it out. "Yes, sir?"

His eyes were black. They stayed on me as I bent to pick up the spilled vegetables. He stopped me with a wave of his hand. "Leave them."

He wore a faded blue shirt, and I could see a dot of blood on the collar from his morning shave. My sister Jane had sewn that shirt for him from a sheet of bleached cotton soaked in cornflower petals until it was the color of the sky—he always wore it with the sleeves rolled up because they were too short. The breeze lifted the front flap where it had pulled free from his belt. He noticed me noticing. "Yes, sir."

"Did something happen last night?"

It was a trick. Whatever it was, he already knew. But the minute I got quiet, I realized everything was quiet. The silence of the air hit me like a brick—there wasn't another soul in sight. "No, sir."

"Are you sure?"

"Yes, sir."

"It was cold last night. Where was your fire?"

"Oh…" My eyes were trained on the dusty patch of dirt darkened by his shadow. "My…my hands were sore. I decided to conserve my energy."

"That sounds like an excellent way to freeze to death."

I didn't say anything.

"Where was your focus?"

I shuffled my feet, kicking up tiny dust devils. "On my hands."

"Where should it have been?"

I kept my head down.

"What are the first four tiers of survival?"

"Focus, shelter, water, and fire."

"How many were you missing?"

I had to look at him. "Two."

"Two. You have to be stronger than that. You have to be stronger, or you can't live out here."

He said it like I had a choice. Like it was a privilege. "I'm sorry." His eyes flickered to my muddy, bloody hands. I didn't explain about the blisters or offer to tell my father where the baby was buried. He wouldn't care. I returned my eyes to the dirt, and the darkness spread. My father wasn't a big man, but he took up space. I always felt like there was a lot more to him than you could see.

His fingers closed over my right hand. He began peeling away the dirty strips of cloth until stark-white gauze peeked through. It gathered in a clump in his hand as it unwound, and when the last layer lifted, tiny white threads stayed behind on my swollen skin.

"This needs attention," he said. "Tell me why."

"Because even a simple infection can kill you."

He nodded gravely. I was still holding one handle of the wheel-barrow, and he pried it out of my grip. The weight left my hand, but I kept it open, hoping for a new burden, anything to do. He twisted my wrist between his fingers. "They're bandaged quite well."

My heart dropped as my brain began frantic calculations of what might come of this crime. If he knew it was Cole, he'd force me to punish him. "I'll be more careful. I'm almost done with the beets, and I want to check on the heifer—"

His other hand settled on my shoulder. "Not now," he said, keeping those black eyes on mine. "They're waiting for us inside."

*Inside* had become something of a foreign concept, and eighteen eyes were on me the minute I crossed the threshold to the main building. It was bright outside, and I blinked in the sudden dim. As the room lightened, I saw all my brothers and sisters staring at me with the same expression. They were sitting in demonstration formation: a wide semicircle of metal chairs. My hands tingled under the thick layer of ointment my father had smeared on my palms before wrapping them in fresh gauze. The attention scared me. There had been no medicine and no bandages the last time he'd split my skin.

Meetings were seated oldest to youngest: Amaris at one end and Benjamin at the other. He still had the rifle strapped to his back. My sisters were dressed like I was—blue apron dresses over white blouses. The boys wore jeans, dark and stiff, with blue button-down shirts.

The floor around our chairs bore years of scuff marks, and that made it the most decorated surface of the room. It was a huge room, so dark, it could trick you into shivering even in the dead of summer. The windows were small. Sunlight stretched like fingers through the glass, but they weren't long enough to touch us.

The chair between Amaris and Seth, my chair, was empty. On either side, their faces were enviably, deliberately blank. My heartbeat pounded in my ears; the room throbbed with it. Something was going to happen. They were here to watch.

Cole sat sort of in the middle, and I centered my gaze an inch above his head. Out of the corner of my right eye, I could see the jumble of Sarah's red curls. Amaris's deeply tanned face frowned in the left. My father's thumb grazed my neck, and I flinched— when his voice boomed, I jumped. A tiny smile touched Seth's lips.

"This won't take long," my father intoned. "We have a lot to do after the time we lost yesterday, and when I am finished speaking, I want all of you to return to your chores immediately."

I chanced a look at Cole. He was staring at my hands, wrapped clean and tight. His eyes darted to mine. I shook my head almost imperceptibly.

"Your mother and I have decided," my father went on, "to move Avery into Hannah's room. Hannah will share with Jane."

I would've been less shocked if he'd put a gun to my head. Hannah's room was a prize, three times the size of the one she was being forced into with Jane. Aside from being the only one of us who could stitch a wound without flinching, I often wondered what Hannah did to deserve it. Cole's face was inching toward confusion, but Hannah was enraged, and her fury made her foolish.

"Why?" she blurted. Everyone shifted in their seats. You didn't challenge our father, even with a single word.

His reply was slow and silky. "Why?"

"I—yes," Hannah said, committed now. "That's my room, so how come Avery gets it?"

"Because I said so."

"Yeah, but *Avery?*"

"Yes." His voice was firm, but it forgave her tone—her disgust. She slumped in her chair. Amaris threw a panicked look toward Seth. My father continued, "Avery needs to get her strength back. She's going to be resting for a few days."

I pressed my lips together. I'd spent months in a tent with frozen hills and troughs digging into every muscle and every bone…

A few days ought to do it.

"When is she getting it?" Hannah asked.

"Now. Nicholas?"

"Yes, sir?"

"Please collect Avery's clothes from her tent and bring them back here."

Cole nodded, but I felt a fresh stab of fear. I didn't like that my father knew I'd be most uncomfortable uprooting Hannah—or that

Cole was the only one I would trust with my things. I didn't want to think about what else he knew.

He turned his attention to the youngest kids. "Sarah?"

"Yes, sir?"

"You, Candace, and Benjamin will finish the harvesting for today. The three of you will cover Avery's quota for the week."

"Yes, sir."

"Are there any concerns about this arrangement?"

There were plenty but none he would hear. A thousand pounds had been added to the room, pushing on us from all sides. Amaris had lost her tan. Sarah's face, young and sweet, was painted with as much revulsion as Hannah's, whose eyes were bulging, her forehead pulsing with red spots and slick with sweat. Cole glanced at her sideways. No one spoke.

"Very good," my father said. "We will have a more formal meeting one week from today. For now I would like everyone to continue their work. Mind the perimeter."

Silent nods all around.

"Watchwords, please."

"Prepare, endure, and thrive," everyone chanted. My own voice rose to join them, a reflex as natural as breathing.

"Rewards will come. To all of us," he added with a note of dismissal.

The room emptied in a muted rush of shuffling feet. Candace

and Benji ran to the door, and Amaris passed through like a zombie. Hannah lingered, but when my father didn't shoot me or bash my head against the wall, she followed the rest of the group out, her shape blackened by the light that poured inside the room.

I didn't move.

"Come, Avery," my father said. "Your mother and I would like to talk to you."

My mother. Jesus. We walked outside, thrust into sunshine that seemed much brighter now. The stretch of dirt to the living quarters had been foot-stamped into a path so hard, the grass had given up growing.

It was cool inside. I allowed myself to be steered down the hall to the point of controversy that was Hannah's room—my room. It was a crisp, square space. The bed had fresh sheets and blankets folded at the foot of the mattress, but the rest of the room was unchanged from the last time I saw it, with Hannah's cave drawings decorating the plaster. It was her habit to pencil finely detailed landscapes on the walls when she couldn't sleep: graphite fields and flowers and galloping horses, all part of a grand fresco she'd probably never finish.

I found myself wondering, wildly, if Jane would let her draw on the walls—it was the only thought in my head. Maybe she wouldn't, and that would be enough to put Hannah and me back where we belonged and stop whatever was happening here.

Next to the door, in a beat-up velvet armchair, my mother sat like an old ghost. Her dress hugged her stomach, still a round balloon, the resting place for her swollen breasts. Two wet circles of milk darkened the cotton.

Worse than how she looked was how she smelled: heady and stale, like something that had been butchered and left to rot in the sun. She didn't look at me. "Hello, Mother."

Her eyes flickered toward the naked mattress, and I walked backward, my legs bumping the frame as I sank down on the bed. The air in the room was just as heavy as the one we'd left—heavy and lined with barbed wire that poked at me, tearing off little bits every time I moved.

"Avery," my father began, wandering to the window. "The people out there are unaware they are fueling the apocalypse. They don't realize they are living right in the middle of it, and, most important, they don't know the world is going to turn on them. They are going to turn on themselves." He pressed his fingers to the smudged glass. "But we do, don't we?"

"Yes, sir."

"It's a sickness," he went on. "They are infected with convenience, with immediacy, with entitlement. When that takes them, what will be left?"

"We will, sir."

"Why?"

"Because we have been chosen."

"Humanity is dying, isn't it, Avery?"

"It's killing itself."

"And who are we?"

"We are chosen. We are the only people who matter."

"Right," he said with a small smile. "That's right." He looked pleased with me, but they were only words—words that had been drilled into my head since before I could talk. There was no magic to them.

I glanced at my mother. Her eyes had slid shut, every breath even and deep. She could have been asleep.

"Avery, it's important for all of us to do well," my father went on, staring at one of Hannah's horse-and-bunny scenes. "To contribute, individually, toward the betterment of the group."

"Yes, sir."

"Why were you sent away?"

My eyes fell to my lap. "To improve," I said as my cheeks grew hot. "To enhance my skills—"

"Because you were weak," my father finished.

"Yes, sir."

"Have you changed?"

"I—yes," I said after a pause. "Yes."

"No, you haven't."

My heart tried to stutter to a stop, but I was angry—I wouldn't let it. "I haven't?"

"No. You've been selfish. You've benefited from the gifts of the earth without giving anything in return."

A breeze from the open window touched my face. There was applewood burning in the fresh spring air, and my cheeks burned too. The smoky scent felt like some secret part of me was flowing through the room for everyone to see, solitary memories of my time alone in the dark. Here, that wasn't good enough, and I grew tearful in my anger. "I haven't, sir. I've been planting and harvesting all on my own. I've survived on the outskirts of the camp. I've met my quota every single day," I went on in a rush, my palms lighting in painful remembrance. "I've been strong—"

"Ah." He smiled again and pressed his thumb against the side of his nose. "That's the key," he said, bobbing his finger at me. "You have gotten stronger. The problem is you've only been strong for yourself. You haven't offered those strengths to the group. So where does that leave us?"

"I don't know, sir," I mumbled.

"It leaves us with one member who is useless to everyone but herself. We can all plant," he said, spreading his arms wide. "It takes no skill to pull food from the ground, or…" He stopped and stared at the wads of white gauze covering my hands. "Start a fire. We are all strong," he continued. "But we have one disadvantage. What is that?"

"We are not many."

"Precisely. It took your grandfather's group years to create what we have. They had more people, more experience. We are only twelve."

My vision was getting as gray as the room. I couldn't clear the veil of milky light that had settled over my eyes. The bed was soft, and the softness spread up my back and into my shoulders, begging me to lie down.

My father wasn't finished, though. "But there are things we can do to change that," he went on, "without weakening ourselves with strangers."

The longer he talked, the less I understood. "I don't—"

"And your mother and I think," he said, with a small smile in my mother's direction, "that you can help." He fixed his eyes on mine, black bleeding into black, and so deep, I was afraid to look at them for too long. "It will take time, but it's going to mean everything to all of us. So I'd like you to take this week and rest. Recover. I want you to eat as much as you want and sleep as long as you wish. Would you like that?"

*No.* It was the scariest proposition I'd ever heard. I'd read stories about prisoners and their last meals, and for months I'd been a prisoner kept out instead of in, but still alone. This felt too much like my last meal, and I was shaking more than I had the day he'd dragged me outside and locked the door as the snow piled at my feet and I beat my fists bloody against the cold metal. The noise in my head was so loud, it hurt, but he didn't hear it. He only heard one thing—the low, lying whisper that emerged from my cracked throat.

"Yes, sir."

# THREE

In Hannah's room, time passed in a weird combination of endless moments and rapid days. For my body, which got to eat and sleep and stay warm, the week went by much too fast, but the thinking part of me felt like I was strapped to a bomb and could count every tick.

The hours dragged between naps and meals, filled in by the sight of my father strolling past wearing a deliberate grin or the other kids rushing down the hall without a glance. Even Cole. It was like they all knew something about me and whatever they knew was so dirty and sick that I was even more off-limits than before.

My mother didn't speak a word to me all week, but every day she delivered hot plates of food to my room: seared steaks and chicken, potatoes mashed in warm milk, salted ears of white corn. She brought them alongside bowls of rough-chopped greens tossed with chunks of hard-boiled eggs. Each meal was more than twice the amount of food I'd usually eat in a day, and so heavy, I'd fall asleep until it was time to eat again.

My raw carrots had tasted better.

Sleeping all day meant I was up all night, and one night all the worry and fear seemed to melt until they flowed out of me, and I was left with an exhaustion beyond anything I'd ever known. From my pillow I could see the barn doors standing partway open. I thought of the heifer inside, the calf getting ready to leave her.

My father had inseminated the heifer himself, a complicated process that required supplies that needed to be frozen and thawed and warmed again. That was late last July, only a few months before I'd been banished to my tent. He'd pulled me from the fields for a week, and my only job was to watch the heifer. Husbandry, he'd said, was all a matter of timing. So I watched, and based on my count, the vial was threaded into her after she'd stood for a day in heat.

She'd cried. With my father's arm all the way up inside her, she made a sound that moved well beyond pain: a mournful lowing that made me want to cry too. He said it didn't hurt her, but she still cried, and as I stood in front of her, a burning sense of shame flowed between her liquid eyes and mine.

Now her time was nearly over, and she was out there alone while I lay between cool sheets, staring at the moon through the window.

Shame rose again and mixed with fatigue; it came to life as tears in my eyes.

I could hear my heart beating in a steady thump, like footsteps. I let my eyes slide closed.

*"The bulls and the heifer are from the same mother,"* my father explained. *"So we can't breed them together."*

*"Why not?"*

*He was putting together a metal contraption, something rigid and painful looking.* *"Because if we do, the babies will be weak."*

*I knew that already. I'd read about it in one of my books, now swollen and creased with age.* Incest, *it was called.*

*"I had to go to a breeder on the outside,"* my father went on. *"But we only needed one thing."*

"One," I mumbled. I was hovering between a memory and a dream, and my heart was quiet. It had been replaced by shadowy voices that wavered in and out. I wanted to open my eyes, but they were too full of the sand of sleep, so I kept them closed, not quite sure if the voices were real.

"This is the one?"

"Yes."

"Pretty girl."

"Thank you."

"You told me you had six."

*"I have enough vials for six. Six tries or six calves, we'll have to see."*

*My father gave the heifer a hard slap on her rump.* "She's a strong girl. She won't let us down."

"What I have doesn't matter."

My eyelids fluttered, and something touched my cheek. Only for a moment, but I felt it; a hand lit on my skin like the flicker of a forked tongue—a butterfly that had grown fat on milkweed and could beat poison from its wings. At the touch I opened my eyes, but the room was dark. There was no one there.

"Hello?" My voice echoed in the velvet black. The burning, stinging pain in my eyes was gone, so I got to my feet and walked to the door. It had been open when I'd gone to sleep. Now it was closed.

I opened the door and saw light, a white pool shining at the end of the hallway. My feet began to carry me before I even knew if I wanted to go. All at once I was small again, Cole toddling along beside me with laughter in his eyes.

But when I got to the end of the hallway, I was alone. I peered around the corner.

The first thing I saw was my father. He was sitting at the small table from the kitchen. I could see half his face, but unless he turned, he couldn't see me.

"How old is she?" a voice asked.

"Nineteen," my father replied.

"Virgin?"

"Yes."

The chair facing me held a stranger. A man. A man with small eyes set far apart and neatly carved lips that were so chapped, I could see dead flakes from where I stood. The rest of his skin was flat and pasty, like he'd spent his life running from the sun.

"I'm not looking to join or anything," the man told my father. He had a high, nervous voice—it teetered in the air, and my father left it for a long moment before delivering his response.

"I'm not inviting you. I'm hiring you to perform a service. You wanted a young girl—"

"But you want kids. And I don't want to say *okay* and then get slapped with a paternity suit."

"Your only obligations are confidentiality and conception. Say nothing, do what is required, and there will be no issues. You will have no rights to any children she bears."

My breath cut off. It just stopped. The words were as good as a hand around my throat, and I stood there with one palm pressed to my chest.

A burning pain came when the air didn't.

"I want to be very clear about this," my father went on. "We don't bring people from the outside. I thought about using one of the boys, but—"

*The bulls and the heifer are from the same mother.*

"—that would not be ideal."

The man paused, drumming his fingers on the tabletop. I stood motionless in the doorway, not because I didn't want to move, but because I couldn't. I wanted to move, I wanted to open my mouth and scream and then run, out the door and through the woods until my feet trampled the perimeter and left it behind forever.

But I hadn't even breathed yet.

"No schedules or anything?" the man asked. "I can have her whenever I want?"

*This is going to be your job, Avery.*

"Yes. And I want you to meet the other children. They'll all be expected to contribute eventually, and they need to understand."

"When—" the man asked, his voice even higher, giddier. "When do we start?"

My father paused. It was a heavy, loaded silence. I could hear my heartbeat again.

Then his voice sounded. It was a handshake. A signature. "Right away."

I took a single step back. Then another, stumbling drunkenly until I hit the opposite wall and slithered to the floor. My feet pedaled against the wood, but I got them under me, hopping soundlessly on my toes until I was back in my room. I shut the door and slid to the floor again.

The entire room was tilting. I had to fight to hang on. My hand was clenched so tight, it hurt, desperately gripping a doorknob that didn't have a lock.

# FOUR

---

Nothing happened the next day.

But that wasn't enough to convince me. Not nearly enough to dismiss the man as a dream. By nightfall I reached my quota of food and sleep—my mind wouldn't shut off, and every shadow had a doughy face. I shivered in Hannah's bed until the air was thick with silence, and then I got up and padded through the halls toward Cole's room. Being ignored by my brothers and sisters was nothing new, but Cole's silence was painful. When I lived outside, he would risk life and limb to sneak out and talk to me, but since I came back, his tongue had been snipped as close as my mother's. He didn't even look at me.

My hands shook as I inched my way down the hall. The boys lived in an older part of the building that sloped below ground level, and their rooms were always freezing. It was supposed to be good for them.

Cole's room sat at the lowest point. It was tiny and full of odd angles. Because it happened to have a hot water pipe running through one corner, he was comfortable as long as he kept the door shut. But when I got there, the door was open. And Cole wasn't asleep.

The room was frigid and dark—it felt dead. Cole sat up the minute he saw me in the doorway. He did it so fast, he smacked his head on the water pipe that was doing him no favors at the moment. I saw him wince and try to free his arms from a cocoon of blankets.

"Are you okay?" I hissed.

"Shut the door!"

"Why do you have it open?" I asked, holding the knob so it wouldn't click when I closed it. "You're going to freeze."

"I already am. Come here," he whispered. I took two hopping steps on the icy floor and crawled under the covers next to him. "I left it open for you."

"You should have left the light on too," I said, reaching for his head—I couldn't see anything, but there was a lump rising under my fingers. I probed it as gently as I could. "Does that hurt?"

He lay down again. "It'll go away."

I nodded and dropped down too, suddenly exhausted. My eyes itched and burned, begging me to let them rest in a way they hadn't since I'd come inside. I felt safe with Cole. "Why would you wait for me to come down here when you've been ignoring me all week?" I whispered, listening to his heart thud in my ear.

"I knew you'd come. I wanted to talk to you."

"You could have talked to me."

"No, I couldn't," he said. I looked up. My eyes were slowly adjusting to the dark, but not enough to read his face. "They told us not to."

"Well, I don't want to get you in trouble," I mumbled, moving my head next to his on the pillow. I tried to sound like I didn't care, but my tone didn't match my face. My cheeks burned in the icy air, and I was grateful for the dark.

He smiled then; I could hear it in his voice. "When have I ever gotten caught?" I tried to nod, but I only shuddered. Cole caught my shoulders. I could feel him squinting, trying to make out my face. "What's wrong?"

My mouth was full of cotton. I couldn't tell him, not when my only option was to leave, and we both knew what would happen then. I tried to move my swollen tongue, but nothing came out.

"Avery..." The way he said it put weight in the air, something heavy and thick. He said it like it just occurred to him that I wasn't playing, that there was something more to be worried about. "What—"

"Cole," I blurted. I didn't know what to tell him, because I wasn't even sure what I should be afraid of. "I...I'm scared. I think they're going to do something to me."

"Who is?"

"Mom and Dad."

"Why would they?"

"I don't know, I just…oh, God, Cole, did they say anything to you? Any of you? About what's going on?"

"What's going on?"

"I mean about why they let me back in. Have you heard anything? Or seen anyone new?"

"Like who?"

"Anyone. Why did they tell you not to talk to me?"

Cole hesitated.

My heart sank, further than it should have. The entire week, I wanted to believe—I tried to believe—that nothing was going on, even though that was ridiculous, because weeklong vacations in bed just didn't happen. Not to me. I wanted to pretend there was nothing terribly, terribly wrong with all this, even though everything about it was terribly, terribly wrong. "Tell me," I said.

"I don't…"

"Tell me why I'm here."

"They didn't tell us," he said quickly. "They didn't tell us why you're back. At least not me. I don't know about Amaris, or—"

"But it's something, right? Something's going to happen to me." I heard the words before I realized I was the one talking, but I was positive what I was saying was true.

"Avery, they won't do anything too bad. We need you…" Cole insisted. My head kept shaking, wildly, and I buried my face in the pillow. "Avery, no, listen to me—there's hardly any of us left."

"So?"

"So why do you think they're going to hurt you?"

I rolled to my back and stared into the thick blackness until my eyes found shapes in the dark; they would start to look like one thing—a barking dog, or the crooked nose of a witch—and then melt into something else. "Dad said I need to contribute to the group. They said they had a job for me."

"So that's good."

"It's not good."

"They let you back in, didn't they? And it's not just you, Dad told us we're all getting new stuff to do. Seth went off grounds twice this week. Dad took him."

I let that sink in for a minute. "He took Seth out?"

"Yeah."

"For what?"

"Medicine, I think. I heard him tell Mom something about pills."

I'd never even held a pill. We didn't take medicine, not without a legitimate threat of death. Sometimes not even then. I shook my head. "No one's been out in a long time. They could be pulling people in from outside."

"Dad would never do that. He doesn't trust anyone."

"Grandpa did it."

"And they all died. It's too dangerous. Why do you think they keep having kids? I'm telling you, it can't be that bad—"

*That bad, that bad, that bad.*

"—and we have a meeting tomorrow, so I don't think you should be scared."

"I am scared," I whispered.

Cole shook his head; I could hear the faint rustle. "They're not going to hurt you, and they'd be afraid to send you away. They'd be afraid you'd tell."

"They know I wouldn't tell. Not as long as you were still here."

His reply was long in coming, and he didn't sound like he believed it himself. "That's not enough."

I focused until I could make out his outline, see the shape of his face. "It's enough."

Cole and I had always been closer to each other than anyone else. I was never sure why, but it was dangerous. It was why we were partners. I didn't remember a time when he wasn't there, and I was always there for him. We lay side by side, and while he clutched my fingers, I waited for an out. I waited for him to offer to come with me right then—to get his stuff and follow me into the woods so we'd both be safe, and we'd never have to find out what might happen. But he didn't offer, and I didn't ask. It was too much to ask anyone.

———————

I was probably about twelve years old the day we got our partners.

Not that I know for sure. We had no birthdays. Time passed with a sort of stagnant sameness, the years dragging us by the necks with no celebrations along the way. That day, my father had gathered the whole group in the meeting room for the very first time since Benji had been born—ten kids, ten chairs—and stood in front of us with his fingertips pressed together and a wide smile on his lips.

"This is what is known as the buddy system," he announced.

It was hard not to wiggle in my seat. The bug bites were murder, and I had poison ivy too. Someone—Hannah, if I had to guess—must have gotten to me while I was asleep, because none of us were foolish enough to wander into ivy or oak or sumac. She and I didn't get along, and it didn't help that my father liked to pit us against each other whenever he got the chance. I often thought it was like a game to him, the way he poked and prodded at the ten of us, knowing we could only explode against each other. Hannah and I were two of his favorite targets. I checked out her arms, where the poison could have tapped above the glove line, but there were no bumps there.

Whatever the buddy system was, it had to be a big deal—they'd made a meeting about it. Next to me, Amaris was slumped in her chair, her face set and stony. At the other end, Benji laughed and swung his tiny feet.

"From now on, you are all going to have a partner," my father explained. "Someone you'll be able to depend on for anything you might need."

I frowned. It sounded…nice. Like the opposite of discipline. We had partners for that too.

"Your mother and I have chosen the pairs very carefully," my father went on. "We're going to think of this as…insurance," he said, a fresh smile touching his lips. "Candace?"

"Yes, sir?"

"Your partner is Seth. Seth, your partner is Amaris."

Amaris's face lightened to an almost smile, but then she spoke up. "How…?"

"I will explain. Amaris, your partner is Benjamin. Benjamin's partner is Avery, and Avery's partner is Nicholas."

None of this made sense, he was giving us two partners, not one, and Benjamin couldn't help me or Amaris, he was barely old enough to walk. But I got Cole too. I twisted my head and smiled at him with my tongue caught between my teeth. He grinned back.

"Nicholas, your partner is Jane. Jane's partner is Peter, Peter's partner is Sarah, Sarah's partner is Hannah, Hannah's partner is…" He smiled. "Candace."

He had us wiggling on the end of a line, everyone glancing at everyone else.

"We all struggle to do our best, don't we?" he asked us.

"Yes, sir!"

"We respect the perimeter."

"Yes, sir!"

"Yes," he said, smiling widely. "But what is the perimeter? There is really no need to be frightened of an invisible thing. What you should fear is what is outside. And what would happen if you tried to reach it. Let's do a practical example." His eyes traveled the room. "Amaris? Can you join me? Bring Benjamin with you, please."

Amaris stood, but Benji didn't want to walk; he slithered to the floor like a sack of flour. Amaris hoisted him to her hip and carried him to the front of the room. He rested his curly blond head on her shoulder.

"Let's say," my father began, "that Amaris breaks a rule and we are forced to punish her. And maybe it's her third or fourth discipline in a few weeks and she's tired of it. She thinks she can do better on the outside.

"So she leaves," he went on, splaying his fingers wide. "She runs away. It's a good solution, right? Well, for Amaris, it is. But, as we all know, survival is a matter of balance. By leaving, she has upset our balance, and since she is gone, she cannot be punished for that. But…" My father leaned over and lifted Benji from Amaris's arms. His chubby little legs kicked, and he smiled, happy to be in the middle of so many faces. "Her partner can. And her partner will. Rest assured, things will be very bad for Benjamin if Amaris runs away. If any of you, *any of you*, choose to leave us, your partner will suffer grievously, and when it is over, they will be more permanently gone than whoever ran away. Maybe," he added, smiling at Amaris, who was now chalk white. "Amaris thinks she can get around it. She can just take Benjamin with her when she runs. But now Avery is in trouble, isn't she?" He turned his smile to me—my blood slowed and froze. "And so on," he said, surveying the room, "And so forth."

No one spoke. I don't think anyone even breathed. Benjamin wiggled and squirmed until my father set him down. His tiny feet were clumsy—he lost his balance and landed on his backside with a thud.

None of us looked away. We sat there silently and watched, waiting to see if he would cry.

# FIVE

---

THE FOLLOWING NIGHT I FACED THE SAME CHAIRS. THE SAME KIDS, just older now. The only other difference was that my chair was gone.

I didn't even realize it at first. When we came into the room, I felt sluggish, too full after the dinner we'd all shared. My family had gathered around the dining table as a group for the first time since I'd been sent away. The meal was rich and heavy, followed by a warm, bumpy loaf of sweet bread dotted with raisins that we passed around the table. The bread moved from hand to hand, and everyone tore off a chunk until it reached Benjamin, who got the last piece. We all got to smear the bread with butter from a shared stick that had been brought in from the freezers, marking the meal as a true occasion. There'd been raw milk, too, rich and thick and creamy. My mother doled out a full Mason jar to each of us. Through all this, no one spoke, even though it was likely the most luxurious thing we'd enjoyed as a group in a long time.

When we filed into the meeting room, I moved toward my seat as usual, but I was yanked back by my father, and as everyone claimed their spots, I realized every chair was full. I wanted to speak, but I couldn't. Something metallic was clinging to the back of my tongue, and I stood mutely with my father as my brothers and sisters congregated before us. His voice sounded in my ear, and I jumped. Someone let out a bark of laughter. Out of the corner of my eye, Hannah smiled.

"Before we begin," my father said, holding my shoulders like he was running a jackhammer. "I'd like to ask someone to share a sign of hope."

Signs of hope were a normal meeting opener. It was an easy question, because anything from a ladybug sighting to a garden-hose rainbow could be waved around and made more important than it was. My personal hope was that my father would let me go and give me my chair back, but his hands stayed firmly planted on my shoulders.

"Anyone?"

"The calf was born today," Jane offered.

"Beautiful," my father replied, and I could feel his smile as my own mouth twitched down. I'd been tending to that cow since she got pregnant, and I was hoping to be there when she delivered her calf. In the whirlwind of the past week, I'd forgotten all about her. "Did you assist her, Jane?"

"Yes, sir."

"Thank you, Jane," I said quietly. I meant it, but I don't think she heard me; the words stuck to my tongue like wads of cotton. But my father did hear me, and his fingers tightened on my shoulders, hard enough to hurt. I was not up there to speak.

"Anyone else?" my father pressed. No one said a word. "That's surprising," he said. "We live on beautiful land that we've earned through hard work, we have plenty of food, and the support of one another every day of our lives. You haven't seen what I've seen, but we have so much more than the people on the outside who are slaves to their machines, people who could not take care of themselves if their lives depended on it. And very soon they will. I know the time for resolutions has passed, but perhaps tonight can be the start of a new state of mind for all of us. A state of openness and awareness of the gifts we've been given. Because if we don't see those gifts, if we don't appreciate them, we will not be able to cope when harder times come.

"I saw a sign of hope this very evening," he declared grandly. His voice was too loud all of a sudden, and the words bounced around inside my head. "I saw my wife and my ten beautiful children, all of us in the same room, all of us healthy and well fed—all of us chosen. That was a very hopeful sign. I can think of nothing that would have pleased me more."

My father's heart was hammering against my back, and every

beat felt like the crack of a whip. I could feel the vibrations in my teeth. The smell of the roast we'd had for supper was clinging to his hands, and I imagined tiny shreds of meat embedded in the lines in his skin. It was nauseating; the whole room pulsed with his heart and his smell, but every time I tried to inch away, he tightened his grip.

"Someone tell me why we have been chosen," my father went on, digging his dirty fingers deeper into my muscles. "Peter, tell everyone why they have been chosen."

"To prepare, endure, and thrive," Peter said without missing a beat. "To bring strength to all we do so we can become something greater than human when humanity is dead."

"Is humanity dying, Candace?"

"It's killing itself," Candace said.

"And are we the only people?"

"We're the only people who matter," bounced back in unison, and it was the only time I'd heard it the way my father did, standing on the other side. It was better than nine voices. It sounded like ninety voices, nine thousand, nine million. It sounded like applause.

"That's right," my father said, and I could feel his smile again. "That's right. And as I stand here tonight, one word in that sentiment is particularly strong. Thrive. We are all thriving. Our land, our bodies, our plans. We do not dread the end. We are looking forward to it, because then it will be safe for us to branch out even more." He pushed me forward suddenly, and I almost lost my balance; it felt like I was wading through syrup. "I want everyone to take a good, long look at your sister," he announced. "She has been away from us for a long time, and we all need to welcome her back. Avery is standing here with me because I believe she embodies another important word: endure."

I was starting to feel heavy, weighed down and sleepy by the food in my stomach, and my father's hands felt like a lead vest. My own hands twitched at the sound of my name. Until that moment I'd felt like an accessory to his speech, like a gavel or a baton. Just something to hold. My eyes bounced from face to face; they all looked wide-eyed and blank, and for a moment, their faces melted into one thing, and I couldn't tell any of them apart.

"And we," my father went on, "have endured. All of us, our whole family. Together we've endured an unspeakable loss that is not easily forgotten. We lost one of our own."

My legs felt like jelly. It took me a moment to realize he was talking about the baby.

"That is what spurred this meeting," he said. "Before I tell you why, I want you to understand I did not bring you in here as children today. We are all responsible for the fate of the group. Every one of you was in that room, every one of you lost something. And it would be a shame—a dreadful shame—to allow that loss to go unnamed or unspoken. It would be a shame to allow it to go unchallenged."

His words put a wrinkle between my eyes, sharp as a knife

jab—he was talking about a death that happened over a week ago, but I didn't have a chance to think about it because that's when I saw Cole. Somehow, he had separated from the rest of the group; he wasn't melted into them anymore, and I could see him, a clear spot in the mist. His eyes were huge with some dawning understanding, and I could see them better than I had any right to from so far away, blue orbs growing bigger and bigger. He was looking right at me, which was the most dangerous thing he could have done. My father was thundering now, shaking my shoulders, and I was so weak that my head jerked back and forth like a rag doll.

"And so your mother and I have decided that we will challenge it," he said, indicating her silent form frozen on the sofa. "But how do we challenge death? We challenge it by not allowing the simple human weakness of age to limit our numbers, because the fact stands that we are still few. We are far too few, and in order to continue, we must consider the next generation. Strength begets strength. It was a strong cow that birthed that calf. But there are certain things we must forgive, and one of those things is the fact your mother bore eleven children and now that time is over. Her body is weak.

"But Avery's," my father said, twisting me around to face him, "is not."

A dull smile crawled across my face—it was nice to be something right, something good. He was smiling, too, and I knew that meant I could stay, and that was enough—it didn't seem important that I pay attention anymore. My eyes were sliding shut when a new voice shattered the air, high and thin. "No—"

I didn't know who it was. I could not speak. I couldn't even move. Through the slits of my eyes, I watched my father's face grow hard, felt his fingers turn to stone, and it felt like I would be stuck to him forever, that he would never let me go. "Avery has proven that she can endure and proven that she can thrive," he said.

"*No!*"

"Be quiet, Nicholas!" My mother's voice cut through the haze, a sharp hiss from behind us.

At that admonishment my father's hand left me briefly to gesture toward the couch. "Your mother has decided, and I agree," he finished with a flourish. "From this point on, Avery will continue our bloodline, and she will bear our children. We are all here bound by blood, and we cannot neglect that bond."

My face felt rubbery and numb—my head flopped back, so far that I could see a dark figure over my father's shoulder, watching us. I could hear that invisible protesting voice growing louder and louder, but my mother did not acknowledge it again.

"Strength," my father whispered, "begets strength." His fingers had turned to maggots and worms against my skin, but I couldn't pull away because he was the only thing holding me up. "Let's see how strong you are."

I felt the world tilt until my feet left the floor. I hadn't been dropped or pushed; I'd been lifted, carefully, like something fine and breakable. My eyes were still open, but they showed me nothing but darkness and light—shadows that fell and lifted, and I heard more voices and names and orders. There were cheers and chants, the sounds of celebration. The shadows grew solid, circling me, and I felt hands on my ankles and fingers on my wrists and then a long tearing sound that left my whole body cold. The shadow behind my father drew closer, twisting into a solid shape, and it was a wretched, horrifying shape that had no face. I felt thick hands touch my skin and then take me from my father's arms. My ears left me then, but for a moment, I could make out that same protesting voice, growing softer and softer and crying out that it was sorry.

# SIX

---

THE NEXT NIGHT, I SAT ON HANNAH'S BED, HUGGING MY KNEES TO MY chest. It hurt terribly, sitting like that, but I didn't care. I needed to be small, curl up until I disappeared or at least until they couldn't find me anymore. A fat, white moon hung in the sky behind my window like a picture framed just for me. I wanted to crawl into that icy silver light and slip away into nothing, vanish with the shadows when the moon set.

A shudder moved through me, and my face contorted into weird expressions that were uglier and more painful than my thoughts. It helped, for a moment, to step outside and see what the Man had done instead of feeling it. Finger-shaped bruises circled my wrists, but I clutched them tightly. My face was wet. I might have been crying, but it could have just as easily been blood, or snot, or drool. It didn't matter.

My door inched open, and all that tension turned into a seizure of flailing limbs. It hurt, every muscle coming alive at once. My hands found the blanket, and I burrowed under it like a child hiding from monsters, monsters that could slink and slide and find me no matter how small I felt. The door creaked, and a voice followed, halting and scared.

"Avery? It's me. Are you okay?"

"No," I whimpered. And I wasn't. I was too late—impotent in size and strength, and all the fiery grit that could have carried us away from that place had been pumped out of me. Extinguished. Fresh wetness tumbled over my lips. "No."

Cole eased the door closed behind him. When I peered over my knees, I saw him, another shadow veiled in darkness until the light found his face. I was sorry when it did. His eyes on me hurt as much as everything else. More. His eyes knew everything.

"Avery?" he said again. "Oh no, you're bleeding…let me get something to—"

"No," I mumbled again. It was the only syllable I was capable of. My lips were puffed and swollen from being clamped between my teeth.

Earlier in the day, in the bright light of morning, I'd been slapped awake by my mother. When I opened my eyes, I could barely move; even the stinging smack had little effect. She loomed over me, her face sliced in half by the sun bleeding through the blinds. I felt my cheek go warm as she jiggled a fistful of pills in front of my nose.

"Here." She dropped down on the bed, jogging every sore part of me. "Folic acid. Iron. Take them." She shook her head in disgust of something I couldn't see. "It's too soon for this. Might as well have inseminated every runt in the barn then sat back scratching our heads when all the babies were born dead."

My head ached—there wasn't enough room around the pain to think. "What hap—"

"Mercy is what happened, and don't get used to it because you're not getting it again." She produced a jar full of orange juice, snatched the pills out of my hand, and began grinding them to powder under the glass. She swept the powder into the juice and shoved it at me. "Drink."

Jumbled memories began to gather in my head: sounds and tastes and smells. And the more I felt, the longer I took stock of my body, the less I wanted to know. The heaviness in my stomach wasn't in my stomach, it was lower down, between my legs—an ache, like someone had been kicking me all night. I propped myself up and winced. "I—something's wrong with me. I can't remember…"

"I know you can't remember. That's the point." She settled back, and the sun cut directly across her eyes. "It wasn't much—just a little something to take the fight out of you. But we can't do that every night. This is going to be your job from now on, so you might as well get used to it. Best you can hope for is that it takes right away, but I doubt it with the shape you're in." Her fingers jammed against the glass in my hand, pushing it toward my mouth. "Drink."

Something dark and filthy took root in the corner of my mind. I didn't want to look at it. My eyes darted around the room, if only to distract my body from feeling anything more, anything new. There was a deep scratch stinging my shoulder. My hips felt loose, dislocated.

"I'm leaving you one—*one* more of these," she said, dropping a tiny envelope on the table. I touched the paper and felt a hard lump. "It's plenty strong, so don't take more than half. And that's only for after—"

"After what?"

"—and only if you can't sleep. If you feel up to it tomorrow, you can go out to the barn and see the new calf."

My throat closed when I tried to swallow.

"You know better than any of them that the calf was work for that cow. That's why we picked you over Amaris," my mother said, jerking her head toward the door. "She'd have taken it as an honor—dropped everything and leapt into bed thinking everyone would fetch and carry for her. But it's not an honor, it's a job. I should know."

The pills gave the juice a bitter, metallic taste, and I gagged as the bigger chunks caught in my throat. The first solid memory came back to me: dinner the night before, all of us around the table. Everyone got a hunk of sweet bread and a jar of raw milk. Mine hadn't tasted right, I remembered, it had an acrid tinge, but I drank it anyway, I drank it, and I...

"It's a job," my mother repeated, yanking the glass out of my loosening grip. "You'd better understand that. They're killing themselves out there. Whole world is going over the edge, and if we want to keep this place going, we need more people."

"Mother, what—what did you do to me?"

"We didn't do anything *to* you," she snapped. "We did something *for* us. All of us. And you might think it's ugly, but it's not. It's just life. We need more of you, so you better set an example for the other girls. You're lucky your father found someone. It could've been a lot worse. Do as you're told and it won't take long. He can't bother you while you're carrying. If you behave, the others will go along when we need them. We could triple our numbers in ten years' time."

My mind spun because nothing she was saying made sense. The words made sense, just not the fact she was saying them. They made terrible sense, but they couldn't be true, because...

"Finish your juice," she told me, getting to her feet. "The good news is your temperature was up this morning."

Now the room was spinning, and that dark, filthy thing was still there, embedding itself into all my thoughts. Impregnating them. "What—"

"It means you're ovulating," she said, and her voice was tired, bordering on kind. "And that's good, because he's coming back tonight."

---

Now Cole hesitated by the door, still bathed in shadows. "I brought you something." Whatever it was rested flat on his palm, but it was too dark to see. He stood perfectly still, like he was balancing an invisible tray. "You're bleeding," he said again.

So I was. And good. Blood elucidated better than tears. Blood was not optional, and therefore not weak. My nose hurt—the Man had hit me after I tried to hit him. Then he'd pinned me down on the mattress so I couldn't swing, stripping away my clothes and pushing harder and harder until I felt something inside of me break, pain so great, I couldn't even scream. Pain that lasted and lasted. Same as the night before.

Except this time I was awake.

Cole took three halting steps. I jerked with each one. By the time he made it to the bed, I was pressed against the wall, digging my heels into the mattress.

His eyes widened. "Av, it's me. I'm not going to hurt you."

"No?" I choked.

"Avery…" His voice turned to jelly, and he dropped to his knees next to the bed. "I didn't know. I swear I didn't, and how…how could I stop them?" Moonlit tears pooled in his eyes and vanished in a blink. "How?"

There was no *how*. He was right. I used to believe my father when he said we were too few, but for me, we were too many. It just depended on which side you were standing.

I swallowed, and even that hurt. Cole's fingers tangled in his hair. "God, Avery—what if you have a baby?"

"I will," I said, my voice ugly and deformed. "They won't stop until I do."

"But we have to—"

"*We?*"

"We have to remember we've been chosen," he jabbered. "Right?"

I shook my head. I couldn't bear to spout platitudes of comfort—not when there were no words for me. "I'm the only one who was chosen," I mumbled. "And it's a bad thing."

"Don't say that." His face was like marble in the cool light. "We all were. We were all chosen to—"

"It's not true," I whispered.

He looked at me, stricken. I'd changed the script—he didn't know what came next. "What?"

"I said it's not true. This whole place, everything. We're—"

"Of course it's true, what do you mean?"

I forced his eyes on mine—he had to see me to understand. "I mean they're not protecting us. They're collecting us."

"I don't—"

"Then listen," I said, scrabbling for his hands. The words were tumbling ahead of my thoughts, but I was afraid to stop. "Listen. The calf was born yesterday. And we—we farm and we raise animals and we butcher them and milk them and we plant and harvest—and now they're doing it with us, they want more so they can get more, it's just like the calf. They're *breeding* us."

His eyes widened without understanding. "They wouldn't—"

"They already are! What do you think happened to me tonight?

They're going to use us to grow babies who won't die, more kids to keep in this place, except they'll be *our* kids, not theirs. They'll tell them the stories to keep them scared—"

"Avery, stop! It's not the same."

"Then what is it?"

"We're safe here," he insisted, and I could hear my father's voice resting on top of his, bending it into submission. "You've heard what goes on out there, you know what people are like now—"

"We never knew what people were like!" The rise in my voice hurt my nose, my swollen lip. "We've only ever known each other, all of us, so how could we know?"

"Because Mom and Dad told us—the people who used to be here," said Cole. "They came from the outside, and they died because—"

"They died because they killed themselves, Cole. And if they didn't do it themselves, Dad did it for them. They knew they were trapped, and they were scared."

"But they weren't like us!" Cole said. "They were weak."

His words washed over me, riding on a wave of grief and fear. I felt starkly alone and, worse than that, foolish. Even though I knew he didn't remember that day in the living room, the blood that painted my ballet shoes red, I always believed some part of him understood that we weren't innocent and this place wasn't immune.

He didn't.

Cole couldn't read—not like I could. Years ago, one of the women on the compound had taught me, back when Cole was still too young to learn. It was a memory I'd kept, because it was safe and warm and covered by an itchy woolen skirt. Her name left me, but she had long hair and smiling eyes, and while my parents tended the fields, I'd sit in her lap, spellbound by the way she made shapes into letters and letters into words. I could still see her long, crooked finger as it traced the page. *Cat, hop, big.* I heard her voice in my ear telling me it was a special skill I was learning, not like hunting or farming, a secret one, and I could never tell my parents, ever. She gave me books I squirreled away, culled by the very people who'd lived and died in those square buildings, so fast, they left their stories behind. And I was grateful, because without them, I wouldn't know about things like school and peppermint ice cream and wooden carousels with one brass ring. I knew that, out there, every birthday got a party, and summer meant swimming and beaches and picnics. Things I never could have dreamed up on my own.

They were hard to think about. The *almost* things. Sometimes it hurts worse to miss something you never had.

"Do you remember our lives being good, Cole?" I whispered. "Ever?"

A shadow of confusion darkened his face. The word *good*—he didn't know that it was something to want, something you could just have. "I—"

"Do you remember when Benji was born?"

He looked at me for a minute. "Yes."

"When was that?" My voice was plaintive…begging. "How old is he?"

"Eight, maybe? Ten? I don't know."

I swabbed blood from my nose and looked at him through watery eyes. "How old are you?"

Cole's fingers dabbed my wet cheek. "I don't know."

I squeezed my eyes shut, a dam against the tears. "We can't stay here." The spongy pain between my legs made it easy to say, but it was something I knew and had known—I'd just never had the words for why. They were tucked between the pages of my books, in foaming ocean waves and clouds of cotton candy. In Christmas and movies and bicycles. The reasons were endless, but Cole couldn't read them, so they didn't exist.

My parents must have known that.

"We're supposed to know how old we are," I insisted, harping on something simple and silly. "We're supposed to *know*…"

He didn't answer me for a long time. When his voice came, it was lower than before, more thoughtful than expected. "You would really leave?"

"If you come with me."

His eyes went wild. It was unfair of me to ask, I knew that. "What about Jane?"

I bit my swollen lip. Shook my head.

The wildness vanished. He looked scared now. He looked scared of me. "What if I won't?"

I didn't respond—not right away. My mind turned to the

thought of my own belly rising—to choiceless children, *my* children, who'd be kept and worked, knowing nothing but how to stay alive and hate to live. Children who didn't even know how to hope for anything else.

Cole's face was innocent, lovely—not even a touch of longing. It shimmered and blurred.

"Then I can't," I whispered.

In all those years and all those books, I'd never told him there was something called *school*. Never fed him tales of ice cream and carousels. I thought it would hurt him to know, because it hurt me. But I should have. I should have scattered all those gleaming *almost* things around him like glass, rolled him in the shards of what our lives could have been. I should have stuck him until he bled.

Maybe my gaze was a scratch—he fumbled on the ground next to the bed. "Look." He held up what he'd brought me, something long and flat. "Chocolate."

Hot tears escaped. "You have to stop doing that."

"Too late." He pushed a lock of hair off my forehead. "Share a sign of hope."

I shook my head, even though it was an easy question.

"Come on…"

"I can't."

"It's easy."

The candy bar was clutched in my fist. "It used to be."

Cole stared at me, a line of worry dividing his eyes. "Avery, you—you're okay. Right?"

"Sure." My voice was dead. "I'll get cleaned up, I'll have a little chocolate, I'll be absolutely fine."

"I didn't mean—"

"Go to bed, Cole."

"No, I—I'm worried about you…" His eyes flickered to the window.

I shook my head; fresh blood stained my lips. "They'll kill you if I leave."

"I know."

"So how can I?"

"I'll stay with you," he said in a rush. "I'll sleep here—"

Bile soured the back of my throat. Having someone—anyone— near me would guarantee I wouldn't sleep. "No."

"Are you sure?"

I rolled to my side, knees tight against my chest, and closed my eyes. I would sleep by myself. I'd get there by thinking about my tent, about the knife that was still inside, and the sleeping bag, and the canteen. That would get me to sleep. By myself.

"I'm sure."

He wanted to say more, but there was no more to say. My eyes stayed shut. But before Cole walked away, I felt him lean close. His voice sounded in my ear.

"Is it true? That it's all a lie?"

I wanted to say yes, to believe it would change anything. "Does it matter?"

"Of course it does."

"Not to you. If it did, you would leave here with me tonight," I said to the wall. "If it did, we'd already be gone."

There was a long moment of silence. When Cole's voice came again, it sounded like he was channeling someone else. "No one is going to hurt you again."

"You can't—"

"I won't let them," he said, still distant and strange. "I promise."

His lips bumped my cheek, and then he was gone. The spot stayed cool in the breeze from the window, and my head filled with the sweet scent of the night air. They were nice words, but that was all they were. Words.

The door closed.

I began to drift, so lost in a memory that it turned into a dream. The kind of dream that only comes once but stays with you forever, sleeping quietly in the corner of your mind and refusing to fade until you can never decide if it's old or new.

But later that night, I knew it was an old dream, as old as my time in that place. It was my own fear tucked inside, waiting to escape.

I was afraid I was already gone.

# SEVEN

———————

WE LEARNED WHAT WAS IMPORTANT BEFORE WE LEARNED WHAT WAS EASY.
But the important things were easy, too, once you knew how to get them.
Like water. Water hides. It stays deep underground, so you have to dig a
little, but at least it's there. Fire is different. Making fire is like magic.

First you need wood. It can't be sticky or damp; it has to be dry, and
you need two different kinds, a hard piece and a soft piece. Something
that's going to fight and something that's going to give.

My fingers curled around the tree branch I'd sharpened to a point.
I held it up for inspection. "How's this?"

My father shifted my grip. "Good." He positioned the stick at an
angle against the flat board propped against my knees and moved it up
and down along the groove we'd carved out. "It takes a long time, Avery.
You've got to be really strong to make a spark. Can you do it?"

*"Yes, sir!"*

*"But it's nighttime and it's cold," he said, painting a head picture like he always did when we trained. "It's so cold, you can see your breath... How long do you have without fire and shelter?"*

*"Three hours."*

*"Right. And the only power comes from the sun and the wind, but the wind can't help you and the sun won't be back until morning. If you don't find a way to get warm, you will die. Are you going to die?"*

*"No, sir!"*

*"Prove it."*

*I set the spindle in the groove and pushed, down and up, up and down. It was hard to see, because it really was nighttime, but it wasn't cold, and my sweaty hands slipped against the stick. It was my first fire test, and I had to do it right or else. Fire-plowing was easy—I'd seen Seth do it lots of times, and he wasn't even as old as me. You just push, over and over, until you wear the soft wood down, push until it crumbles into a pile that gets hotter and hotter. It has to get hot enough to fight back. And when it does, you have to be ready to drop those hot crumbles into a bundle of weeds and leaves and blow and blow and blow until it starts to smoke and glows orange and then red, and then...*

Lights. There were lights behind my eyes that didn't make sense. The air was too thin and too cold to belong to the morning. My eyes squeezed tight against the glare.

*"That's it, Avery."* My father sounded happy, but I wanted to cry my

*hands hurt so much. Push, push, push, and there was no smoke, no glow, and I couldn't remember it ever taking Seth so long. My palms were dotted with shards of dark wood, but if I told my father, he'd get the hot needle, and I'd rather keep the splinters. He got behind me and pushed hard on my shoulders, hard enough to bend me in half. "Faster, Avery, that's not good enough!"*

*The wood wouldn't burn. But my arms did—I stopped, and my father barked my name so loud that I jumped; the spindle skidded out of the groove and poked me in the knee. The tiny hole started leaking blood, and my father grabbed my hands and shoved the pointed wood back into place.*

*"Push! As hard as you can, Avery, push!"*

*I pushed and I kept pushing, and all of a sudden, I saw my mother on the ground in front of me, her face white and pouring sweat. Her stomach was big again, it rose under her graying nightgown, and she was pushing too. I heard Amaris yelling the same words at her that my father was yelling at me: push, push, push! There was blood dripping from her legs onto the leaves, and my hands were bleeding, too, ripped to shreds from the blisters and the wood, and my father and Amaris still yelled, and my mother and I still screamed. But we pushed, both of us, until the pain moved from my hands to my belly. All at once my mother was holding the stick, and I was bleeding into the dirt, a slick, bluish baby resting on my chest.*

*My father's big, calloused fingers reached down and nudged the baby's cheek. "He's not good enough, Avery."*

*"No..." I was panting, and everything hurt. The baby let out a feeble cry.*

*"Give him to me."*

*"What are you going to do?"*

*"I have to take care of him."*

*"No, he's mine—"*

*"He's weak."*

*"No..." As I moved to touch the baby's face, the stick in my mother's hand suddenly flared to life, her face shimmering behind the heat. It wasn't the nice, smoky smell of campfires; it was oily and acrid, and the black smoke singed my nose. The baby stirred in my arms, and I tried to shield him from the...*

smoke

Smoke.

*"Push!"*

The voice yanked my father's hands from my shoulders and erased the blood from my legs, but it didn't silence the burning stick. The air was pulsing and bright, and I wasn't even sure if my eyes were open. The crackling, popping sounds were still there, joined by a light scattering of feet, a long scraping sound, and then something heavy hit my door.

At that my eyes flew open for real, in terror of what I might find, but the room was empty and pitch-black—even the moon was gone. Time had turned in for the night and left me on my own. I threw the covers aside, and my bare feet hit the floor. The burning smoke had followed me out of my dream. It was leaking under the door, rising toward the ceiling in gray curls.

My steps were shaky and full of dull pain. Someone was screaming on the other side of the door, a lot of someones. My fingers touched the doorknob. It was cool, but when I twisted it, the door wouldn't open.

"Amaris?" I called, slapping the wood. "Amaris, what's happening? I can't get the door open—"

"No, get out of there!" Hannah—far off. "Jane is—"

I heard the squeak of a door and another voice—Candace, still sleepy, and rational in her confusion. "Did somebody run away?"

Something behind the door popped and sizzled. I yelled, "Amaris!"

"No, leave it there, take Sarah, and get outside!"

"Where's Benji?"

"I'm over here!"

There was a long, wailing shriek. More banging followed, the crash of breaking glass.

"Don't! She—"

"*Who ran away?*" Candace screamed. That was followed by a harsh, barking cough and a meaty thud. A different voice responded without words—it only screamed.

"Amaris!" The door wasn't locked, it was stuck. I turned the knob and rammed the wood with my shoulder, but it held fast. The voices to the right were fading, but the screams on the left were not. They were horrifying, painful, and I joined them with a scream of my own, my voice catching on the words. "Help me!"

"*Cole?*"

It was a beckoning, searching tone—he wasn't with them. "Cole," I cried, beating at the door. "Cole!"

"Hannah, go! Get them outside!"

"The doors are burning!"

A crash. Another scream that started long and then cut off.

Something exploded, and I felt the shudder as the blast hit my door—the bottom lit with an eerie, pulsing glow.

"*No!*"

Amaris's words were swallowed by the roar of burning wood. "Peter! Somebody…dead…I think Cole—Avery…"

Her voice trickled and died. I beat at the door, landing solid, flat blows that resonated dully on the splintered wood. "Amaris? *Amaris!*" The crackling was louder, and I pounded harder, tearing at the rough boards until my palms slid across the grain in a sticky smear. I stared at my hands—they were a mess of torn skin and dark, bloody splinters. The door groaned in response to my pause, and I stepped backward so quickly, I tripped and landed flat on my back. The heat was dizzying; I could *see* it, a heavy shimmer denser than the air. I crawled to the window. My hands scrabbled against the glass and left red prints, but the screen wouldn't budge.

The glow that had started behind my eyes was real now. It was eating the door with hot tongues that licked the underside of the wood. I pulled my nightgown over my mouth and nose and yanked one end of the bed away from the wall. My fire-plow was under there, the spindle lying neatly in the groove. I snatched it up, using the sharp end to jab at the screen until the point tore a hole in the mesh wide enough for my fingers. I wedged my hands into the gap, ripped the screen open, and squeezed through.

It wasn't a graceful escape—I fell out the window shoulder first, and the rest of my body twisted and slithered to the ground. Rocks and gravel dug into my feet as I ran toward the front of the building, toward where I'd heard the voices. My eyes combed the pulsing dark for people, movement, anything. I was running full tilt when I tripped over something and fell face-first into the dirt.

Broken glass glittered on the ground—I had landed on the bent frame of another screen that hadn't been ripped but shoved through the window. When I pushed myself up, I had to blink three times before I could understand what I was seeing.

"Jane?" I whispered.

She was lying on her side, one hand flung over her head like she was trying to answer a question. "Oh no, no, no...Jane?" I tapped her cheek with my fingertips and rolled her to her back. Her eyes were open but blank, like those of a doll, and there was a sticky pool making mud around her head. She'd probably landed the same way I did.

But it's a long drop from the second floor.

I jammed my fists into my eyes until stars danced in the blackness. Blood from my hands printed her cheeks, and I tapped her again, even as I noticed more: the grotesque length of her neck, the loose roll of her head. Things that told me not to bother.

The window behind me shattered in a shower of glass and puffs of black smoke. I jumped to my feet and broke into a clumsy, shambling run, away from Jane's empty gaze, taking gulping breaths that sounded like sobs. I clutched my fire-plow to my chest. "Sarah?" I managed. "Benji? Cole?"

Windows were popping like balloons, spraying glass everywhere. I ran until I was out of reach, skidding to a stop next to the gate to the fields. Suddenly, the building seemed to sigh in defeat. The right eye of the compound wilted like melting plastic, and the fire escaped in a burst of rage that crawled across the breezeway to eat away at the other side. A plume of black smoke rose like a tornado, and the hair on my arms crackled in the heat.

I took a last, desperate look, and then I turned and ran as fast as I could toward my tent, because I knew that Cole would run there too. Maybe they all had.

I almost made it. I wasn't even fifty feet away when the world exploded.

# EIGHT

I FELT THE BLAST BEFORE I HEARD IT. AN INVISIBLE HAND PICKED ME up and threw me in a wide, graceless arc, and I landed on my back just in time to see a mushroom of flames rise in the sky. There was no air. I'd been thrust into space; my lungs were flat and my head filled with hollow vibrations.

The main building had collapsed into a two-hundred-foot firepit. The rest of the compound stood bravely, engulfed in flames bright enough to obliterate every star in the sky—other suns warming other places.

I crawled backward on my elbows for a few yards before I tried to get to my feet, and even then, I couldn't. The world had gone vertical, so I flipped over and climbed, digging my hands and knees into the dirt. The afterimage of the mushroom was printed on everything, blocking what little vision I had. My ears were still buzzing, but I kept climbing.

My trip through the air had twisted me around, but I knew I was still on planting land. Beet tops scraped my knees, and cucumber leaves snatched tiny bits of skin from my arms and legs. There were broken tomato stalks, and pieces of fence wire, and…

For the tiniest moment, I thought the explosion had snatched the baby out of the earth, ripped him from his cradle grave—but the skin under my fingers was too firm, the shape too big. I saw Jane again, her blank doll eyes, and I squeezed my own shut as I crawled over the silent form. I faced the fire, borrowing the light, and there was nothing left to do but look. I opened my eyes.

*We have to remember we've been chosen.*

Maybe we had.

"Cole?" I whispered, touching his cheek. His eyes were closed; he was all splayed out. I pressed my hand to his neck. "Cole?"

His pulse thrummed against my fingers. I shook him, turning my whisper into a scream. I slapped him as hard as I dared. His head rolled boneless in the dirt, but his eyes opened and even looked normal for half a second before they turned up and showed nothing but white. I grabbed him under both arms and started to drag him backward. I could just make out the pitch of my tent, and I got us there in seconds. The fire ate up the entire horizon.

Sweat was soaking my hair, pouring down my face in torrents as

I eased Cole to the ground. The second building fell in an echoing crack, but that wasn't what made me jump. Something else did. Something high and whining and tuneful, like a song. I could see a different kind of flashing, organized flashing, and then there was something rolling down the only road in and out of our compound. Something big and red and loud.

"Oh my God…"

The big, red car stopped. Another one pulled in behind it.

"Oh no…oh, please. Cole," I moaned, dropping down next to him. "Oh God. Please wake up, please…"

He didn't listen. I pinched his cheeks and got no response. My fingers clawed at the neck of his T-shirt, and when I dragged my knuckles across his sternum, digging into the bone, his head rolled on its own. My water buckets were still perched at the corners of the tent. I picked one up and dumped it on his head.

His eyes shot open, and he let out a low, choking gurgle. I clapped my hands over his mouth. Across the field, dark shapes were running toward the fire, and there were more flashing lights as more cars arrived in a line. I reached for the tent flaps, fumbling with the ties.

Cole's voice was heavy and slow. "What—"

"Everything's on fire. We have to get in the tent."

"Where's—"

"Now!"

His eyes were open, but when he tried to sit up, he flopped over sideways. I grabbed him under the arms again and crab-walked backward, dragging him through the flaps. I tied them shut with shaking hands.

"Avery, what—"

"The compound's on fire." I peered through a tear in the canvas. Thrashing white snakes were spitting water on the flames.

"Wh—which part?"

"All of it," I whispered as the pulsing grew brighter despite the water and the shouts from the men in the cars. "All of it…"

"Where is everyone else?"

I glanced over my shoulder.

"Where's Jane and Benji and everyone? Did they get out?"

"I don't know."

"We have to find them!" He sounded closer to normal, but when I turned to face him, he was slumped against my sleeping bag, his eyes half-closed. "We have to make sure they're okay—"

"We can't. There are people out there…"

"Who?"

"From outside. They must have seen the smoke," I murmured. "They're trying to put it out."

"We have to—"

"No!"

He cringed and put one hand over his head. He wore the bloody print of my hand across his mouth and chin; his own fingers were tipped black with soot.

"No," I repeated, willing my voice not to shake. "We need to stay here until the fire's out and those men leave, do you understand me?"

"But what if—"

"They're fine. They're probably hiding. Once the fire's out…" I glanced through the tear again. "Once it's out we'll look for them."

"But what then?" Fear and confusion were making him tearful. His eyes darted wildly. "What are we going to do?"

"We're going to stay here." He shook his head until I gripped his shoulders, leveling my gaze on his. "Cole, hey—look at me. Just look at me. We are fine. We know what to do," I said carefully. "We were chosen to know, right? To survive?"

His head rose and fell, not quite a nod.

"So maybe it's not *the* end, but it's *an* end, so what do we need right now? I want you to tell me."

"I can't…"

"Yes, you can. Start with number one. What's the number one thing we need?"

"Focus," he whispered.

"That's right, and you need it bad, kiddo. What else?"

He blinked hard. "Focus," he said again. "Shelter…water…" His voice faltered and died.

"And fire," I whispered. He nodded miserably, curling up next to me like he used to when we were little, when he would sneak into my room in the middle of the night.

But I flinched. I didn't mean to—I couldn't help it. I couldn't stand the feel of his skin against mine. I pulled away, and Cole fell back against the sleeping bag.

"We're fine," I went on, pushing dripping strands of hair away from his face with the tips of my fingers. "Focus on being okay right where we are. That's all we need to do."

"How did you get out?" Cole asked. "I never—how did you know?" His voice was heavy. I didn't like it, the heaviness. He didn't sound right.

"I went out the window," I told him, taking his hand in mine. I could smell the fire on him, on both of us. The same blackness that tipped his fingers blotted out most of my skin. I was nearly invisible in the dark. "And I heard Amaris and Hannah and Peter and Benji— they're okay. Probably everyone's okay. I bet they went to the storm cellar."

"They'll be safe there?"

"They'll be fine. How did you get out?" I asked him.

He shook his head. "I just…I was talking to you, and then I…I went outside. I can't—"

"It's okay." His eyes flickered once and closed. I wished for some kind of light so I could see him better, but our land was so flat, you could watch fireflies dance from a mile away. Smoke had begun to roll in billows over the grounds, forced to flee as the water took out the flames. "Once it's out and they leave, we'll find everyone else. We'll figure out what to do."

"I did it for you."

His voice was so low, I wasn't sure I heard him right. "Did what?"

"You asked me to help you," he mumbled. "I was helping you. I was waiting for you. The tent's our place. Remember?"

"Sure." I tugged the top flap of my sleeping bag over him. Cole seemed relieved by my agreement. I sat next to him and pulled my knees to my chest. He smelled like clean, black soil and grass mixed with the smoke that clung to us both. Fine lines of white vapor followed my words, but I didn't feel cold. "We just have to wait."

# NINE

---

THE FIRE BURNED ALL NIGHT, WAVES OF ORANGE AND BLACK THAT briefly turned to white smoke before finding more pieces of our lives to devour. My thoughts drifted in the swirling ash, inviting me to put it back together. In my mind's eye, I gathered the falling dust like a snowball, packed it tight until it turned into the ballet slippers I'd stuffed under the floorboards, into Hannah's pencils, and the animals in the barn, and all the rooms crammed with things that were supposed to last us the rest of our lives.

Morning came, tinged gray with a dirty mist the sun couldn't break through. I sat up painfully, remembering all at once that I would have more to fear if my family were still alive than if they weren't. The fire had temporarily erased the bigger tragedy, the one I wanted to forget anyway, but I knew that would never happen, even if the whole world burned.

My mouth felt dirty and dry. I took a mouthful of water that tasted ashy, and when I spit it out, it was black. Cole was all bunched up in the sleeping bag. I'd spent the night rolled in a tight ball to fight the chill, but it was warmer now. The sun was working even if I couldn't see it. I left Cole where he was and peered through the hole in the tent.

The minute I did, I knew I'd slept or maybe I had yet to wake up. The compound was gone. All of it. There was nothing but a vast expanse of blackened flatland. My mind flashed in a million directions—I wondered if the fire had gotten far enough to overtake the storm cellar, I wondered if the men had been able to get to Jane's body before the flames did.

I wondered if anyone else was alive.

Behind me, Cole twitched in his sleep. He was alive. I was alive. That was enough. I crawled through the flaps of the tent. Two of the red cars were still there, and now there were others—black and white cars that had the same kind of flashing lights on top, box-shaped cars with crosses painted on the sides. At least a dozen people were combing the black hole in the ground.

My first absurd urge was to run screaming to them, to grab Cole and beg those people to help us, please. To take us away from there, away from our father. I'd rather hedge my bets on the outside than spend the next twenty years being ground against a stained mattress so I could deliver another chosen child on it nine months later.

My mouth watered with want. A craving for something unknow-able. Something I couldn't predict, because I'd never had it before.

But my parents might be with them. There might be a story in place. Who we were. Why we were out there.

I tried to breathe, and it got caught in my throat.

*Focus.*

My first urge. My first absurd urge.

Maybe not.

I took another breath—it tasted like ash and hurt my ribs. I glanced back into the tent. A sliver of Cole's sleeping face peeked through the canvas. He wouldn't go. He'd never go.

But the compound was gone. And his partner was Jane. Jane was dead.

I turned and looked into the woods. The southern edge of the perimeter was only a hundred feet away.

We would disappear.

We *could* disappear.

The people milling over the wreck of the compound were closer than I'd thought. There were two men standing near the gate to the footpath that led to the field, practically on top of where Cole and I had buried the baby. I saw two more men pushing what looked like a bed on wheels toward one of the square white cars. There was something on it, all covered with a sheet. When they got to the car, they lifted the bed and pushed it inside. I scanned the faces, and the shapes. Nothing was familiar.

My eyes landed on another bed covered with another sheet. My gaze caught on it like a thorn from a briar. Cole and I *had* talked last night. I'd been too mixed up when he'd mentioned it, but now I remembered. Before I went to sleep, he'd snuck into my room and sat on my bed. He brought me chocolate, and I poured out everything that had happened, everything I'd seen and heard. And he was afraid I would run, that I'd leave him there...

*"They'll kill you if I leave."*

*"I know."*

*"So how can I?"*

But I'd never do that. And no one knew Cole was with me. I looked at him again, and just turning my head hurt. Everything hurt. Pain that was deep and embedded. Pain that was implanted. It would never go away.

I dropped to my knees and barged back into the tent. Cole didn't move. My fire-plow was lying on the ground. I plunged my hands under the foot of the sleeping bag, positive I'd find nothing, but my knife and cooking pan were exactly where I'd left them. My magnifying glass was under the rock I used as a table, along with a ball of wire, a length of string, and the remains of the gauze Cole had stolen for me. My canteen. Plastic bottles of water. A dozen dented tin cans. Three paperback books.

There were two satchels stuffed in the corner. Jane had made them from the same cornflower-blue cotton as my father's shirt. One of the bags was half-full of old clothes, but the other one was empty. I crammed the pan and the bottles and everything else on top of the clothes, and then I yanked at the ties connecting the tent canvas to the poles until half of the heavy, damp sheets fell onto our heads.

Cole's eyes opened, floating in a milky haze. "What...?"

"We have to leave," I said shortly, kicking one of the poles. It fell, taking a chunk of black dirt with it. "We have to get out of here before they see us."

He blinked up at me. "Who?"

"The men, the ones who put out the fire."

Confusion bruised his features. I could see the night fall into place, and it was so much more than he could process fresh from sleep. "Oh, wait...we have to find every—"

"They're gone," I said, letting a sob bleed through. "They didn't make it. The explosion—"

"Wha—no!" He sounded furious, and for a tiny moment, I thought he might hit me. "That's not true, don't say that!"

"The armory blew, I saw it—"

"*Shut up!* You said they were okay. We have to look for them, we have to—"

"We can't. If those men see us, they're going to take us—"

"They can't take us—we can't *leave*..."

"Yes, they can!" I leaned in, propping the canvas up with my hands. "I want you to be quiet and listen to me." I waited until his eyes settled on mine before I spoke. "They're dead," I told him. "The armory exploded. They're dead."

"But you said—"

"I was wrong."

Understanding dawned, but it didn't bring agreement. "No."

"They're dead, Cole. There's nothing left, so let's just take whatever we can and go."

"Go *where*?"

"We'll set up camp in the woods," I said, rolling a sheet of canvas as tight as it would go. "But we have to get out of sight. We have to get off the grounds."

"They can't be dead," he moaned. "Not everyone..."

"*Cole!*" I wanted to slap him. "They're gone, there's nothing we can do for them, and if we stay here, those men are going to take us." I kicked another pole. "What are the rules? Tell me the rules. What has to happen today?"

He blinked, and his eyes cleared a tiny bit. "This—I...we have to use today...to do whatever is going to keep us alive tomorrow."

"Yes, good." My hands fumbled on the canvas ties—any minute now someone really could see us, my father could emerge very much alive and grab both of us, one under each arm, and make this start all over again somewhere new. The people in the field had a clear view now that the sun was up. I didn't think the police could take me away, but I wasn't sure about Cole. He was younger than me.

I just didn't know how much.

"It's...we'll be fine," I told him. "We'll come up with a story, we'll figure out somewhere to live, and—"

"Out *there?*"

I said nothing. I finished rolling the tent and stuffed the canvas into the empty satchel. Cole was still packed in the sleeping bag on the ground. "Get out of there and roll it up—"

"*Mason!*"

It was a shout, a man's voice, loud and close. I yanked Cole's arm so hard, I heard something pop, and we both ducked down. "Run," I ordered. "Don't look back, just run."

But neither of us could run—not really. We broke into a shambling trot, dragging the tent and the sleeping bag, and it was very much like being frozen in a dream—the one that grabs hold of your ankles and slows you down just enough for the monsters to get you.

"Over here," I hissed, stopping at the base of a forked tree.

We got behind the tree and peered through a space in the trunk. The men were harder to see, but they still weren't that far away.

"Roll up the sleeping bag," I whispered, shoving the tent canvas deeper into the satchel. The cloth was rough against my sore fingers. As I tightened the ties, a sudden rush of tears threw me off-kilter—such grief over bags. The fabric was sturdy in my hands—well-made—they were both filled to bursting, but they were stitched tight, expertly. "Jane," I blurted. I bit my lip, but I couldn't catch her name before he heard it.

Cole's head dropped between his shoulders. He had the sleeping bag strapped to his back, and he bent over to pick up one of the
packs. When he felt the fabric, a shudder moved through him.

"I don't think they saw us," I whispered, shouldering my own bag.
"But we need to get into the woods…"

For a minute it looked like he might do it. Then he stopped and
peered out to where the compound used to be, his eyes showing as
much life as Jane's had.

"Cole?" I said. "You ready?"

He shook his head slowly. "We had it backward." He gestured
toward the ruins of our home, the tight groups of strangers combing
the remains. "It was us. We killed ourselves."

"No," I said, hitching up my bag. "Not all of us. Let's go."

# TEN

---

THE AIR INSIDE THE WOODS WAS WET AND GREEN, BUT IT WASN'T choked. We could breathe it. Once we got moving, Cole either caught my fear or found some of his own, and that made it easier to hurry. We slipped and skidded over damp leaves for miles, carrying the bags and the tent and the monsters, real and imagined, that skimmed our shoulders and bit at our heels. It was a giddy, terrified march—neither of us looked back, and as we got farther away, the monsters melted in the sun and our fear fell, taking the adrenaline with it.

Cole shuffled next to me in a cloud of disbelief—every so often, he stopped and stared at the trees with his mouth wide open, like they'd somehow abducted us. The forest mascots had woken up, we were already slapping mosquito bites, and chiggers stuck to us like burrs. I was still wearing my bloody nightgown, my hair tangled all the way down to my waist. Every step I took drove needles and rocks into my bare feet.

"Stop," I said, letting my bag drop. We'd stepped into a small clearing, relatively free of scrubby underbrush. My shoulders protested the shift in weight and produced a deep achiness that stretched to the small of my back.

Cole bumped into a tree, his eyes wide and blank. "Where are we?"

"I don't know," I told him, "but we need to figure out where we're going." It was close to noon; the sun was almost directly overhead. I knelt and swiped at a wide patch of dirt that was free of shadows. When Cole saw what I was doing, he ran back into the tangle of trees and returned with a stick as long as his arm—by then I had a clean, flat circle about three feet across. He handed me the stick.

"Which way should we go?"

"Away," I mumbled, jabbing the stick into the ground. "Far away." The shadow fell, long and thin. I dug my fingertip into the dirt at the very top. "Sit down for a few minutes."

Cole turned and looked me full in the face, probably for the first time since he'd left my room the night before. "You're a mess."

"I'm fine."

He pulled a water bottle from his bag. "Close your eyes."

I did. The water felt like heaven on my skin. It ran red and black with blood and smoke, and what I swore would be my final memories of that place. I let it all drip to the ground. Cole wiped away the rest of the grime and placed his hands gently on my cheeks, probing the bridge of my nose with his thumbs. I could smell the fire on his fingers, and I jerked away. "Don't—"

"Your nose was bleeding. You're all swollen. Does that hurt?"

"No…"

"Then sit still."

I tried, but the jerking returned with his touch. My feet pedaled, and my hands slapped his away.

"Avery, stop! What's the matter with you?"

"Nothing, I just—don't touch me."

"You might have burst something," he said, pulling away. "That was a lot of blood."

Peter had burst something in his nose once—a vessel or a capillary. It bled until he turned the color of cream and could barely stand up. Mother had to cauterize it. She curled a wire to a soft end and held it in the fire until it glowed. His scream was like nothing I'd ever heard, but it didn't bleed after that.

The replay of that incident must have been painted on my face. "I don't have any wire," Cole said with a little smile. He dampened a handkerchief and came at me again, gently wiping at the flakes of blood clinging to the underside of my nose.

The cloth was cool against my skin. The morning air had melted from gray to gilded, bright streaks that lit us up through the trees. The fire was gone, officially.

I pushed his hand away. "Have some water."

Cole dropped to a flat rock with the bottle and took three measured gulps. He had dried mud caked on his clothes, but he looked relatively untouched by the fire. I was wearing it. I rummaged through my satchel and turned up a spare dress and blouse, two undershirts, and a pair of jeans Peter had given me. No shoes.

I stripped off my nightgown and used the wet handkerchief to wipe blood off my legs. Cole was staring at his hands, rubbing his sooty fingers with the hem of his shirt. I yanked the jeans up over my hips. "Anything yet?" I asked, nodding toward the stick.

"I think...yeah." Cole made another indentation in the dirt while I pulled an undershirt over my head. The tip of the shadow hadn't traveled far, but it was enough to tell us that the world was still spinning. "East," he said, tapping the new mark. "And we came from that way, so—"

"We'll go west."

We walked all day, mostly without speaking—every step pulled us further over the edge of escape, even though we were still tethered and both knew it. We could be yanked back at any moment.

Our eyes moved constantly, searching for flowing water, for food. Mulberries weren't ripe until summer, but they were still edible— tangy, with only the faint promise of sweetness. We gobbled them until our fingers bled juice and our lips darkened to purple gashes. We found pecans, too, and Cole chewed dandelion leaves, but the taste was too earthy for me.

"We better set up shelter before we lose the sun," I told Cole. My stomach was starting to tighten from fruit and water. "We need to get a fire going."

Cole didn't respond.

I squinted up at the red sky and the treetops dipped in melted gold. "I thought we'd have found something by now."

Cole had stopped walking. His eyes were wide, staring at nothing as he absently ran his finger under the strap of the bag on his shoulder. "Jane made these," he said.

I stopped too. "I know."

"Remember Dad's shirt?"

"Yeah..."

"Sleeves were too short," he mumbled. The bag slid off his shoulder and hit the ground like a lead slug. It was the most he'd said since we left the clearing. He'd kept slightly behind me as we walked, the way I used to when my father brought me into the woods and I wasn't sure of the way. But this was different—neither of us was sure of the way. It would have been nice to have Cole next to me.

"What'll we do?" His voice was low and hoarse. "When we find something?"

"Depends on what we find," I said, tugging at my own straps.

"I guess."

"We're not finding anything tonight. Let's just set up here. I packed cans in one of the bags. I don't know what's in them, but it'll be better than nothing." I looked at my shredded palms and then shrugged out of my pack. "I have the plow, but my hands are a mess." I found the board and spindle and pulled them free. "Would you start the fire?"

Cole looked at the fire-plow, but he didn't take it. Instead he burst into tears with a ferocity that scared me, collapsing like a pile of sticks as he sobbed into the blue bag. He cried, and I stood there, one hand pressed to my mouth.

After a minute I knelt and touched his shoulder. "Cole…"

He jerked away from my touch more violently than I had his, curling into a shaking ball. I felt empty just watching him. Cold. I had no tears—I'd used them all on myself. When it came to grief over what was lost, my father was right: I had nothing to contribute.

I left Cole where he was and spread one of the canvas sheets on the ground under a wide tree. I took two more pieces and tied the corners together. After a few throws, I managed to hook them over an overhanging branch. I put a rock in each corner to widen the base, collected my bag, and brought it inside.

Ten minutes later I had a circle of rocks and sticks perched over a jumble of twigs and dry weeds just outside the tent. I picked up the fire-plow. There was blood caked in the grain from all the other nights fire didn't come without sacrifice. Again, my hands bled, but eventually the weeds caught, then smoked, then roared to orange life, the embers squirming like maggots. I walked over to where Cole was still lying on the ground. "Cole? Come on, let's get in the tent."

He didn't move. I got my arms under his and dragged him backward. He slumped between the folds of canvas.

My rifling fingers found the cans at the bottom of my pack. I stacked a few on the ground, ignoring the way my hands were shaking. "Are you okay?"

His eyes were like two bloody gashes. "How do you know they're all dead?"

My fingers tightened on a can. "I saw them—I saw them being carried away. And I saw Jane on the ground outside her window. Her neck was broken."

He swallowed hard. "Are you sure?"

I remembered the pool of blood that haloed her head, her blank doll face. "Yeah," I said, blinking my own eyes like her dead gaze was contagious, blinking hard enough to hurt.

Cole wouldn't look away. "She's the only one you saw?"

"I told you, they took the rest of them on those beds—"

"That doesn't mean they were dead."

"They were, Cole, they were all covered up—"

"I think we should go back."

They were plain and uncomplicated, but his words stunned me as much as my wanting to leave had stunned him. "What?"

"I want to go back. I want to make sure."

"Yeah, well, I don't." I picked up a can and rubbed the top briskly across a chunk of rock.

"I have to. Just to check—"

"There's nothing to go back to."

"Not for you," he said, and there was an edge of accusation in his tone, blatant and fiery. "You wanted to leave, you're—"

"I'm what? Tired of getting beaten up?" I spat. "Scared of being raped again?" His eyes narrowed at the word, like I'd started speaking a different language, another concept alien to him. "I've read things, Cole, you haven't, and that's what it's called when someone has sex with you and you don't want to. It's called *rape*," I hissed. "And if you ever bothered to step out of what—what they told us is normal and what they told us we have to do, you might know that. And I'm not..." My voice broke, and I mashed my lips together to keep the tears at bay. "I'm not," I said again.

Splotches of red bloomed high on his cheeks. "You're not scared?"

"I *am* scared," I said, slamming the can down next to the fire. "I'm as scared as you are, but I can't go back to that place."

"We all got hurt, Avery. It wasn't just you. I know that what...what happened was bad, but you don't—"

"No, *you* don't," I said, pushing dry wood into the fire. "You don't understand. Go back if you want, but nobody's telling me what to do anymore."

The fire crackled and popped in its little stone house. I hated it. I hated that we needed it. Turning away from Cole, I curled up on the canvas floor, ignoring the timid warmth carried on the breeze.

I stayed there for a long time, and the only thing I heard was the jagged rhythm of my own breathing. Cole didn't speak and he didn't move. I was touching sleep when his voice came again. "Avery."

I didn't respond.

A rustling followed, the awkward and clumsy gathering of too-long limbs. Cole lay down behind me.

"Don't touch me!"

"I won't," he said. "I'm sorry."

I waited a beat. "Are you?"

"I'm scared. I'm really scared."

"I know."

"And I'm sad—about everything. But mostly because you aren't."

"What does that mean?"

I couldn't see him, but I felt him deflate. Something like disappointment colored his words, though they were more carefully chosen. "It's almost like—like this isn't enough. I know you…I know you wanted to get away from Mom and Dad, but our whole family is gone, everything we had, and you're still not…"

"Not what?"

"You're not—you just don't seem sad."

But I *was* sad—in some abstract way that was still liquid in my mind. I was sad for lying to Cole, for making him believe they were all dead when I really didn't know, I was sad because it was just like my father said—I was selfish.

My voice emerged, creaky and choked, but still lying. "It was an accident, Cole. And it's not like we ran away from everything like it was. There's nothing left."

"What if there's nothing out there either?"

"We're going to have to find out."

"And then what?"

"I don't know." I sat up so quickly that Cole rolled away, and I reached for the can next to the fire—the top popped off easily. I dumped the contents into my cooking pan expecting beans, or maybe pasta and sauce—something substantial. Instead, a wave of golden juice splashed my wrist, followed by yellow rings that sizzled and hissed on the hot metal. We both stared at it. "Pineapple," I said, finally.

The ghost of a smile waved across Cole's face before it was blown away by the cooling breeze. "What are we going to do?" he whispered.

I pulled the pan off the flame. "We're going to have pineapple for dinner," I told him. "Tomorrow we'll do something else."

# ELEVEN

___

COLE AND I BROKE THROUGH THE WOODS AND FOUND A ROAD ON OUR third day out. We walked on it until a car stopped, and a toothless man with a grease-lined face offered us a ride. He barely glanced at me, but when his eyes settled on Cole, they took on a hunter's glint, like he wanted to eat him alive. We ran, ducking back into the woods while he screamed at us to stop. He was old and slow, and we could hear him wheezing from twenty feet away. We stayed hidden in the brush until the door slammed and the rumble of the car faded into space.

When it started to get dark, we tried again, but then it was a truck that stopped, a truck full of boys who kept their eyes on me and didn't even look at Cole. They coasted alongside us, and we ignored them until one boy reached out and let his fingers skim my bare arm. I let out a panicked scream that scared them more than they scared me. Cole yanked me off the road, and we walked in the opposite direction for a mile until we were sure they were gone.

After that we stuck to the woods. When it began to storm, we were grateful for the cover and even happier to stop walking for the day. The windblown rain forced us to get more creative with the tent than just hanging it from a tree. We set it up next to a steep rock face, propping the canvas with the biggest sticks we could wrestle into the ground, and got soaked in the process. Our wet clothes were spread flat near the glowing flames. I loaned Cole the dry jeans and an undershirt and forced myself to put on my nightgown, ignoring the bloodstains as I did. My hair was still damp, and the chill seemed to penetrate every inch of my skin.

Cole sat on the other side of the fire and watched me heat up our canned dinner. I had no idea what it was. The pan looked like it was full of glue, but we were too hungry to care. He was staring at me with a weird smile on his face. "What?" I asked.

"What?"

"Why are you smiling?"

He stretched out on the tarp. "I was just thinking."

"About what?"

Cole smiled again. "Seth and Amaris."

My stomach gave a painful lurch. I drew my knees to my chest. "What about them?"

"They were doing it, you know."

Rain pounded the canvas, and the drops that splashed inside made the fire spit. My finger touched a hot spot on the pan, and I yanked it back with a hiss. "They were not!"

"Uh-huh."

"How do you know?"

"I saw them." Cole propped himself up on one elbow and squinted at me in the dark. "Twice, but I bet they did it more than that. I caught them once in the barn and once in Seth's room."

I remembered Seth's big, ruddy face—the way he always smelled sweaty. Amaris had tiny hands and feet, and even when she walked, she looked like she was dancing. "I don't believe you."

Cole shrugged. "His room was right next to mine. They weren't quiet."

My stomach tightened again, and I tipped the mush that might have been chicken from the pan into the tin can he was using as a bowl.

"You don't want any?"

"No." I flopped on my back and wiggled into the open sleeping bag. "You're being disgusting."

"This is disgusting," Cole said, frowning into the can. He still ate it, though, tipping the gloppy mess into his open mouth. It was gone in two swallows. When he was done, he shoved the can into the corner of the tent and stretched out next to me.

"Ugh, *Seth*..." A shudder racked me from head to toe, and I tried to pretend it was for a different reason—I didn't like the conversation, but I was still fighting the revulsion of my own body and Cole still wasn't talking much. It had only been the last day or so that he'd started to sound normal again. After that first night, he hadn't brought up what happened to me. Half the time I didn't think he even remembered. I wasn't going to remind him.

"So he's disgusting, but Amaris isn't?"

"No, if they were doing that, they both are."

"It's not like they had anyone else around."

"Jesus, Cole...that does not make it okay."

I could feel a slight bristle in his voice. "Am I disgusting, too?"

"Right now? Absolutely."

"Shut up."

"You asked." I was being honest. We were both pretty gross, but it was a state we were used to. I pulled the sleeping bag tightly over my shoulders. My nightgown was thin, and the damp chill pushed my skin into tight knobs; Cole was covered in them too. "Get in, quick."

"Are you going to bed already?"

"I'm tired. You can stay awake if you want to, but I'd rather not freeze to death."

"You're tired, I'm starving," he grumbled under his breath. "I'm done with these cans. We're killing something tomorrow." He wiggled next to me, closed the sleeping bag over both of us, and zipped it up.

I said nothing. We were almost out of canned food, anyway, relying more and more on the nuts and roots we found. The cache of cans back at the compound had been massive, three rooms full, not to mention the fruits and vegetables and livestock. Out here we just had snacks. We'd combined our supplies to one bag apiece, with the bulk of the space taken up by the sleeping bag and rolled-up tent canvas. The few cans we had left, we saved for the nights, because it was easier to sleep when we had something in our stomachs.

"Do you think it'll rain all night?" Cole asked me. He lay just behind me, the entire length of his body pressed against mine. I didn't love the arrangement, but I didn't say anything. I couldn't. We only had the one bag and each other—it would have been worse to put those words between us. It became clear early on that my tactile contact issues would have to wait until we were better settled. I could cringe all I wanted, but the truth was we had to stay close if we wanted to stay in one piece. Cole couldn't be snatched away by a greasy old man if we were both in one sleeping bag, and if a bunch of kids in a truck tried to grab me while I slept, Cole would be the first to know. It was also convenient when he woke up crying, or I did, which seemed to happen every night. Spreading flames danced behind Cole's eyes. My father's shadow darkened mine.

We both had bad dreams.

"It better rain all night," I said, working my fists into my eyes and yawning. "I set all the water bottles outside."

"Good idea," Cole said.

"I know."

"Mantra?"

"Go ahead."

"Today we brought strength to all we did—"

"So we can become something greater than human when humanity is dead," I finished with him. We said the mantra every night, just like we had when we lived at home—not quite a prayer, because for us there was no one to pray to. My father, in some vague, undeclared way, had been the highest power our whole lives, but now he was gone, and for some reason, the mantra felt more helpful now, truer. We weren't forced to say it, but we were living by those words. We had to believe them.

Cole laughed suddenly, a short, hard burst. "Remember—do you remember Benji getting his leg stuck in the well?"

He'd been doing that for days, tossing out old, odd memories like he was carrying them around in a box that needed to be lighter, like he'd be punished if he didn't. Or maybe he was punishing himself just remembering.

"He was lucky that's all he did," I said with a smile. I'd been with him when it happened. Candace was too. It was an old well, tiny and flush to the ground, and Benjamin had stepped right into it—it looked funny because one second, he was walking along next to us, and then, he was just gone. He hadn't been hurt, but it took all us kids forever to get him loose. Benjamin wouldn't let anyone call our parents, because it was around the same time Peter had his nose cauterized, and Benjamin was convinced they'd have to amputate. "It was a miracle he could walk after being bent like that all afternoon."

Cole didn't answer right away, and when he did, his voice was quiet. The laughter was erased, because that's where the story stopped being funny. "He lost his shoe," he said softly.

"Right," I said, and my voice was just as low. "I remember." Losing his shoe had been the biggest tragedy. Clothes we could make, but shoes were tougher, and God help you if you lost something that had any wear left in it. Benjamin had stretched both arms into that well, we all did, and we came up twenty feet too short to rescue the small brown oxford that swam in the leaf-choked water. He'd gotten the switch for that. Twenty whips.

"I remember," I said again.

Cole let out a little breath that sounded like a whimper. "He… he had to…"

I shook my head against his. "Don't think about the shoe. Just think about Benji and you'll be able to sleep."

Cole didn't say anything more after that, but I reached behind me and put my hand on his cheek until his breathing evened out and grew heavy. I tried to match it to my own, but I was shivering, and I couldn't get comfortable.

The rain beat steadily against the roof. I drifted and dozed for what felt like hours before real sleep finally came, but even when it did, even when I started to dream, I could still see Benji's face.

And I could still feel the switch in my hands.

By the next day, there were no more woods. For a while they were just thinner—straggly, stubborn hairs on a balding landscape. Then there were long stretches of open space where we had to use the road's shoulder. By early afternoon our cover went from thick trees to scrubby underbrush, and then there was nothing at all, just dry, dusty land with a black ribbon to walk on. The blacktop was like roasting coals, and the shoulder was bristling with thorns. The soles of my feet were shredded. Cole cut the bottoms of his jeans away, and we wrapped my feet in the cloth, but it didn't make walking any easier.

There was nowhere to rest, so we didn't. We walked all night and saw nothing until the sky started to glow in the distance. Silhouetted against the light was a giant building, so stark gray, it made both of us jump. For a minute it was as though there never were any people, just the compound itself, following us all along, waiting to swallow us up again. But, after a blink, the feeling disappeared. The building had big cars butted up to the walls like pigs at the trough. We found some kind of machine there, a glass box full of food hooked together in metal curls. We pressed all the buttons, but the flashing sign kept asking for money. While Cole tried to shove his arm through the slot on the bottom, I found an outside door that said BATHROOM. Inside, it smelled like years of rot, with rust on the faucets and a big hole above the sink. But there was water—cold water that washed the blood and grit off my feet before I rewrapped them in denim. I collected rolls of toilet paper from every stall and held our canteens under the reddish water that streamed from the sink.

The rusty tint of the water reminded me that I would know soon if more than just the two of us were shambling down that black road. I'd been watching myself closely, looking for signs, but I couldn't find any. I wasn't throwing up, my belly was flat, and nothing felt swollen or tender. I prayed relief would come swiftly, even though if I started bleeding, there would be no way to hide it. I didn't care. It could pour down my legs and paint the road red and I'd still be happy to be empty.

The farther we walked, the more cars sped by, but no one was interested in giving us a ride now. We were filthy, visibly so, and even the forgiving pink of dawn and dusk couldn't make anything pretty out of what the sun did to us in between. Our skin was burnt and peeling. We wore days of sweat and grime and not much else.

Around midafternoon on our eighth day out, we passed through a tiny town with a few houses scattered along the road. The houses were caked with veins of dirt but lit up and almost pretty against the deep-blue sky. The grass had long been baked away, and you could read the direction of the wind on the bare, dusty lawns. We saw no people. About an hour later, the big road split into a bunch of smaller ones, and we turned from our westward route for the first time, toward a sign that read WICHITA. A real word attached to a real place. I felt a rise of panic bubbling in my chest. I saw it on Cole's face.

A few hours beyond the sign, we came upon another cement building, this one flooded with cars and trucks: a congregation of metal. I found a bathroom and pulled Cole inside. It was dark, with the stink of rot and urine, but it was also cool. We blinked in the sudden dim, and as the darkness faded, we both saw it at the same time.

There was a mirror above the sink.

The glass was dirty and coated with rust, but the sight of it made me suck in my breath. The compound had no mirrors. *Reflections serve no purpose*, my father whispered, my eyes trained on that water-stained square. *It's a distraction. Distraction is a weakness.*

The mirror waited on the tiled wall, but neither of us moved, not right away. We both knew that once we did, we'd see something else we'd never seen before. Then my denim shoes began to slide over the floor, and Cole's hand was in mine. We walked toward that mirror like it was an altar. Or something that might bite.

I knew I had hair the color of corn silk because it hung all the way down to my waist, but I'd never seen my face clearly. Sometimes, if I bounced my reflection off the surface of a puddle or caught the light in a windowpane, I could get an idea, but those were only ghost images, nothing real. The mirror was streaked with soap and dotted with water spots. I approached myself with a swirl of excitement spinning in my belly. I always knew how I felt…I wasn't sure if I was ready to match that up with how I looked.

Cole had the only blue eyes I'd ever seen. Everyone else in the family had brown, ranging in shade from my father's obsidian beads to Amaris's beautiful amber gaze. Just like the caul, the clear coolness of Cole's eyes was something I always thought was his alone, something that set him apart. But the first thing I saw when I looked in the mirror was that my eyes were blue too—almost the exact color of the bags we carried. They looked huge in my face, startled, like something wild that had come up from underground and didn't understand light.

Cole's skin was peeling, but he'd gotten brown under the sun. My cheeks and forehead were shiny and flushed, dotted with freckles a few shades darker than my hair. I blinked, and the mirror me's big eyes blinked back. I smiled and so did she.

Beside me Cole was just as enamored, and I smiled again, because for a moment, everything was so surreal and weird and wonderful. I caught his eye in the mirror, and the two of us stood there twisting our faces every which way and laughing—pantomime dipped in hysteria. It was terrifying and delightful. It felt like a gift. We gazed at our splattered newborn reflections with glass eyes that danced and lit and knew how much this meant. Cole's mirror image looked at mine. His fingers touched my cheek.

"*What* are you all doing?"

We whipped around, too quickly to erase our bizarre expressions. A woman in a faded cotton dress stood in the doorway, framed in bright sunshine. Her dress was sleeveless, and her arms seemed to burst from the holes like risen dough. She wasn't smiling.

"Him," she said, pointing at Cole like he had done her a great offense. "What's he doing in here?"

Cole's eyes widened as the levity faded away. He turned to me.

"I—we…just needed to use the bathroom," I said.

"Well, that's all fine and good, nature's call and all, but he can't be in the ladies' room," she said, pointing a flabby finger at Cole. "And you two ain't usin' the bathroom, you're makin' faces in the mirror. Are you on drugs or what?"

"No, I…" My cheeks burned as I saw what she saw. My apron dress—just raw muslin with nothing underneath. Cole in his cutaway jeans and no shirt. "We didn't know he couldn't…"

"You didn't know he couldn't go in the ladies'?" she repeated in a voice appropriate for a toddler. "Well, shit, welcome to America, darlin'. Boys ain't allowed to go where girls do, you get me? So you and your boyfriend—"

"He's my brother."

"Your brother?" She snorted. Her eyes darted between us, doubting and curious. They landed on my feet, all wrapped up in blue. She stopped then; for a split second, everything nasty left her eyes. "I think you were up to something else—"

"No, we—I'm sorry. We just want to clean up." The woman's face didn't soften. "Where can he go?"

"How 'bout the little boys' room right next door, that make sense to the two of ya?"

"Yes, sorry. We just want to clean up," I said again. Cole broke into a shambling trot, wordlessly pushing past the woman, leaving me frozen by the sink.

"Fuckin' kids…" she muttered. "Brother, my fat ass." One of the metal doors squealed open, followed by the heavy thud of said fat ass landing on the seat. I turned back to the mirror. A hard pinch had appeared between my eyes.

The handles on the sink were loose, but the water went on. I rinsed my hands and face as fast as I could, raising tiny muddy streams on my skin. Then I ripped off my denim shoes.

I made it back outside before the woman made it off the toilet, and I found Cole hiding around the corner from the bathroom. He was soaked from the waist up, like he'd taken a half-dive and then changed his mind. His T-shirt was balled in his fist.

"Put that on," I said, shoving him ahead of me around the side of the building.

"Avery…" His eyes were stunned, his hair dark and dripping water down his cheeks. "We shouldn't be out here—"

"We're fine." I yanked the shirt from Cole's hand and tugged it over his head.

"But—"

"Forget it. Come on," I said as we stepped off the blacktop. There were more buildings ahead, more doors and more people, moving like ants. Cole was right. We didn't belong here—everyone would know.

"Slow down," Cole said, catching my hand. "You're running."

I had to. The cement was hot, and my feet were already cooking with blisters. The woman in the bathroom had nothing on her feet but flat slabs of rubber that went between her toes.

"And we need to eat," Cole said, jogging to keep up. "We haven't since yesterday morning… Slow *down*."

"I know we do, I know," I said, my voice pitching up. "We just… we have to get…"

"What?"

I stopped midstride, my eyes wide and frozen. Cole walked right into me, but I barely noticed. We weren't on the road to somewhere anymore. We were *somewhere*. The streets were neatly cut, lined with trees in boxes and buildings with fancy lights in every window. A girl about my age walked past me, and her arm brushed my bare shoulder. I jumped and she gave me an odd look. Her eyes were beautiful, deep brown with no crease above her eyelid. I'd never seen eyes like that before. Her skin had a glow to it I hadn't seen in my own when I looked in the mirror. Her eyes hovered over my dress and landed on my bare feet. What she saw made her move faster: a trail of bloody heel prints on the cement, red crescents, following me.

The air was loud; it was *stuffed*. Puffs of white vapor trailed from the cars, puny little clouds of nothing that terrified me in some huge, unknowable way. I couldn't squelch the thought that all that haze would rise like a fog and choke us, leaving us to claw our way through the oily air.

My throat closed. I could feel my heart thumping in my chest like it wanted to escape. Everything around us was neat and sharp with corners and lines. There was nothing natural about this place. The trees weren't even allowed to grow out of the ground. But that wasn't the worst part.

The worst part was the people.

They looked just like me. They looked like Cole. When you stripped away everything, Cole and I didn't look chosen. We looked like what we were: dirty and confused and terrified. I could feel it fall away, that last thin veil of protection, even though I knew in my thrashing heart that it had never really been there at all.

It pooled around my feet, and when my knees buckled, Cole grabbed me by the arm and yanked me into a thin space between two buildings. My shoulder bumped the rough brick, and the air in my chest emerged in a peal of laughter.

"Breathe," he said, putting one hand against my forehead. My hair snagged on the brick, bringing pinpoints of pain in my scalp. "Avery, look at me. Breathe."

But I couldn't breathe, and I couldn't beat back the frantic giggles that poured out whenever I tried to. Tears streamed from my eyes; my chest ached with shallow gasps. Cole pulled a half-full bottle of grainy water from his pack and poured it over my face. I let out a thin shriek.

"I'm right here," he said, his voice low and unruffled. "Calm down."

The water put the brakes on my pounding heart. When the laughter slowed, I took the bottle and drank a little. It tasted familiar, like dirt, which made me feel better.

A shadow fell over the late-afternoon sun, blotting us out and throwing a spotlight at the same time—out of the corner of my eye, I saw a man in a baseball cap. He was staring at the two of us squashed between the buildings. Water dripped down my face and made mud on my bare feet.

"Don't move." Cole's voice was barely a breath in my ear. I was still watching the man. I saw the faintest trace of anger color his face, saw him bubble and melt into the woman from the bathroom, ready to yell, to pull us from where we didn't belong. Cole must have read his intent, meant to camouflage us further, because before I could blink, he took my face in his hands and kissed me.

My heart picked up again, reacting wildly to everything my brain couldn't comprehend. Cole pulled me against him like this was something we'd done a million times. I started shaking as the last of the hysteria melted away. He held me tighter.

The shadow passed.

I broke free and shoved Cole so hard, he hit the opposite wall. "What are you doing!?"

"Sorry." He didn't look sorry—his color had risen, and he was grinning from ear to ear. "I knew that would work! I walked in on Mom and Dad once, and I ran like—you okay?"

"No!" I said, pulling a real breath. "You didn't have to do that!"

"I just wanted to get rid of him. I didn't mean..."

"Get away from me," I said, shoving him aside.

"Avery, Avery, I'm *sorry*," he said, finally sounding it. "Come on, please? We can't fight."

I wiped my wet hair away from my face and took another jagged breath. "Don't do that again."

We inched out of the alleyway and started walking, moving past a little shop window that had pictures of fat sandwiches encased in glossy rolls. Saliva hugged the sides of my tongue. Behind the window people were milling around holding real sandwiches, lifting bags from shelves, and grabbing plastic-wrapped cookies.

I could see Cole in their movements: his quick, slender hands, adept at snatching up whatever he wanted without anyone noticing... my eyes caught the wondering look on his face as he stared through the window.

He was watching them too.


"What did you get?"

"Lots of stuff." Cole's eyes were bright and dancing under his tumble of hair. We'd squeezed into another narrow space between two buildings. There was a metal roof that stretched over the middle part, and we'd wedged flattened pieces of cardboard between the walls to make a little house for ourselves.

"They had sandwiches in this glass thing…I got thr—no, four," he said, pulling warm, foil-wrapped packages from his backpack. "Juice…apples and carrot sticks, and…candy," he added with a sheepish grin that made me laugh. He added some weird-looking things that turned out to be sticks of cheese to the brightly wrapped pile and topped it with two oranges, garish in the dark. "That's it."

I took a sandwich and peeled away the wrapper. It was gummed up with bright yellow cheese, and honestly it looked horrible, but I bit in hungrily. The cheese was melted into a scrambled egg and a thick slice of bacon, sandwiched between something that wasn't bread, more buttery and delicate. I ate the entire thing in four bites and ripped into a second. We didn't think about rationing, or tomorrow, we just ate and ate, food that was too plentiful, too wonderfully salty and sweet and rich. We finished with the oranges, which were their own treat— sticky and fragrant and bright. When we were too stuffed to move, we collapsed in a heap on the cement. We were on the outside, but we were safe and we were full—for the moment, that was enough. The streetlights revealed a soft fall of rain, but the shine didn't reach us.

"Hey." Cole pinched my cheek, and I realized my eyes had fallen shut. "Don't fall asleep on me."

I moved just enough to slide inside the sleeping bag, bunched up next to Cole with my head resting on the rolled canvas. It was almost comfortable. My eyes closed with the sound of the zipper, and the night grew dimmer as the world went home. I was on the cusp of sleep when Cole's voice reached me, but just barely.

"They taught us so much." He wasn't talking to me. The words were tinged with something deeper than sadness, more futile than regret. "So much. We never would have made it this far... We are chosen... We are..."

Something stirred inside me as I listened to him. The stirring was low, a tiny flutter deep in my belly where I still felt fullness and I still felt pain. It swirled and rose and pushed upward until it touched my lips, a foreign sensation I knew from somewhere but couldn't quite place—I'd felt it before, but it was so long ago that I'd forgotten.

Just before I fell asleep, I realized what it was. I was happy.

# TWELVE

---

For me, the line of demarcation that separated me and Cole from who we were and what we would become was drawn the minute we looked in that mirror. The simplicity of that moment fooled us; even without the smoke, the mirror did the trick. And it did it so well that we didn't realize that the sight of ourselves, our real selves, wasn't a greeting—it was a goodbye. Our dirty faces in the dirty mirror—something otherworldly and forbidden—christened us into the new world, and in that world, we weren't survivors; we were scavengers. We were homeless. And that was a different thing altogether.

*Homeless* meant starving on the days we weren't clean enough to go into a store to steal food. *Homeless* was exhausted with no place to lie down. *Homeless* felt damp and sticky, and it smelled like sweat at the end of a hot day. Our father had told us we'd be invisible on the outside, and believing him was our biggest mistake. We were never more evident. Being outside with nowhere to go made us repulsive and dirty—something to be stared at.

You can't survive in a city, at least not survival the way we understood it. You can only cope. Cole and I couldn't hunt or gather food, we weren't keeping warm or sleeping under the stars. We were digging through trash cans and stealing—*shoplifting*, several signs informed us—committing arson, and trespassing.

We were always running. Our preparations meant nothing, and our skills were useless. We had to throw away what we knew and learn different things. We learned to prepare to be chased, to endure hunger and weather, and to thrive not at all.

Nothing was ours.

But after a while, we began to find a pattern to the chaos, tiny cracks we could slip through. Early morning was the best time, the most secret time, with the most gifts. There was a little shop at the end of one street, and while the store didn't open until nine, the door was unlocked at seven. When the lone employee arrived, he stationed himself in the back for two hours, and as long as we got there the minute he trudged into the back room, Cole could slide in and grab anything he wanted. We found a library with a basement full of discarded books, cool air, and overstuffed chairs that were perfect for napping. Twice we managed to hide and sleep there all night. The park had bathrooms and water fountains. All those things were good, and we accepted them as good enough—until we found the school.

The only reason we tried to get in was because it was pouring and the library was closed. The school was a long, redbrick building, and as we huddled in the breezeway to escape the soaking gray rain, Cole pointed at something with a dripping hand. I followed his finger to a huge circle of blacktop with a field in the middle—and the silhouette of a tiny structure on the other side.

It was probably an accident that someone left the door open. When we walked inside, our feet slipped and skidded on white tiles, and we stood shivering in the echoing chill. There were wide wooden benches and shelves full of clean towels, folded T-shirts, and shorts. Another door, slightly askew, revealed a sink and a toilet. On one side of the room, the tiles didn't stop on the floor. They climbed right up a wall divided by partitions and studded with showerheads.

The water worked. At the first turn of the tap, we didn't care about getting caught or even think about staying. We just ran the water as hot as it would go, and as the room filled with steam, Cole dug up a half-melted bar of green soap stuck to one of the plastic shelves. He snapped it in two, and we each claimed a stall, replacing cold rain with hot water, soaping ourselves over and over until there was nothing but lather in our hands. I rubbed the last of my bar into my hair and scrubbed until the suds slid down my face, stinging my eyes.

We swathed ourselves in shorts and oversized T-shirts that let us ignore how skinny we'd gotten and pushed the benches together, padding them with the sleeping bag and folded towels. Then we fell into a sleep that was leaden and dreamless with nothing to disturb us, inside or out.

It was acclimation—survival by degrees. I have no idea how long we stayed there, how many nights we slept on those benches or how many meals we crept into town to steal. It felt like years—an endless stretch of time lined with unknowns. For Cole, the unknowns were not as big and not as many. He took present victories, like being dry and being fed, as success, and tomorrow didn't matter. But I couldn't enjoy them because there was too much I didn't know. If our family was still lingering at camp, putting up walls or lying in ash underneath them. If they knew we got away. If they'd planted a living, growing seed inside me. I didn't know. And it was eternity to wait and watch and plead for answers that never arrived.

"We need money," I said to Cole one night. The sky was brilliant, inky black, the moon a silver hook in the darkness. Someone was having a party at the park near the school. Music traveled on the breeze with the fragrant smoke of a barbecue, marrying in a lullaby that was beautiful and desperately sad. "We can't keep taking things."

Cole was lying in the grass, chewing on a long piece of red rope candy. I'd just finished cutting his hair with the tiny scissors on my knife, and it waved over his forehead. "Where do you get money?"

"Maybe we can find jobs."

"We can't do anything."

I laughed at that for no reason—it wasn't funny. I'd been professionally homeless long before we set foot off camp. Cole couldn't even read. There was so much in front of us, roping the moon seemed easier.

"I think we're doing okay," he added, offering me the candy. "Don't you?"

I dropped down next to him. The music mixed with laughter, and it sounded so pretty, I felt tears stuffing my throat.

"What?"

"You think this is okay?" I asked, flinging my arm toward our little stolen house. "Sleeping on benches in a giant…bathroom, stealing food…"

"We're trying," Cole said. He nudged my shoulder when I didn't respond. "What's the matter?"

I shook my head against the grass. "Nothing."

"What?"

A sob escaped, bursting free with the words I didn't want to say or even think about. "I stopped bleeding."

He looked at me without understanding. "When were you bleeding?"

My fingers knotted together. "It's like—animals go in heat, and girls bleed. It's the same thing. And if you don't, it means you're—" I couldn't say it. "And I haven't since we left. I stopped."

Cole sat up. My hands had drifted to my belly, my fingers digging into the skin, clawing at whatever might be inside.

He stared at me, eyes wide. "Avery?"

My hands moved to cover my face, and my shoulders shook, more of a gag than a sob, a full-body spasm.

"What does that mean? Are you going to have a baby?"

"I don't know. But I'm not bleeding," I said, keeping my eyes on the endless night. "I know what that means."

Cole reached over and pushed my shirt up to my ribs. "Mom got fat," he said, touching my stomach. "You're not fat."

"You don't get fat right away."

"So we have to wait and see if you do?"

"I can't wait," I whispered.

"There's no other way to tell?"

"Doctors can tell," I said, racking my jumbled files for bits of information I might have read. "And I think there's a test you can buy, but you need money. We don't have any money—"

It took a minute for it to happen, but it did. Cole's eyes lit, brightening with the idea that he might be able to fix something again. It happened because I said the wrong thing.

"When we go in, find the one you want, pick it up, put it back down, and walk away. I'll be behind you, but don't look at me."

"I know, I know—" I said, nearly tripping over a burly old man shuffling ahead of us. He stopped suddenly, and I darted around him, clipping his heel without stopping to apologize. Cole had snatched me a pair of the same thin rubber shoes the woman in the bathroom wore, and they were hard to walk in. "Don't linger, don't leave too fast, don't look at you, I know."

"Just use your brain this time " he said, glancing at the approaching storefront. It wasn't our usual store. We had gone there first thing in the morning, but it didn't have what we needed. The blow nearly killed me, and in Cole's opinion, I'd immediately done something without using my brain. In a burst of bravado, I returned to the store after it officially opened and asked the man at the counter where I could buy a pregnant test. He was short and slight, with bright-white hair and oversize glasses, and his face registered something I couldn't quite place when I said that. But then he smiled. His voice was kind as he suggested I try the pharmacy a few blocks down. Then he patted my hand and told me that pregnancy tests were in the family-planning aisle. I'd thanked him, and when I got outside, I marched past Cole with tears in my eyes and told him we were never taking another thing from there ever again.

We were within reach of the pharmacy door when Cole put his hand out to stop me. "I'm going in," he whispered. "Wait about a minute." The door opened by itself. He stepped through, and it swallowed him whole.

I swallowed too. The old man I had clipped was having a coughing fit a few feet away, and every time he hacked, I jumped. His watery eyes caught mine for a brief second before they squeezed shut, and those short, painful barks came again. Barely thirty seconds had passed when I lunged for the door.

Inside it was cool and quiet, with a hum of low voices and soft music. Cole was standing next to a rack of magazines. His fingers flipped nimbly through the pages of one with cars on the cover. He didn't look up.

I walked without any real direction toward the heart of the store, away from any eyes that might be up front. There was an aisle of diapers that I hurried out of and another of soap and shampoo. Then I turned, and the universe smiled on me. Right in front of me was a white placard that read FAMILY PLANNING. The aisle had all kinds of boxes and bottles, too many for my eyes to take. I forced myself to walk slowly, looking only for the words I needed.

I found them on the bottom shelf. The words *pregnancy test* paired with other letters, other words. *e.p.t. Clearblue. First Response.* I had no sense of Cole being anywhere near me, but I was afraid to touch anything in case I made a mistake.

Someone in the back of the store coughed, loud and rattling. My hands shook. There were tests that gave the news with smiley faces, pluses and minuses, and thin blue lines. There was one that said the words in plain English: *pregnant* or *not pregnant.* That's the one I picked up.

I examined the box, trying to figure out how it even worked. Then

I replaced it on the shelf and straightened up. A man in a white coat passed by and smiled at me. I smiled back.

Then I turned and walked back the way I came.

When I got to the front of the store, Cole was gone. The magazine he'd been reading was slightly crooked in the rack. The woman behind the counter was helping someone else, and I made a quick dip toward the racks of candy and gum, running my eyes over the bright colors before heading for the door.

It slid open. I had one foot on the sidewalk and one on the black rubber mat. One outside, one in. Halfway home. But halfway wasn't good enough, and I had left my other half behind. When I heard his voice, high and protesting, I knew it was over.

They came from the back—Cole and the man from the sidewalk, the old man with the cough. He had Cole's elbow in one hand, and he swung his blue bag in an easy arc in the other. It hung heavy at the end of the strap.

"We're just going up front to look in the bag, son, don't get excited," the man said. "Pretty sure I can handle you myself, but we might have to call someone if—"

"Cole!"

My voice shattered the air. Everyone's eyes swung toward the door where I stood, half outside, half in. Cole squeezed his eyes shut, but the coughing man smiled.

"Ah," he said. "There's your friend."

# THIRTEEN

_____

AFTER COLE AND I WERE ARRESTED, I THREW UP TWICE. ONCE IN THE car, and once on the slick, polished floor of the police station. We were handcuffed by then, and Cole stood woodenly beside me as I splashed his shoes with vomit for the second time. The woman behind the desk pursed her lips and called for a janitor. I didn't apologize, because I couldn't speak.

"Send someone with sawdust out to my car too," the old man with the cough said, his voice weary but not feeble. His name was Officer Rodolfo, and in the back office of the pharmacy, he had patiently explained that he might not arrest us if we cooperated with him. We didn't. He kept asking us questions we didn't understand, and it felt safer to say nothing at all.

"Drunk tank?" the woman asked, her eyes bouncing from me to Cole.

"No."

She looked at us again, squinting. "Juvie?"

"That remains to be seen. They haven't been very cooperative, and neither of them has any ID. What they do have is snipped tongues, so first we're going to see if they want to change their minds and tell us who they are, and if they don't, we'll have to do something else to figure it out. Right, my boy?" he asked, nudging Cole.

Cole didn't respond.

"Right," said Officer Rodolfo. He sounded exhausted. "Right as rain. Put 'em in a room. I'll be right there."

A meaty hand grabbed my elbow. Another policeman, younger but huge, steered me and Cole down the hall.

He deposited us in a pantry-sized room with a table and two metal chairs, the same kind we had at the compound. I felt my stomach clench painfully for the third time. Cole sat next to me, his face the color of bleached muslin. The policeman brought in a third chair from another room. I expected him to stay with us, but he didn't, closing the door with a hard click.

Cole looked at me, and his eyes were huge. "Avery—they know about us. I know they do. They know about the fire. What if they ask us what happened, what if—"

"Shh—no, they don't. Don't say anything," I said. "If we have to talk, I'll do it. Don't say a word." My head was churning with fear mixed with the sickly sweet smell of vomit rising from our shoes. I was thinking about the fire, too, but in my head, the scenarios were far worse. If my parents or any of the kids were alive somewhere, the police might know about us. They could already be looking for us. Cole would know I'd been lying.

He'd want to go back.

Everything about that was terrifying, but another part of me was desperate to know how safe we were, if everyone did burn or if there were still roots that could grab us—it was a question that had been weighing on me worse than whatever might be growing inside me, the other unknown. It gave me nightmares. In them Cole and I were small. We were in the living room with that man and woman, still smiling, their feet all splayed out on the floor. And my father—

"Okay!" a voice boomed. I jumped. Officer Rodolfo plopped heavily in the chair across from us. He still wasn't dressed like a policeman, and that made him scarier somehow.

"Guess what? I'm not even on duty, but I don't think you're going to talk to anyone else, so we're going to try this again," he said. "Cooperate and you'll be home in no time. Keep your mouths shut and we'll have to do it the hard way. Makes no difference to me, but I guarantee it'll make a huge difference to you."

He leaned back in his chair and pointed his pen at Cole. "What's your name?"

Cole said nothing.

"Well?"

"Nicholas," I said quietly.

Officer Rodolfo twirled the pen between his fingers. "Is that your name or his?"

I looked at my hands, bound in silver. "His."

"Can he talk?"

"Yes, sir."

"Then how 'bout we let him say it?" Officer Rodolfo said, turning back to Cole. "Come on, son, with feeling… What's your name?"

"Nicholas," Cole whispered.

"Nicholas what?"

Cole blinked and looked at me. Officer Rodolfo didn't budge. "Nicholas what?" Officer Rodolfo repeated.

Long pause. "He doesn't know what you mean," I said finally.

"He doesn't know what I mean?" he repeated, swinging his head toward me.

"No."

"How fascinating. Well then, how 'bout you tell me, since you seem to know everything. What's your name?"

I cleared my throat. "Avery."

"Your *whole* name."

"That's it."

"No, that's not it. You got at least two names, and I want both of them. Is this your boyfriend?"

"He's my brother."

"Wonderful! That means we're only one name away from finishing one question. Nicholas and Avery what?"

Cole was chalk white. I stretched my fingers and gripped his hand under the table. "We don't have another name."

The officer put the tip of his pen in his mouth. "How old are you?"

*How old?*

*Nineteen.*

"Nineteen."

"Uh-huh," he said, scribbling in his pad. The pen had made a blue dot on his lip that bobbed as he spoke. "You?" he asked Cole.

Cole threw me another panicked glance. I counted backward: me, Seth, Hannah... "Sev—sixteen," I said.

The officer's hand slapped the table so hard, it rocked back and forth. "Answer for him again and you're each going to be questioned alone and I'm going to stop being nice. Where do you live?" he asked Cole.

Cole looked at the table.

"I can't hear you."

"Nowhere," he whispered.

"Oh, this is getting better and better. No last name, no home, just wandering through town to steal a bagful of junk food and a pregnancy test. I guess that was for you?" he asked me.

I pressed my lips together.

"Where are your parents?"

I said, "Dead."

"Where do you live?"

"Nowhere."

"Where did you come from?"

I fell silent again. I could feel Cole tightening next to me, a winding, twisting rope pulled taut and thin.

"*Where did you come from?*" Officer Rodolfo boomed. "Because I'll tell you something right now, what you did was at least a misdemeanor, and if we find out you've done it before, it becomes a felony, which is big shakes, in case that's something else you never heard of. I'm not playing games with you kids, I—"

"Eight days out, due east," Cole suddenly snapped.

"Shut up!" I hissed.

"No, no, no, don't shut up now," Officer Rodolfo said. "Due east?"

"Yes, sir," Cole said, his chin jutting forward. "That means—"

"I know what it means. What town?"

"I don't know."

"Eight days' walk or drive?"

"Cole, don't—"

"Walk," he said, his voice loud and getting louder with every word. "We walked west for eight days, we kept the sun on our left, and we've been *careful*. We only took the test because she can't wait anymore!"

Officer Rodolfo straightened up and put his pen on the table.

He didn't speak for a long time. "Are you two fucking with me?" he asked finally.

I looked at Cole; his eyes were bright and shiny. "I'm sorry," I said miserably. "I don't know what that means."

"I'll give you a general definition. Most people," he said, tapping his fingers on the table, "give distance in miles, not days. I don't know many who'd even be able to point 'due east.' They generally know what town they came from."

Neither of us spoke.

"So that leads me to believe that you're fucking with me. Or maybe," he said, returning the pen to his mouth, "you've been fucking with each other. Pregnancy test…you won't talk…"

It was like he'd delivered a punch to my stomach. The memory of my father selling me and my womb to a stranger returned swiftly, very vivid and very alive. But I barely had time to notice, because all of a sudden, Cole exploded with a molten fury that forced angry tears from his eyes. "Shut *up*! Don't you dare say that to her, don't! I'll k—"

The officer was up in a flash. He grabbed Cole by the front of his shirt and yanked him six inches out of his seat. "No, you don't get to tell *me* what to do, son. You two have thrown yourselves into much deeper shit than you needed to, and if you mouth off to me again, I'm going to toss both your asses in—"

"Leave him alone!" I screamed.

Cole was beet red, hovering in Officer Rodolfo's grip. He released him suddenly, and Cole dropped with a metallic clang back to his seat. The room was dead silent.

"Okay," the officer said in a much quieter tone. He wasn't agreeing with me; it looked more like he was trying not to hit us. "Here's what's going to happen. I'm going to take you up front, one at a time, and we're going to take your prints, just like they did back in kindygarden. Then you're going into separate cells as Nicholas and Avery Doe, and there you'll sit until Monday morning, when and if the judge is ready to see you. And you better be good and ready to give him the truth, or you won't have to worry about your housing problem for a while. Do you understand?"

We didn't, but we didn't get a chance to answer. Officer Rodolfo threw open the door and hollered down the hall for someone to get us the hell out of his goddamn sight.

The younger policeman rolled my fingers over a thick black pad and inked the impressions onto a card, like a row of oversize bugs. He told me to sign it—I printed my name carefully on the line.

"Do you want to call anyone?" he asked, staring down at the five letters I'd written.

"Who?"

"Whoever you want," he said. "And they can post bail. Do you want to?"

I shook my head. "I don't know anyone."

Cole was gone. They'd taken him first, and by the time they hauled me out of the tiny, airless room, he'd already been tucked away out of sight. When the policeman was done inking my fingers, he took three pictures of me, and then he put me in a cinder-block room with a barred door and a long, padded bench. The metal clang of the door echoed in my head well after his footsteps faded away. There was a toilet attached to one wall, but that was the only other thing in the room. I sat on the bench with my back against the cold blocks for a long time, but no one came back.

After a while I started to doze. I kept thinking I was talking to Cole and getting jerked awake by my own mumbling. I pressed my hand to the wall and pretended he was on the other side. I knew that wherever they had put him, he was talking to me too.

"Focus," I murmured, closing my eyes against the harsh light. I pretended I was back in the woods, and I thought about what my father would have told me to do, even though I hated to summon any part of him.

The bars covered the window in the door, painting the floor with long shadows. It was a trapped situation. I was cornered, buried in debris. Fighting would only push me deeper. The conditions had to change. He would tell me to wait.

"Endure," I mumbled, identifying the most crucial task. "It'll get better or worse. Better and you climb out. Worse and you fight."

There was no sun to watch. I had no idea how long I was in there, but the bench grew harder the longer I sat. At one point there was an explosion of whoops and cheers from the hall, and I covered my ears against the noise. In the hollow white rush, I repeated every mantra I knew, even though my throat was dry and it hurt to talk. I could hear feet rushing past the bars, but I didn't look up. More feet, close enough to rattle the floor, approached, and the door suddenly slid open. Then I did stop. Stopped and curled into a tight ball with my legs drawn to my chest.

Officer Rodolfo stood in the doorway, staring at me with the same look I remembered seeing on Peter's face the first time he got his fire drill to work. It was an astounded look, caught somewhere between wonder and victory. For a minute I didn't recognize him.

He was smiling.

# FOURTEEN

---

Officer Rodolfo ushered me down the hall and into another room—a big room, with a long table and a mirrored wall. His steps were so light, it felt like I was being flown across the shiny floors. When he opened the door, the first thing I saw was Cole. He was sitting with a Black woman who was probably about my mother's age, but the warmth in her expression made her seem far younger. She wore a long skirt and a bulky sweater that looked painfully hot. Cole jumped up and ran toward me. No one stopped him. That scared me more than if they had.

The woman from the front desk was there, too, standing in the corner with one hand pressed to her mouth. A strange, dumbfounded delight colored her face, like we were statues come to life. I put my arm around Cole, and his forehead landed on my shoulder. He seemed determined not to look at anyone.

"Sit down, please," the woman in the sweater said. The kindness in her voice was in her eyes too. They were a soft brown, and she had thick black hair, tied in a twist that fell down her back. "You can sit together," she added.

We shuffled toward the chairs without breaking form. We *were* statues, frozen in a different disbelief than whatever was gripping everyone else in the room. Cole's fingers were white on my arm. We bumped a chair, and it fell over in a terrible clang. Cole clutched me tighter. The woman smiled.

"My name is Amelia," she said once Cole and I had worked out the mechanics and managed to sit down. "I'm a caseworker for the Kansas Department for Children and Families. Officer Rodolfo and I would like to talk to you a little more. But first things first," she said, smiling warmly, "you're not in trouble. There's no need to be frightened, and I don't want you to worry if you aren't able to answer the questions we ask you. Just do the best you can. Okay?"

I said nothing, bouncing my gaze on all the faces in the room. Cole had burrowed into my side.

"I think I already know the answer to my first question," Amelia began. "Are you hungry?"

I still didn't respond—but Cole did. He nodded quickly, automatically, before his head went back to my shoulder, like he was ashamed.

But Amelia seemed pleased. "I thought so. Kelly is going to have lunch sent over for you." Kelly was, I guessed, the woman from the front desk, because when Amelia said that, she jerked to life and hurried toward the door, like she was desperate to do something for us.

"In the meantime," Amelia said, fixing her eyes first on Cole then me. "Please understand that you are in no danger. No one is going to hurt you. I'm here to be an advocate for you. Do you know what an advocate is?"

I looked at her. Cole didn't move.

"An advocate, very simply, is someone who is on your side," she said. "My job is to make sure you are treated well, you have everything you need, and that you're safe. We're going to do our best to help you, but it's important that you answer our questions if you can. Okay?"

I looked at Cole. He was staring blankly, his blue eyes occasionally darting around the room and landing on nothing at all. I nodded.

"Good," Amelia said. "Very good. Avery, I'll start with you. You and Nicholas have been traveling together?"

I nodded.

"Just the two of you?"

"Yes, ma'am."

"For how long?"

"I don't know." I looked at Officer Rodolfo, waiting for his palm to strike the table. "A long time."

"When did you arrive in Wichita?"

I fell silent.

Amelia leaned over, ostensibly to put her hand over mine. I

yanked it away before she could touch me. She smiled. "How about something to drink?"

Officer Rodolfo disappeared into the hall and returned with two cold, red cans, plunking them down in front of us. I grabbed mine with both hands. The liquid inside was dark and full of bubbles, and I choked on the first gulp. Cole didn't touch his. I tried a smaller sip, and the coolness took some of the sting out of my throat.

Amelia pointed at my chest. "My daughter has the same shirt. She lettered in track her senior year."

My eyebrows tugged together. Peter could track, he was the best at it, even when he was little. But the way she said it made me think *track* meant something different to Amelia. My shirt was white with a blue design on the front—we'd found them in the shower room at the school.

"Can you tell us where you've been staying?"

I shrugged once, jerking my shoulders. "We—um…in the little house behind the big—the *high* school," I remembered just in time. "We didn't break anything. It was unlocked."

"I want to leave," Cole said all of a sudden, his voice harsh and loud. "I—we want to leave."

"You will," Officer Rodolfo said.

"When?"

"As soon as everything is sorted out. And I think we can find a better arrangement for you than the high school locker room," Amelia added. "How does that sound?"

Cole shook his head, and I agreed. It sounded horrible. It sounded like another last meal—my father offering me a week in Hannah's bed like it was free.

Like we wouldn't have to pay for it in the end.

"No," I said. I pushed the red cans away with shaking hands and slid my chair back. "We don't want that. Just let us go. We'll be fine on our own."

"You're used to being on your own, aren't you?" Amelia asked.

"Yes," I said without thinking.

"You walked more than thirty miles on your own."

Cole took a breath that sounded like a whimper.

Amelia wandered over to the long mirror and ran her hand along the edge. "That's something else we want to talk to you about. Where exactly you walked *from*. You see, there was a very bad fire that destroyed a small group of buildings about thirty miles from here several weeks ago. Due east," she added. "People died in that fire, but since we don't know who lived there, we don't know who they were or if anyone might have gotten away."

My hands tingled. In the mirror, Cole's eyes were cast down, his expression impossible to read.

"It was an unusual sort of place," Amelia went on. "No one really knows much of anything about what went on there. Stories floated around about people living in the old Clovelite factory, even though it was pretty beat up. But it was owned land, so there was really no need for interference. The people who lived there didn't seem to need anything. Private people.

"So, for that reason, we don't know if anyone survived the fire, and the investigators have been combing the grounds to try and figure out what happened." She stopped, facing the mirror.

"How did the fire start?" I asked quietly.

Cole's whole body twitched. The room was hot, airless, but his hand on my arm was like ice. His fingers tightened on my skin. Amelia turned and looked at us. "They don't know."

Heat rose in my cheeks. It didn't matter how they thought the fire started. I didn't even know why I asked, because it didn't matter to me either. I could still hear the low crackle and see Jane's dead eyes. I could feel the heat of those bright tongues darting underneath my door. I was going to be on fire for the rest of my life.

"Like I said, the people who were there were very sheltered. They must have been very afraid," Amelia said softly.

I sat stiffly in the metal chair. Next to me, Cole was making a weird huffing noise that sounded horribly guilty. Then he spoke.

"Did any of them get out? Is anyone alive?"

Officer Rodolfo cleared his throat. "That's what we're trying to figure out. We don't know how many people were there in the first place. It was a very hot fire, and it spread fast. Seems the cu…the, uh…the people who lived there had a weapons stockpile in the main building. Went up like the Fourth of July."

My mind was spinning, trying to fill in the dense black holes punched into that night, but all I could see were Officer Rodolfo's hands. They were rough, calloused, and in a quick, blazing instant, I was standing in front of my father again…

"Avery?" Amelia said softly.

I blinked. "Yes?"

"What happened to your hands?"

My eyes fell to my hands. The skin had been too tender to stand up to the glass and heat that night, and it had hardly been coddled since. They hurt, I realized, trying to make a fist. My palms were a thick sheet of dead, cracked skin.

"We weren't there." The words left my mouth like molasses. "We weren't."

But Cole was shaking his head with a resignation that was painful to watch. He pressed the thumb and forefinger of his left hand into his eyes and sort of tipped forward, hooking his free arm around my shoulders in a clumsy embrace as his own started to shake. I let him. Let him feel it. I wished I could join him, but the only hope for us was that there was no hope for anyone else. We didn't have that yet.

"I'm sorry," Amelia said.

I nodded.

"You were so fortunate to escape."

I found her choice of words interesting. *Escape*. Until then, I was pretty sure I was the only one who thought we'd escaped. Cole just thought we lived.

"No one has come forward," she said. "Is it possible that anyone else might have gotten out?"

"I don't know," I whispered. Cole looked at me, stricken, and I revised quickly. "I mean, no. Just us."

"Do you know how the fire started?"

"No," I said, glancing at Cole.

"I know it's difficult, but I'd like you to help me understand what sort of a place it was. Who were you living with?"

"Our family," I said, keeping my eyes on the ugly wooden table. "Our parents and our brothers and sisters."

"How many brothers and sisters did you have?"

"A lot," I said, my voice going dead. "Amaris. Seth. Hannah, Jane. Peter. Sarah. Candace. Benjamin."

"Was anyone else there that night?"

"No."

Next to me, Cole stared at his fingers like he was counting. I put my hand over his.

Amelia glanced at Officer Rodolfo. "What did your family do there?" she asked.

"Trained."

"For what?"

"The end."

Amelia paused. "Did you ever leave?" she asked. "Your property?"

"No."

"Do you know why?"

Cole's head was still bowed to the table. I felt my own judgment getting shaky, ripped to bits under gentle scrutiny. I wished he'd look up. "Because," I said. Cole's arm tightened on my shoulder. "It wasn't safe."

Officer Rodolfo made a low grunting sound, but Amelia didn't seem to notice. She leaned forward. "What sort of things did they teach you?"

*Good things. Bad things.* I thought of all those nights crouched in the tent scraping fire out of wood, all the hunting, and the hours and hours spent hoarding our supplies, canning, stocking, preparing. I thought of Cole and the baby as black shapes against the sun, and the light cutting over my mother's face as she told me it was better not to fight it...

"They taught us how to take care of ourselves," I said, blinking hard. The shadow passed, uncovering my eyes. "How to...do things."

"Like what? Forgive me, but I'm trying to understand. Nicholas—"

"Cole," I said, a little too sharply.

"Cole," she said after a pause. "I'm sorry. Cole, when you were initially brought in, you were asked to sign an inventory of your possessions. You told the officer you couldn't read or write. So I'm wondering—"

"They taught us what's important," Cole spat, finally lifting his head. "Anyone can read. You think that's important?"

"Cole—" I started.

But Amelia held up her hand. "What is important?"

"Knowing how to live when the rest of the world is dead," Cole went on in the same harsh tone. He sounded like our father, whether he meant to or not. "Our grandfather predicted it. It's coming. His followers chose to die rather than face it, but we're stronger. They taught us what to *do*. You think you could read your way through the end and still make it out alive? Avery can read. You think that's what makes her smart? It's not. We're smarter, we're *better*, because we know more than that. All of you, with your little…little computers and cars, and none of that will help you, *none* of it."

"Help us with what?"

He shook his head. "I'm not going to tell you. If you were supposed to know, you'd have been—"

I brought my hand down on his leg with an audible smack. "Cole, stop…"

"I want to *leave*," he said, and he sounded like all of us when we'd had enough, when we were rain-soaked and starving and cold. He sounded exactly like it felt. "Just let us go, we don't—"

"We can't let you go. Not yet."

"Why not?" I asked.

"Because we have more to tell you, but you have to promise me something first. You have to promise you'll stay calm." Amelia's face was still soft, but there was a hint of something more, something I didn't like. "Can you do that?"

"Do you promise to let us go?" Cole asked her.

"I promise that you will leave the police station today," Amelia said, and it was a careful dodge, a calculated one. I wasn't sure if Cole noticed, because he nodded. After a moment, I did too.

Amelia made a steeple with her fingers under her chin. "Something came up when we ran your fingerprints," she said slowly. "And if it's true..." She paused, and I was struck by her expression— all of a sudden, she looked like she was going to cry. "If it's true, we will have a lot more to talk about," she said, clearing her throat.

My lungs felt painfully full, but I was too scared to breathe. The air sat in my chest, pressing against my ribs until I thought I'd pass out. Under the table, Cole took my hand.

"I want to show you some pictures."

Officer Rodolfo brought forth a big, flat book and flipped it open. Each page had a clear envelope with a picture inside. He pulled two glossy sheets free and placed one in front of me and one in front of Cole.

"Does anything look familiar?" Amelia asked quietly.

"That's you," I said to Cole, pointing to the picture in front of him. He squinted at it without much interest, but Officer Rodolfo grinned and clapped his hands together so loud, it made me jump.

Amelia was watching me. "Are you sure?"

"Yeah," I said, studying it. "I think so." He was only a baby in the picture, but I was pretty sure it was Cole. I had exactly one photograph from the compound. It may have been the only one ever taken, and it was mostly of people who were long since dead. Cole had been caught in the background, only a baby then too—a chubby little thing with a headful of reddish-brown waves. I still had it. It was stuck between the pages of one of my books; I'd used it as a bookmark for years.

"What about this one?" Officer Rodolfo asked, nudging the second picture closer. It showed a little girl with a thin face framed by two curtains of white-blond hair. Her eyes and her mouth were sad. I shrugged.

"This is a photograph of Celeste Bishop," Amelia said. "It was taken on her fifth birthday. Twelve days later she disappeared from her front yard. She was never seen again.

"This," Amelia went on, sliding the other picture next to the one of the little girl. "Is Noah Reid Pierce. He was eighteen months old when he vanished, about a week before Celeste. He and his mother were at the park with their dog, and the dog got away. His mother left him in the sandbox while she caught the dog. It was no more than a minute or two, but when she got back, he was gone. He would be sixteen today. He hasn't been found either."

I shrugged again. "Looks just like Cole. But…"

Amelia was watching me. "But what, Avery?"

"No, nothing," I said quickly. "I just…I was wo—wondering how you could have a picture of him, of Cole, if…" My voice faltered and died. I looked at the picture again, burning the image into my head so that when I looked up, when I looked at my brother, I would see that I was wrong. I would see nothing of that little boy in him. I opened my mouth to take back my words, but they came out the same. "He looks just like Cole."

"That's because it is Cole," Amelia said, producing a large, stiff piece of paper from under the table. It said MISSING in big, bold letters, and the picture was different, but it was still Cole, same eyes, same hair, same everything. He even had on the blue and white shoes he was wearing in the picture I had. Next to me Cole was blinking very fast, his hand groping for mine again, scratching at my skin. His other hand batted at the picture of the little girl like he wanted to push it away but his body wouldn't listen.

"And this," Amelia went on, rescuing the picture and sliding it in front of me, "is you, Avery."

I swallowed, staring into the girl's eyes. Dusky blue, too big for her face. "No, it's not."

"You recognized Cole."

"I made a mistake."

"Did you?"

"Yes, because I remember when Cole was born, so these can't be us. I—he was born *en caul*, and I *remember*—"

"You were only three years old when he was born," Amelia said. "That's very young to remember something like that."

"It's not us."

"Are you sure? Are you sure you're not just remembering things you heard?"

"No, it's on—the caul is buried on our land. It blessed us. That's why my grandfather named him Nicholas, he…"

Amelia was watching me closely. "Avery—"

"It's not us," Cole cut in, but all the anger, all the defiance was gone. He was wilting under the frozen gaze of his own one-year-old eyes. "It's…no…"

"We're going to run a test to be sure, but your fingerprints matched. Both of you. There is a database…a list…of missing children. They keep things like fingerprints in case something like this happens, so we would know it if we found you. Noah was kidnapped in Washington State, and Celeste disappeared right here in Kansas. To find a fingerprint match between both of these children and both of you, together, almost fifteen years later…"

She fixed her eyes on Cole, and he withered in his seat, an animal caught in the crosshairs. "When a child goes missing there is always some amount of attention. Sometimes there's a lot of it. There was a huge, *huge*, search for Noah. It went on for years; I doubt there's a single adult in America who doesn't know his name. If we're right, if Noah Reid Pierce and Celeste Bishop are in this room, we're going to have to handle things very carefully." She turned to include me in her gaze. "You're both going to have to brace yourselves."

"But you're not listening to me," I told her. "It's not—"

Amelia silently produced another MISSING picture. The same little girl was on the front. Her pale hair was flying, and her face glowed underneath. I looked closer. Her eyes weren't my eyes. They were clear and unafraid, bubbling with the ignorant joy of a life undamaged. The camera had caught her in her own little dance, forever frozen in an endless twirl.

Her tiny arms were spread wide. She was smiling.

There were pink ballet slippers on her feet.

# PART TWO

# FIFTEEN

WHEN I THINK BACK ON IT NOW, THE DAY NOAH AND CELESTE WERE found, it feels like a movie. The cameras, the lights, the interviews… they were all things that happened, just not to me. I couldn't have said it then. I didn't know what a movie was like yet. But I could have said that it felt more vibrant than real life and more surreal. I won't speak for Cole, but a part of me broke off the day they told us, a seed I could hold but couldn't plant. I wasn't who I became, and I wasn't who I was when I disappeared. I was a hybrid person, caught in limbo between what I thought I knew and what was true.

There was so much about myself that I *didn't* know that the words and phrases assigned to me had no meaning. Cole and I didn't grow up in a family, we were *abducted* into a *cult*. It even had a name, bestowed by the world we shunned, because we weren't nearly as secret or smart as we thought we were: Clovelite. So named for the old plastics factory that we'd molded into our home; we were local legends, and we didn't even know it. We became a real legend, Wikipedia official. Celeste Bishop and Noah Reid Pierce, survivors of the Clovelite cult that was taken down by a much smaller apocalypse than we'd been expecting.

Turns out we weren't prepared for everything.


"You knew about us?" I asked Officer Rodolfo hours later, after our blood was drawn and pictures of Cole and I had been sent for something called *age-progression analysis*. My voice was strained, too high, like my throat was caught in a trap.

"The Clovelite preppers? Sure, we knew there were people living there," he said. "Latham kept tabs—they were the closest."

"Preppers?"

"Yeah—sorry, colloquial term. Survivalists, I guess you'd say. People preparing for the end of the world."

His fingers made rabbity gestures on either side of his face, bending quickly up and down. There was too much amusement in his voice for me to take that without offense. "You say that like it'll never happen."

"Okay, when?"

"Soon. We don't know the exact date, but soon, and it's something we pre…something we're ready for. Modern society is dying."

"I'll consider myself warned. You're lucky no one picked a date," he added, jotting down a note on my fingerprint card. "Otherwise you might have ended up in a tracksuit with a belly full of Kool-Aid."

"I don't know what that means. But just because we don't know the date doesn't mean there isn't one," I said, narrowing my eyes at him. "We were protecting ourselves."

"Sure were."

"If you knew about it, why didn't you…" I didn't know how to finish. *Rescue us* popped into my head, but no, that was wrong, wasn't it? We didn't want that.

I halfway hoped he'd read my mind, see where they'd failed and be sorry. But he didn't. "You weren't doing anything wrong," he said with a small shrug. "Not that we could see, anyway. Living out in the woods, farming your own food. There was no reason for us to bust in on you."

I thought again of the dead couple on the living room floor, their twisted feet and the blood on my ballet shoes. The rancid, oily bonfires, and the rooms that were off-limits. The baby buried on the edge of the field.

"You can't go after a recluse for wanting to be alone," he added.

"What's that?"

He looked at me for a beat before he answered. "Some people," he said, "just do better on their own."

*Recluse* sounded good—it sounded like a goal, something I was and could be again once we got away from all these people. There were other words I would come to know intimately, like *programmed* and *abused. Brainwashed.* It was a slow road to understanding what those words had done to me.

Most of the bigger cities surrounding the commune had known about us for years, but, according to Officer Rodolfo, we were officially categorized as "strange but not dangerous." They had no inkling of the children being kept there, the stolen ones, and we couldn't offer much help. Cole and I could only speculate as to why our parents bore some and stole others, but once the story was as complete as it could be, all I could do was step aside and watch it unfold, reel after reel. Without being part of it at all.

I couldn't make many connections then, but my shock, the detachment, forced me to understand more than I wanted to. Leaving the dark tunnel of the compound didn't free me from fear, which was always my greatest wish—not only to run, but to forget. That hole had been dug too deep. I'd spent years learning that there was nothing *but* fear, nothing happy, nothing hopeful, just preparation because things would always get worse. And even without the end, the worst still came, again and again. That thinking was engrained, and it followed me out. There was a lot to panic about when I learned about Celeste Bishop, but nothing was scarier than discovering I had lived most of my life playing someone else.

---

Our father hadn't lied. We had been chosen. First by him, when we were still small and soft—chunks of clay he could mold into whatever shape he liked. He narrowed our world to a field and some trees and made us more important than we were. But when we got out, the world was huge, and we were still chosen. We had everyone's attention from the moment our names were uttered, the day we sat in a brightly lit hospital room with hordes of reporters in the lobby. The whole world hoped to get a glimpse of us, our father's unfinished masterpiece—rough and unexpected, but still something. Still alive. After years of being told we were important, we finally were.

But before all that, Celeste Bishop lived with her mother in a tiny four-room house in the southeastern corner of Kansas. Celeste had her appendix out when she was three, and I wore the white ghost of her incision near my hip. In Washington State, practically inches from the Canadian border, Noah Reid Pierce lived in a sprawling six-bedroom house with his parents and his older sister. The scar that cut Cole's eyebrow in two was born when Noah smacked his head against the side of a glass coffee table. Those were the things that gave us away, the little things—eventually our blood would say everything they expected it to about both of us, but we didn't have to wait for that. They knew enough to take away our names.

We were in that glassed-in hospital room when they told us they were sure. Cole got upset. The room was too small for how upset he got. It was one thing to lose your entire family in a day, quite another to lose yourself and still be breathing. The news took no time at all to sink in because we'd heard it before. The difference was that now we had to believe it. I didn't cry or scream. I just slid to the floor when my legs gave out and sat there while Cole's flailing arms knocked over a long metal pole, a tray full of cookies and juice, and a young doctor who stepped too close. No one tried to stop him. Eventually he dropped down and crawled over to me, and then I did cry—for both of us. We sat on the floor, clinging to each other, and everyone watched, and no one did a thing.

"What's going to happen to us?" I asked Amelia, hours later. We were still in the hospital. Cole had been given a pill to put him to sleep.

Amelia sat on the edge of my mattress—Cole was in the other bed, still and silent. We'd arrived wearing the various cuts and bruises you learn to live with when you're just looking to stay alive. They were not classifiable injuries in our world, but here we were beat up enough to earn a bed apiece in a room that was closed, locked up, and guarded by a policeman.

"Nothing is going to happen tonight," Amelia told me. "You're going to sleep, and—"

"What's going to happen tomorrow?"

She took one of my hands, sandwiching it between hers. "I want you to believe me when I tell you you're going to be fine," Amelia said. "Better than fine—you're going to be free."

Hot tears started as a lump in my throat that slowly dissolved and trickled down my cheeks. "We won't. It's not safe out here. Not for us."

"Avery—what's out here," she said, indicating the sprinkling of lights that dotted the dark sky outside the window, "is not what you've been told. And I can say that until I'm blue in the face, but I can't make you believe me. It's something you have to learn."

I swallowed hard; my throat felt dry and sore. "I don't think I can."

"Do you know what an agenda is, Avery?"

"Like a schedule?"

"Well, yes, but what I'm talking about is more than that. The people who took you and Cole had an agenda. They wanted to build an army to fuel their belief that the world was going to end. To me, that sounds like a movie, but they really believed it. They needed other people to believe it too."

"But you don't know that it's not true," I said.

She shrugged. "You're right, I don't. But what they did, taking you and raising you in those conditions, preventing you from having a normal life, was not preparing you for anything. It was abuse."

"They told us," I whispered, "that we were chosen."

Amelia looked at me. "I believe that," she said finally. "Maybe not the way they did, but you're here, aren't you? You and Cole both."

"Why us, though?"

"I don't know," she said, getting to her feet and pulling the blanket tight around me. "And that's too much to think about tonight. Try to rest. I'll be back in the morning."

I shivered, staring at the back of her soft, brown sweater as she slipped out the door. The air was cool and thin, the room too big to stay warm. I wished for my sleeping bag, anything familiar to curl up with.

I settled for Cole. The curtain that wrapped around his bed was as good as a tent, our own little box. I lay down next to him. He was warm with sleep, the kind that rescues you from waking and doesn't bother you with dreams. It was a long time before I was too.

"Vitals?"

"Normal."

"How'd they measure?"

"Under fifth. He's five-four, a hundred and one, she's five even and eighty-two…"

"*Four* news vans out there now, Amelia…"

My eyes opened with the creak of the door as Amelia slid inside and greeted me with her warm smile. Someone had pulled the curtain back to assault us with daylight that was unwelcome and painful. My lower back felt dented from being pushed into the bed rail, my entire body was an S-shaped cramp. Cole lay facing me, his blue eyes glassy and blank.

"Hey, guys," Amelia whispered. "How'd you sleep?"

"Okay," I mumbled.

"I brought you some clothes." She didn't bat an eye at the sight of Cole and me wedged into one bed. "I figured you wouldn't want to leave in a hospital gown."

I rubbed at the sleep caked in my eyes. "Thank you."

"Breakfast will be here soon. Avery, you look a little more awake. How about a shower?"

I climbed out of bed slowly. Cole was holding my hand, something I didn't notice until he wouldn't let go. I uncurled his fingers as gently as I could, and Amelia led me into the bathroom. I tugged at the neck of the gown the nurse had bullied me into after they'd cleaned us up the night before. She'd also given me something that looked like mosquito netting and was supposed to pass for underwear. I told her I never wore underwear, but she'd made me put them on anyway.

Amelia was riffling through a paper bag. "Everything's in here, clothes, underwear, socks… I had to guess on your sizes, but we'll get you some better things later. The shower," she said, leaning past me to push a curtain aside, "is right here." She turned the water on full blast, and the noise filled the room, bouncing off the tile walls. "You've got soap, shampoo, but if there's anything I missed, just yell, okay?"

I nodded, squinting in the steam. My head felt hollow, and there was a tinny, metallic taste in my mouth, like blood.

The hot water reddened my skin. I filled a washcloth with soap and lathered myself all over, scrubbing the cloth over my face before dousing my hair with gobs of shampoo. It tangled under my fingers, but the clean scent was worth it. Despite the line of showers at the high school, there was always a stale, mildewy smell seeping from the tiles, something dank and wet that clung to me like a second skin.

When I got out, I pulled a comb from the bag and tried to untangle my hair but only succeeded in making it worse. I brushed my teeth instead, relishing the taste of cold peppermint in the hot steam. The mirror above the sink was frosted with a gossamer veil that hid my face. I didn't wipe it away. I was afraid I might look different now that I knew my name was wrong.

When I was dressed, I padded out of the bathroom and found Amelia perched on the edge of my bed. Cole's side was empty.

"Everything fit okay?"

"I guess," I said, tugging at the waistband of the jeans that wanted to slide down my hips. "Where's Cole?"

"One of the officers took him down the hall to get cleaned up. Figured he'd prefer another guy over me. I'll fix your hair for you, if you want," she offered.

I blinked. I'd fixed fences and tentpoles, but never my hair.

"Sit," she said, patting the bed.

She misted my head with something that smelled light and clean and began tugging the comb through my hair one section at a time, looping the smoothed strands over my shoulder. "You have pretty hair, Avery. The color is really something."

"Thank you."

"I was hoping I could talk to you a little more—while Cole is out."

"About what?"

She paused. The comb caught on a small knot that pulled my head back. "The pregnancy test."

My heartbeat was cold and fast. "What about it?"

Another knot, another tug. "It was for you?"

Acid shot up my throat searching for an exit, but the bile only soured the back of my tongue. "I don't want to talk about that."

"Avery, I'm so, so sorry. This is very painful, I know that, but I want to try and keep anything else from hurting you. If I ask you some questions, do you think you can answer them for me? All you'll have to say is yes or no."

*No.* It sounded too easy.

"Just try," she coaxed. "I'll ask the two most important questions first. If you answer those and don't want to say any more, that'll be fine—okay?"

*No.* "Okay," I whispered.

"I want you to know that if your first answer is yes, you really did nothing wrong."

I felt guilty and I hadn't even heard the question.

"It's just—you were secluded during a very important time of your life. And you were around other kids who were too. Now, in a regular family dynamic, there are certain safeguards in place. You didn't have a typical family, so if you did have a...relationship you might be ashamed of, it's really not your fault.

"So, did you need the test because—did it have anything to do with any of your brothers?"

"You mean Cole?" I spat.

"Any of them."

"No," I whispered.

"All right." Her voice said I was lying. "Just one more question. Was this…was what led to you needing the test something you wanted to happen? Or did someone do something to you?"

"You're tricking me," I said, my eyes bubbling with sudden, hot tears. I'd almost forgotten—in all the mess and confusion, I'd almost left the panic in another place, something to deal with later. She was giving me too much to hold. "You're asking me two different things."

"I'm sorry, I—"

"*No*, and *yes*, and that's it. I'm not saying anything else." I buried my face in my hands until tiny stars danced in the galaxy behind my eyes.

Amelia's hands rested on my shoulders. "Avery?"

I shook her off. My wet hair was soaking through my shirt.

"You're not pregnant."

I raised my head slowly. "I'm not?"

"No."

"Oh." It was a terrible, ungrateful word, but it was the best I could do. I said it again. "Oh."

I'd had an abscess once. A hard lump that took root in the small of my back. It grew for weeks, and my skin got hotter and redder with each day that passed. The pain was incredible. When I could no longer stand up straight, my mother laid me on the kitchen floor, stuck a needle into a flame, and sank the sharp end into the hottest, reddest part of my skin. My fingers were clenched against the floor, bracing myself for the inevitable, more pain, pain so bad, it would kill me. But it didn't. The needle released me from its grip, and the relief that came as she coaxed the infection from my body was so great, I cried, all that poison oozing out and taking the pain with it. It was the most blissful moment of my life.

*You're not pregnant* was better.

It took me a minute to understand she was speaking a fact and not a hope. She said it like she was giving me a gift. "I'm really not?"

"The doctor ran a test when they took your blood last night. I can have him tell you if you want."

"No," I said, and then I was laughing, a hysterical bubbling laugh that sent tears streaking down my cheeks. "I'm just—"

"You're just what?"

"I'm just happy," I managed, my smile huge and watery. "Thank you."


My hair was twisted in a complicated pattern that fell down my back before I finished searching my mind for lingering fear and crying it out. Amelia was fitfully patient; she didn't hurry me, but I could tell she wanted to.

"We're going back to the police station," she told me when we finally left the room.

"Okay. Can I take this off?" I asked, tugging at the hooded sweatshirt she'd given me. "It's hot."

"No," she said. "Not yet."

When we'd walked through the hospital the day before, there were people everywhere, but now it was empty, eerily so. Our footsteps echoed down the hall.

"Where is everyone?" I asked.

She hesitated, and it was heavy, the pause. Full. "There are some reporters outside. We don't want them to see you."

"Why not?"

Another pause. Too long to be anything but a lie of omission, something to shut me up. "The van is right outside, so there's nothing to worry about."

She was very worried that I might worry. After finding out I was alone in my body, I doubted I'd ever worry again. We hit a dead end, and there was nowhere to go but out. Amelia touched my wrist. "Avery…"

"What?"

"Put your hood up."

There was no option to object. I pulled the hood over my head. She opened the door.

One second later I knew exactly why I should have been worried.

Amelia's face was steely. Her movements demanded no argument, not from me, not from anyone. She pulled my covered head to her shoulder, shielding my face with the notebook she held in her hand. Her other hand rose, pushing past the crowd of shouting people shooting questions like bullets.

Their aim was perfect. Words flew through the air, and each time they hit me, I was certain I'd be crushed, stomped to death by the weight of those voices that demanded so much. I brought my arms up to shield my ears.

But they weren't talking to me.

"Celeste! *Celeste*, over here!"

"How did you and Noah get out?"

"Was it a mass suicide?"

"Who was the leader?"

"How did the fire start?"

"Did anyone else survive?"

They were pushing, pressing on me from all angles. I kept my eyes on my feet, clad in new white sneakers. They looked like someone else's feet, too graceful to be mine. Quick, flashing pops snapped the air like lightning. When we got to the van, I kept my face down, and Amelia helped me climb inside. Cole was crouched on the floor behind the front seat.

"Climb in the back with your brother," the driver told me. I bumped his shoulder as I squeezed through the space between the two front seats. He wasn't much older than me, and he seemed wholly uninterested in the contents of his back seat.

Amelia joined the driver up front and slammed the door. The van started to move, and I was thrown sideways into Cole, who was dressed exactly like I was: jeans, white shirt, black sweatshirt. When I tugged my hood off, he reached over and grabbed the tail of hair that hung down my back.

"What'd they do to you?" he mumbled. "Do you know where we're going?"

"Police station," I said, sitting up on my knees to peer out the windows.

"I meant after."

"I don't know. Why were all those people—"

Amelia's voice cut through the air. "It's almost ten thirty."

"I was ready at ten, Mellie. You weren't," the driver told her.

"I couldn't bring them out together."

He glanced in the mirror over his head. The crowd was still in sight, still milling, still hungry. "They're at the station too. We're going to have to bring them in together."

"I know. Go faster."

"Just drive us back to the woods and let us out," I mumbled.

Cole pushed his hands through his hair. His face was white, shot through with hectic patches of red high on his cheeks.

The van jerked to a stop. "We're here," Amelia said, turning to face us. "Hoods up, heads down. Don't talk, don't look, just keep moving."

The driver got out first, spreading his arms wide to create a buffer of space between us and the new pushing, screaming mass. Amelia took my arm, and the van driver grabbed hold of Cole. The four of us moved in a line very much like a drill formation—maintain strength in unity, even when you are few.

There were more than reporters lining that sidewalk; there were people with phones pointed at us like guns and so many voices, it was impossible to pick out a single one. The crowd morphed and screamed until it looked solid, an entity with one face, and a gaping, open maw that wanted Noah and Celeste. We were hundred-year-old trees being ripped from the ground, babies who had a warm home inside a comfortable place and weren't willing to leave it for the inconvenience of birth. We were rooted and cocooned, and I held Cole's hand tightly in mine, our feet marching swiftly to escape the maelstrom we didn't even understand.

# SIXTEEN

We were seated at a long table, Cole and me on one side,
Amelia, Officer Rodolfo, and the kid from the van on the other.
Amelia was smiling. It was a strained, hopeful smile. A calculated
and painted expression that looked like it hurt her as much as she
was about to hurt us.

"Cole," she said.

"Yes, ma'am?"

"Your parents are coming to get you."

Silence. There was so much wrong with that sentence, it almost
slid past me. I almost laughed, because it was almost funny. *Your
parents are coming to get you.* But no, that wasn't right, because our
parents were dead...

*I hope...*

When the rest of it sank in—Cole, *your* parents are coming to get *you*—my confusion deepened. The words rattled around in my head without fitting together.

"What?" he said.

"Your parents," said Amelia. Her face, her static smile, instructed him to be happy about this. "They're so...I think they're in shock. Your mother—"

"My mother is dead." His expression was anger carved in ice. "*Our* parents are dead."

*I hope...*

Amelia's smile faltered, but she held on. "No, honey. Your real parents."

"Our parents are dead."

"Their names are Brian and Katherine Pierce," Amelia went on, as though an introduction would solve everything. "And you have an older sister named Eve, and two little brothers, twins, that you—"

"My sister's name is Avery," he said, gripping my hand. "We're two of those who were chosen and the only ones who survived."

"Avery has family too," Officer Rodolfo said. That was news to me. He wasn't smiling, and I felt some vague appreciation of that. Everything was vague. I was in shock too. It was the only camaraderie I could find with Cole's real parents.

"Yes," said Cole. "She has me."

Amelia's smile died. Just then, I hated her. My hate was thick and bloodred, it got tied up in sticky knots that slowed my heart, and I didn't even care that she was the one who told me it was beating alone, that there was no baby. Anyone could have told me that.

"You lied to us," I whispered.

"No—"

"You said we were getting out."

"You are. Cole's parents are coming, and—"

"But you didn't tell us *that*!" I shouted. "You didn't tell us you were taking him away!"

My voice cracked and died in the heavy air, leaving a corpse of silence. Van Driver looked like he was on my side. Officer Rodolfo looked at the table.

"I'm sorry, Avery," Amelia said after a moment. "But you must be returned to your families. I thought you realized that. Most people would be happy—"

"We're not *most people*. We've been the *only* people, our whole lives."

No one spoke, and for a moment, it felt like we might get away, like we *could* get up and run. There was no script in place; they hadn't thought this through either. Amelia was shooting glances at the door. It was a thin, wooden door. It looked like nothing.

But next to me, Cole was shaking so badly, his chair was squeaking. "What about Avery?" he asked.

"Avery is going to be given a place to stay until her family is located," Amelia said.

"And Cole?" I said. "You're just going to let these people *take* him?"

"They're his parents. He's going home."

"I don't want to go," said Cole. "Not without Avery."

"You have to," she told him.

"Why?"

"Because you belong with them. You're only sixteen—"

"What about me?" I cut in. "Do I *have* to go with anyone?"

"No," she said slowly. "But—"

"She can come with me," Cole said. "I'll go if Avery comes too."

Amelia threw a stricken look at Officer Rodolfo. "I don't think—"

"Son, your family is coming to take you home," Officer Rodolfo told Cole in the same voice he'd used to arrest us the day before. "The whole world has been looking for you for fifteen years, your parents have been through hell—"

"So have we," Cole said, tearful and loud. "And yesterday you said—"

*Yesterday.* One day. Years at the compound, months on our own, and nothing happened. It was these snippets of time that were ruining me. My father was right—there was no warning.

The end was swift.

The door opened a crack, and the receptionist poked her head through. "They're here."

Cole's whole body jerked. I pressed a hand to my mouth. "What, now?" I managed. "They're here now?"

"Avery," Cole choked.

"I'll come out," Officer Rodolfo said.

"No!" Cole shouted, warming to fight or run. He jumped to his feet.

"Cole, look at me," I said, tugging on his arm.

"Listen to me, Cole," Amelia said.

"No, don't listen to her, look at me." I pulled him back to his chair and pressed my forehead against his, gripping his face in my hands. "Calm down," I whispered.

"We have to get out of here, we have to—"

"We have to be smart. Do not lose control. What do we need?"

Every breath he pulled was ragged and choked. I pressed his hand to my chest and took a long, deep breath, nodding as I did. He followed, and we sat there for a full minute, our chests rising in tandem, ignoring Amelia's gently irritating pleas until the air felt like an ally again. Cole's free hand gripped my wrist, the same hand that had danced me down the hall years before—bigger, but still the same. We weren't dancing now, we were being dragged—hauled and pushed toward another moment that would change us forever.

And he would remember this time.

"Tell me what we need."

"I don't know!"

"Remember…remember the baby," I coaxed, close enough that the others couldn't hear.

"That wasn't im—"

"It was, Cole. I lied to you, it *was* important, it was so important, and so is this." I closed my eyes, curling my fingers against his cheek and trying to breathe. "We got through that together. Try and remember how. What do we need?"

"F-focus," he said. "But I don't—it's not supposed to happen like this!"

"Shh…close your eyes." His eyes slid shut, bright droplets clinging to his lashes. "We're in the woods," I whispered. "It's nighttime. And it's cold. We don't have our tent, we can't make a fire, there's nothing to protect us. So first we focus to prepare our minds. Then what?"

"Then, um—"

I could hear steps in the hallway. Officer Rodolfo's voice over the sound of someone crying.

"Focus," I breathed, pushing his hair back. "You only hear me. We're the only ones here. Why do we prepare?"

"So we can endure—endure anything."

"And thrive. No matter what, right? If we do those things, we can save ourselves."

"Not from this!"

Now I was crying, because I was lying to him, and I knew it was a lie, and so did he. "Yes, we can," I said, my arms tight around his neck. "We have no fire and no shelter, but if we lie down together and hang on to each other, we'll be able to stay warm. So that's what we'll do. Because we're the only people who matter. We're the only ones left."

"You need to be back with your family, Cole," Amelia said. "You need—"

"Shut up!" I shouted.

She did, for a second. "We're trying to help you."

"Then leave us alone! You can't just *take* him," I insisted, ripping off the elastic wrapped around the end of my hair. "You didn't even tell us, you didn't—"

Officer Rodolfo came back in. Cole jumped up so fast, his chair flipped over. Before I could move, he dragged me out of mine, gripping me like a shield.

"Let's all calm down," said Amelia. "Let go of Avery—"

"No."

Amelia pressed her fingers to her temples and nodded toward us. Van Driver crossed the room and took me by the wrists. He wasn't rough, but I let out a thin shriek, and Cole shoved him, hard. The momentum sent Cole and me flying backward, sprawled out on the ground.

"Don't touch her!" Cole screamed, pedaling his feet against the shiny floor. Our legs smashed into more chairs, raising a tremendous clatter as we swam through an aluminum forest.

"Please," I whispered. "Oh, please…" I didn't know who I was talking to, but I kept saying it, begging some invisible entity. *Please let us go, please be wrong, please wake me up.* Cole was my last thing, the last part of me. They'd already taken everything else.

He stood and lifted me along with him, holding me up—maybe to make up for what he'd done, or what he didn't do, the last time things had gone so terribly wrong.

Maybe he knew it was his last chance.

"Cole…"

"I'm not going! We're not who you think we are."

"You are. You have to."

"No, I don't, I—"

"Noah?"

The voice was barely more than a whisper. It should have been swallowed in the din, but somehow it broke through my panic and Cole's rage and silenced us both. It was a woman's voice, and when she spoke, the entire room stopped. Stopped like we'd been frozen, like she'd turned us all to stone. I couldn't see Cole's face. He was holding me aloft at an odd angle, my toes barely kissing the ground.

Katherine Pierce stood stock-still in the doorway. I'd never seen her before, but I recognized her immediately. She had reddish-brown hair, pale, creamy skin, and Cole's eyes. They were the only part of her that moved, the only part that hadn't been suspended by the sight of what she thought she'd never see again.

Cole hugged me closer. His heart was throbbing in his chest, like something trying to escape. We were a portrait of chaos; no one spoke and no one moved.

Then the woman took one step. Then another, sliding across the

floor. But she didn't see me, even when she was in front of us, searching Cole's face with bright bewilderment through a gloss of tears.
Her hand fluttered toward his cheek, and he flinched, a reaction that
brightened her eyes further.

"My baby..." she whispered. "Brian, look. It's him."

A man I hadn't noticed at first walked toward us. He was tall,
with a smooth, young-looking face, confused by all the gray in his
black hair. He was looking at Cole with the same expression of awe,
like he might disappear in a puff of smoke. Cole was holding me like
I might too.

The man named Brian blinked. "My God. Noah..."

I felt the rhythmic motion of Cole shaking his head. "That's not
my name."

Katherine's hand went to her mouth, barely catching the sob that
bubbled free. "Noah. Oh, baby, what did they do to you?"

"Why don't we give you a few minutes?" Amelia said in a voice of
practiced mediation. "Come with me, Celeste."

Cole's lips moved against the back of my head. "That's not her
name. She's not going anywhere."

There was no nod and no discussion, or maybe there was,
behind our backs in the stationary silence, because the next thing
I knew Officer Rodolfo had yanked me out of Cole's grip like a bag
of feathers. The motion, the sudden off-kilter jerk, sent me back to
the commune, back to my father handing me off. I screamed and no

one understood, because instead of letting me go, Officer Rodolfo dragged me halfway across the room.

The tips of Cole's fingers skimmed my sleeve. "Avery…no! Put her down!"

"Just for a little while," Amelia was saying.

I threw back my head and screamed, pounding my fists against the doughy arms that were carrying me back to the only moment that was worse than this. I couldn't live them both at the same time.

A hot ball of lead settled in my stomach.

"*Let her go!*" Cole screamed. "Don't touch her, don't!"

The heat lowered and pushed until the ache between my legs lit with fresh remembrance. I twisted and kicked, but Officer Rodolfo was burlier than he looked—my fists and feet had no effect on him. We were almost to the door when I landed a solid blow to the side of his neck, and he grunted. He hauled me up until I was hanging over his shoulder, one arm pinned beneath me. "Watch yourself," he mumbled.

"Help me! Help me, Cole, *please!*" It was barely a sob, the raw and pathetic plea I managed to cough out. My next scream died in my throat and burned there until I was too choked to speak.

"I'll stay, I'm sorry, just let her go!" Cole shouted.

I kicked upward, hard. Amelia grabbed my ankles.

"Bring her *back*," Cole screamed.

Cole's parents got tired of waiting for us to leave—their fingers had been itching for too long. They pounced, grabbing at him until all I could see were his eyes wedged between their shoulders, his protesting voice muffled in white cashmere. "No," he spurted, trying to wiggle free. "Avery, no—"

"We'll bring her back," Amelia said, smiling her plastic smile as her hands pinched my feet together. "Promise."

"*Please!*" Cole screamed. His voice was hoarse, his face red and hectic, both hands flying to his head. "Don't do this, please don't take her away from me—Avery!"

My fingers reached out, groping at thin air. The door slammed behind us.

# SEVENTEEN

"AVERY?"

Amelia's voice was distant and strange, like I was hearing her underwater. The words blurred, and I blinked hard, as though that would help me hear better. "What?" I whispered.

"When Noah and his parents are—"

"Cole."

Her eyes, frozen in static sympathy, wavered a bit. "I know how painful this is."

I laughed, one loud throaty bark. "No, you don't."

"I…I appreciate it, then," she said. "But you have to realize that Cole—Noah—is their child. The last time they saw him, he was a baby. They spent fifteen years not knowing if he was cold, or scared, or hungry—they had no idea if they would ever see him again. Last night they got a phone call that hurt too much for them to even hope for. Do you understand?"

She wouldn't look away. I squeezed my eyes shut. "Cole is my brother," I said. My voice was strange. I barely recognized it, and I wouldn't understand...I wouldn't *appreciate*...that I was tapping into a level of fortitude I didn't even know I had by even having words to speak until much later. "He's been my brother since he was a baby. I spent fifteen years making sure he was never cold, or scared, or hungry. They're taking him away, and I don't know if I'll ever see him again. Do *you* understand?"

Amelia pressed her fingers together. "He needs to go home."

*I think we should go home.*

The fire was still alive when he'd said that, still eating whatever we could have gone back to when we'd had one horrible chance to make one horrible decision.

"They've agreed to let you say goodbye."

I nodded faintly. *Goodbye.* That word had never meant much, because I'd never had anything I wanted to keep. But now...

*Goodbye,* I thought. *Goodbye, Mother; goodbye, Father; goodbye, sister; goodbye...*

"Where is he?" I asked.

Amelia led me down the hallway with her hands on my shoulders.

"I'm going to call you Celeste while we're in there," she said as we approached a closed door. "Kate is very overwhelmed. Using your real name will make it easier for her to see your connection to Cole."

"She already has the easy part," I mumbled.

"No," Amelia said, almost to herself. "She doesn't."

She opened the door. Cole was inside, huddled on a squashy green couch. Kate was next to him, practically sitting in his lap. He looked up when we walked in. She tightened her grip on his shoulders.

"Kate, I'd like you to meet Celeste Bishop," Amelia said, choosing to erase any memory of our first meeting. "Celeste, this is Noah's mother, Kate."

Kate's eyes darted toward me, but when they met mine, she looked away. "I don't have to leave, do I?"

Amelia smiled smoothly. "I thought we could go down the hall."

"No," said Kate, her eyes tight and snapping. "She's one of those...those people."

"Kate, Celeste was abducted, same as Noah. She has no ties to the cult."

"I don't care. I'm not leaving him with her."

"She's my sister," Cole spat, wriggling feebly in a cage of white sweater and gold rings. "Her name is Avery."

"Honey, no," Kate cried, cupping Cole's cheek. "She's not your sister. That's what I'm trying to tell you."

"Kate, I know it's difficult, but Celeste and Noah were raised as siblings. It would be healthier if they had the opportunity to say goodbye privately. Like I said," Amelia told her when she didn't respond, "we're only going down the hall."

The carpet was patterned in big squares. I kept my eyes on the square under Kate's feet, her gold shoes shining against the weave. *Rabbit*, I told myself. *She's a rabbit, and if you're not careful, she'll bolt.* My father's voice instructed me, *Stay still as a statue. You don't have her yet.*

I waited, watching, until the toes of her shoes slid backward. She got to her feet.

"Five minutes. And then I'm leaving here with my son." I could feel her eyes on the top of my head, prickling my scalp.

There was a muted padding of heels on carpet. Amelia held the door open for her and then turned back to us.

"Take as long as you need." She took Cole's hand and put it in mine, sandwiching us together before she slid through the door. She paused when there was still an inch of space, and she used it, that tiny crack, to break through her own facade. Her words were an afterthought or a fearful thought, but they sounded honest. "I'm sorry."

The door closed.

Cole and I looked at each other, our hands still linked. I sat down next to him.

His eyes on me burned. "They hurt you."

I shook my head. "No."

"You were screaming."

"I was scared," I said, pushing his hair away from his eyes. "I was...remembering."

His eyes were wide, brimming with something I didn't recognize until he spoke again. The words shook and rose and fell. "I can't go with those people."

"Cole—"

"They're going to take me."

"Listen to me." My own eyes were darting around the room, searching every suspect object, every foreign thing I didn't understand. "It won't be for long." My voice wavered and caught on every other word. "It won't..."

Two tears slipped down his cheeks, but he broke into a sunny grin that morphed into a grimace so fast, I almost missed it. "How do you know?"

"Because they can't keep you forever. Only until you're a little older. I'll wait for you."

"What if someone takes you too?"

I stilled, my tongue frozen to the roof of my mouth. I hadn't thought about meeting my own strangers, people from the outside who could lay claim to my life and looked just like me. "I won't go," I said after a moment. "They can't make me. I'll stay here until you come back and then we'll start over."

"Start over?"

"Yes. Somewhere else. Somewhere safe."

Cole motioned to the empty door. "They told me everything... everything is a lie. You're not my sister."

"Don't listen to them," I said. "It doesn't matter what they say, *we* know. I'll always be your sister, and you'll always be my brother. They can't undo that."

"I hope not," he whispered.

My vision swam with hot tears. What I was saying to him was true, though I don't know if he believed me. But it had to be true, because I'd read about love. Not the married kind, which I'd never seen between my parents, save for the occasional rise of my mother's belly, but regular love, the kind that is gifted to most people in the simplest of ways. I didn't know parents were supposed to love their children. It never occurred to me to love my parents, and I didn't. I know I didn't, because right then, in that moment, something flooded through me in a wave of unbearable pain and unspeakable bliss. The feeling was new and unknowable, and it turned me into a puppet, all strings and wooden parts that reached for Cole and pulled him toward me. He arrived without complaint, burying his face in my neck, and for the first time since we'd run, my heart didn't rise in panic, however brief. Because he was mine. Someone I was just then realizing I'd loved from the beginning. Someone who had always loved me.

It was horrible.

"I can't leave you alone," Cole moaned against my shoulder.

"You aren't leaving me alone. You're coming back, right?" His breath hitched, and I clutched him tighter, nodding for him. "Right?"

"What if—"

"Just say yes. Just say you will, and that's all. Please."

Cole nodded, his head moving against mine. "Yes."

I pulled back slowly, wiping my cheeks, and tried to smile. Cole reached for my hands. He gripped my fingers tightly.

*He took my wrists in one hand and held them over my head. He was strong—maybe not strong for a man, but strong enough to overpower me. When I kicked, his knee pinched my leg down. When I tried to scream, he mashed his forehead against my mouth. Moving...*

My vision doubled and then tripled until everything was a blur. I looked down at my feet, a burning, tickling pain crawling through me like ants.

"Avery?" Cole was shaking me. "What's the matter?"

*Moving on top of me. Pushing hard enough to split me in two. Feathery, penciled horses galloping over my head.* I blinked hard. "Nothing, I just...I was remembering."

"You said that before. Remembering what?"

The truth was lodged behind my tongue. "What it was like to be alone," I said instead. "And...and the walls in Hannah's room. The way she drew those pictures on them." I stopped while the words were still shapeless, just a kaleidoscope. Moments.

"And the fire?"

"Yes," I said. "The fire too."

He took a breath that looked painful; he seemed to be speaking to himself. "It was an accident."

My heart slowed somewhat, even as his eyes darted around the room. I caught his hand. "I know it was."

"So let's forget about it, okay? It was our place, and our people. Let's just let them die. No one deserves to know about us. Don't talk about it," he said in a rush. "Not to anyone. I promise I won't either, not ever."

My fingers tightened, asking their own question. "Cole?"

"Just promise you won't, please? Promise you'll forget."

I looked at him, still tangled up in fear and pain. Still held together with string. Nodded.

The worry line I knew so well, etched in the smooth skin between his eyes, cut deeper. "I'm sorry," he whispered. His eyes were bright, losing to whatever was battling to come out. "This whole thing was my fault—everything. I'm so sorry."

"It wasn't—don't be sorry."

Those bright eyes looked into mine. There was confusion there, something tugging at him that I couldn't see. He blinked, and the brightness slipped away. "Then I'm sorry," he said carefully, "for the things you have to remember."

I nodded hard and couldn't stop. I nodded until Cole gripped the back of my neck and pulled my head down to his shoulder. We stayed that way for a long time, and I tried my hardest to feel and see and file away as much as I could: the sound of his breathing, the beat of his heart. It's a moment I still go back to, and I like to think it was real, every part that I remember.

I hope that some part of him remembers me too.

# EIGHTEEN

When it was over and Cole was gone, I sat by myself in the long, mirrored room. Less than twelve hours had passed since we'd woken up in the hospital bed, and I still had a gnawing ache in my back where the railing had dug in. I liked it. All my other senses had left me, so it was nice to feel something. Even something that hurt.

I fiddled with the loop of blue fabric around my wrist. Cole's parents had tried to make him leave his backpack, but when they told him that, his eyes got fiery and bright. He'd taken it off and grabbed the hanging end of the left strap, tearing it free with a long, low rip. Everyone in the police station watched as he took my hand and wound the strip of cloth around my wrist again and again, tying it with a knot so tight, I'd probably need a knife to cut it off.

But I wasn't going to cut it off.

"Avery?" Amelia's voice sounded at the door. "Are you ready?"

I looked up. My eyes were popping with black spots, like I'd just come in from the sun, but really it was just the part of me that wanted to shut off, the part that wanted everything to be dark. There was a similar static in my ears, the rushing hollow that only comes after tremendous noise.

"There is not a great deal of information to disclose at this time." A faceless officer was speaking from his position at the outdoor podium set under the eaves to avoid the spray of gray drizzle. There were a dozen microphones attached to the wooden stand and dozens more held aloft in the crowd. "However, we can confirm that on the afternoon of June twenty-fourth, Sedgwick County law enforcement apprehended two teenagers who were later found to be survivors of the five-alarm fire that struck the Clovelite plastics factory just outside Latham, Kansas." I watched his face on the television screen behind the desk. It blared the words a half second after I heard them from the steps of the police station. The officer was oblivious to the rise and fall of the crowd. It swelled with every word, fed but not sated.

"Investigators are still working to determine the cause of the fire and the exact number of fatalities that occurred. However, we were able to positively identify, and do confirm, that the individuals in question are Noah Reid Pierce and Celeste Bishop, both of whom had been missing since 2008. We are—" He held up one hand against the barrage of questions that punched through the damp air. "We are happy to report they are both healthy and doing well, and based on the information they were able to give us, it appears the fire was accidental and not a planned suicide as previously speculated. We are unable to confirm any additional information at this time. We would like to thank the Pierce family for their statement, and we echo their request that the public give them privacy during this emotional time."

"Avery?"

I blinked. The mirrored room was gone. There was an acrid, oily smell in the air that made my eyes burn. We were moving, I realized— the floor was vibrating underneath me, and I bounced around in the open space of the van. "What?"

"I said you'll like this place," Amelia said. The windows were dark and rain splattered, illuminated by flashes of dirty-yellow light every few seconds.

"What place?"

"I told you back at the station, remember? I've set you up with a friend of mine. She runs a facility, a private place for women," Amelia told me as Van Driver piloted us through a maze of loops and turns. "It's a wonderful program, and you'll be safe there."

*Safe from what?* I didn't dare ask. I didn't have room to be afraid of anything else.

"It's only temporary," she said without turning. "Just until we're able to inform your family that you've been found."

Not found. Taken. Me and Cole both.

His departure had been anything but smooth. No one would tell me anything—not where he was going and not when I would see him again. His mother had kept an eagle's grip on his shoulder, her nails sharp and shining pale gold.

My eyes were glued to those nails. Cole flinched when they poked his skin. "Can you, um—where are you taking him?" I asked her.

"Don't worry about that, honey," said Kate. She was all sweetness and light in her sweater and heels, dancing over the same patch of floor I'd thrown up on. "You'll be back with your own family soon." She turned to Amelia as if to confirm, and I saw the tiniest quiver rumple first Amelia's face then Kate's.

But Amelia's voice was just as sweet. "Kate, I'm sure you'd be willing to let them keep in touch—"

"We'll see," said Kate, tugging Cole closer. "Right now we need to concentrate on putting our family back together."

Cole had been silent up to that point, but when she said that, he jerked away from her and pulled me into his arms so tightly, I thought my ribs would crack. Someone near the front desk started to cry, like this was their tragedy. There were delighted sighs and a smattering of clapping hands. I pulled back and rested my forehead on his. "Soon," I whispered.

Cole's father stepped forward. "Come on, Noah."

His voice demanded no argument, which wasn't fair—they got to keep him. Officer Rodolfo and Cole's father had to physically drag us apart. Suddenly everyone in the room found other things to look at.

"It's just for a little while," I said, choking on the words. My hands scrabbled for Cole's before his father yanked him backward. "Remember what you know, remember what you need to do—"

"Let go of her, Noah..."

"Let *me* go!"

"Cole, please," I whispered. I squeezed his hands and tried to broadcast what I couldn't say, things no one had taught us. "Please. Remember what I said."

"Let go of him," his mother said briskly. It looked like she wanted to smack our hands apart. His father gave another yank, pulling him toward the door.

"Cole!"

"I'll come back!" he screamed over the hump of his father's shoulder. "I promise! Stay here, Avery! Don't go anywhere! I'm coming back, so stay—"

The door slammed.

"We're here."

The side of the van slid open, revealing me again to no one this time. I set one foot cautiously on the ground. It was rough blacktop, cracked and dotted with loose, tarry chunks and drizzle. Night had fallen, finally, and the black sky rolled with dark, smoky clouds, oozing across the moon like spilled ink.

The pavement rose and stretched toward a house, a real house, with a wide porch and staggered squares of yellow light. The compound had been neatly cubed, but this house was tall and rambling, with rooms jutting out at odd angles like someone had stuck them on with no regard to how they might look. The whole thing was surrounded by a chain-link fence that sat well outside the perimeter.

*We fear the perimeter.*

My head turned, searching for the words that hadn't come from the outside but in. I waited for more, for clarity, but there was none. More drops fell.

There was a moderately nicer wooden fence blocking off a side yard. Mud-caked toys lay abandoned in the wet grass. Plastic lawn chairs were stacked four feet high on the porch, and a sagging loop of mosquito netting hung off the railing.

I swallowed hard. "Where are we?"

Amelia caught my hand. "Come inside," she told me. "You'll see."

I pulled away. This wasn't a place anyone wanted to see. It was a last resort.

But I had nowhere else to go.

Our feet clumped up the peeling porch steps. The rain was carried sideways by a stiff wind, and I slipped on a slick patch of blue paint. I lurched forward; Amelia caught my arm.

"Careful," she warned.

"Careful," I whispered.

Amelia produced a key from her pocket and slid it into the lock.

A series of high-pitched beeps followed the click of the door. Amelia stepped inside and flipped open a tiny flap attached to the wall. There were lighted buttons underneath. Her fingers moved nimbly over them, and the beeping stopped. Amelia shed her wet jacket and hung it on a hook by the door.

"Come on in," she said.

"I don't—"

"We just waxed the floors up there, close the door, Mellie!"

The words echoed in the damp darkness, and I automatically stepped into the vestibule, though the voice carried no sting. It was a girl's voice, rich and melodious, full of body. Amelia ushered me in and shut the door.

"Thank you!" the voice sang.

"Are you spying on me again, Ronnie?" Amelia called.

"I spy on everyone."

Amelia started walking, and I still had nowhere to go, so I followed her. We crossed the shiny wooden floor into a hallway, and the foyer suddenly branched out. It reminded me of a butterfly, the way it was long in the middle and opened on both sides. A huge desk took up the length of the room and blocked two sets of double doors: one right, one left. The left-side doors were made of frosted, wavy glass, and behind them I could see blurry colors, dancing shadows. The doors on the right were plain wood.

Faint strands of music, plaintive and slow, drifted from behind the desk. It sounded like the scent of grass on my skin, like fire-warmed breezes and being alone in the dark. The melody wrapped me up and pulled me forward, and without it I might not have moved.

Amelia walked up to the desk and leaned across the shiny top. I lingered a few feet behind her. "I see you got the cameras working again," she said to the air.

"Uh-huh. Toby fixed them this morning."

"*Toby* did? How?"

"He was highly motivated." A bright-red head suddenly popped up from behind the desk, and its owner smiled at us, flashing slightly crooked white teeth. "Mission critical. The Wi-Fi was out too."

"Ronnie…" Amelia said glancing sideways at me. "Can you tell Zoe we're here?"

"I already did. I told her you were here and ruining the floors." The girl turned to me and smiled again. "Hi."

My eyes dropped, focusing on the toes of my shoes. "Hi," I mumbled.

Amelia pulled me forward. "This is Avery," she said. "Avery, this is Ronnie. She's the front desk supervisor here."

"It sounds a lot more glamorous than it is," Ronnie told me.

I didn't know what to say, so I kept looking at my shoes. They weren't white anymore, not pristine. They looked like my feet again. My throat felt dry and rough, and I became aware of too much to look up. I had a fistful of my wet shirt bunched up in one hand. The loop of fabric on my wrist was dirty. It itched. I moistened my lips before I raised my head.

"Where is here?" I asked.

A peal of laughter sounded behind the glass, and Ronnie's smile warmed. A line of tiny television screens glowed next to her, gray screens that showed the rain and the porch and the van, still idling at the curb.

Amelia nodded toward the door to the right. "I'll show you."


Zoe was Zoey Pyne, but only to her parents. "Zoe," she said, "no *y*. Zoey makes me sound like I should be hosting a kids' show in the seventies. Welcome to Haven House, Avery, it's nice to meet you."

I glanced at Amelia.

"Avery," Amelia confirmed. "We thought you'd prefer to keep your name. Would you like to?"

I nodded before I wondered why she was asking such a weird question. Despite what was becoming unbearable fatigue, my whole body was crawling with nerves. I wanted to get out of there.

"Don't worry about anyone finding out who you are," said Zoe. She reminded me of a statue. Her skin was like polished marble, gleaming and nearly colorless, and she was the tallest person I'd ever seen. I only came up to her shoulder. She had a slick of shiny brown hair that fell to her chin and a face that was wholly unremarkable, save for her lips; they were lush and pouty, painted a deep shade of crimson. "Not here. We have a nondisclosure clause among residents." I must have looked blank, because she kept talking. "It promises anonymity within our space. No last names, no private details, nothing. No one is allowed to question you about your situation, and you cannot question them about theirs."

I swallowed and it hurt. "Why would they care?"

We were holed up in a tiny office at the end of the hall. Zoe was sitting at a small, cluttered desk. She rifled through a mound of papers, and I thought she was going to make me write my name on one of them, like the police officer had, but instead she pulled something silver and flat from underneath the pile. She pointed it toward a television in the corner. "That's why."

The black screen brightened to reveal the officer at the podium, booming the names *Celeste* and *Noah* like they were presents he was dying to hand out. Zoe clicked a button, and the picture changed to Cole's parents, red-faced and crying. A third click revealed something that sent thousands of buzzing black dots into my eyes: me and Cole being ushered into the police station with Amelia and Van Driver by our sides. I saw a pale strand of hair escape my hood, the briefest glimpse of Cole's eyes. Our hands were tightly linked. I didn't remember holding hands.

"You're on every channel," Zoe told me as Cole's baby picture flashed on the screen. "That's why Amelia had you cover your faces. One look and the public is going to be all over you. I'm sure you don't want that."

I tore my eyes away from Noah and Celeste. "No."

"We can help. Even with our usual safeguards in place, we're prepared to be extremely careful with you."

"But if I don't go around telling people, how would anyone know who I am? No one is going to recognize me from that," I said, indicating my own five-year-old face lit up on the screen.

Zoe nodded. The television flicked off. "You're a smart girl, Avery."

"I don't understand what I'm doing here."

"You're here because you need protection right now. The media doesn't know where you are, but if they find out, it will be much, much worse than just your face getting out."

"All this is," Amelia cut in, "is a safe house. It's a place for women who don't have anywhere else to go. Young women just like you, women with their children—"

"But I don't want to—to be *put* anyplace. I'll be fine on my own." The word *safe* kept bouncing around in my head in Cole's voice. *This is the only safe place.*

Zoe was watching me. "Will you?"

"Yes," I snapped.

"You don't have to stay," Amelia told me. "We can't force you, but maybe we can tell you a little more about Haven before you decide?"

I took a deep breath. I didn't know if they believed me or not, but they shouldn't have. I was so tired, I wouldn't have made it out of the parking lot. "Go ahead."

"Haven House is a private shelter," Zoe said. "I own it, I run it, and I get to decide who stays and who doesn't."

"What is your criteria?"

Zoe glanced at Amelia, a tiny smile on her lips. It made me mad—I was tired of everyone acting like I was supposed to be completely ignorant.

"It varies," Zoe said. "We look at each situation individually. Suffice it to say we try to offer some sort of solution to every woman who comes through the door. If we can't be the ones to help her, we try to find someone who can."

"I don't need any help."

"What if someone else does?" Amelia asked.

"What does that mean?"

"There are two reasons I brought you here," Amelia said. "Let me make it perfectly clear that I'm not trying to frighten you or imply anything about what you've been through. I'm simply going by what I know. Okay?"

I shifted in my seat and fiddled with the blue fabric on my wrist. It was still wet. "Okay."

"There are still a lot of question marks surrounding you, Avery. You came out of a major crime scene, and it was probably a crime scene long before it burned down. Have you stopped to wonder whether or not there were other children like you there? Other children who were taken?"

I didn't answer for a moment. Sarah's red curls flashed in my mind's eye. The way Amaris's olive skin deepened to a gorgeous brown every summer when the rest of us turned pink. I tried to pull apart all our differences and see who might be the same. "No," I lied. "And I don't know how I can help you with that."

"You can help us by being available," Amelia said. "By answering whatever questions you can. Noah—Cole—will not be available. His parents don't want him interviewed, and we have to respect that. But if you agree to help us, no one is going to grill you, and no one is going to hold you accountable for information you might not have. We hope to hear from your family—"

"Where are they?" I asked suddenly. "How come no one came running to get me like they did Cole?"

Amelia pulled her chair closer to me. "I wanted to wait until tomorrow—"

"Tell me now."

"Your mother is deceased," Amelia said, point-blank. I felt nothing at the words. If anything, I was relieved. "She passed away about five years ago. She was raising you alone, and it seems that your father was never named. Right now we're looking for extended family—grandparents, aunts and uncles..."

"Don't bother."

"I understand you're used to being on your own," Amelia said. "But knowing when to accept help is just as important as knowing how to take care of yourself."

I looked around the room, and my eyes were burning again, tears mixed with the fierce, desperate need to sleep. "What's the other reason?"

Amelia glanced at Zoe. "There were twelve of you, right? At the…"

"At the compound, yes," I said. "Ten kids and our parents."

"You and Cole survived the fire," she said after a moment. My reference to our parents threw her. "That's two. So far, police recovered six sets of remains from the scene. That's eight."

It was unnerving to hear the same math I'd done a million times parroted back at me. To have my secret fear brought to the outside. "They're sure?"

"So far."

I took a deep breath, but it shook.

"When we found you, you thought you were pregnant. You told me it was not consensual. That made me think that, perhaps, there was someone there who was hurting you."

My head lowered. I didn't speak.

"It was a very bad fire," she went on. "We're almost positive you and Cole were the only ones to make it out alive. But the almost…the almost is what bothers me."

"You think they...do you think they're going to come back for me?" I whispered.

"They who, Avery? Who are you afraid of?"

"I'm not afraid."

"If someone else in your family did survive, would you want to see them?"

"No," I said quickly. It was too quick—the words blew away the protective layer of dirt I had piled on the truth. My answer proved I'd been lying about what I saw that night. But Amelia seemed pleased.

"That's good," she said. "That's important. Because you were raised in a cult, Avery. You were brought up to believe things that are simply not true. These types of people, survivalists, they're not uncommon. You can see them on reality TV any night of the week, but the people you were with were fanatical. And the one thing I know about cults is that they don't like it when there is interference from the outside. They don't like to lose members.

"Now, of all the people," Amelia said slowly, "in all the world, the only ones who could possibly match your name to your face are the people who took you. Not even your biological family could do it. And your name is out there now. I don't think we should take any chances."

I looked down at my lap. "The commune was supposed to be safe, and it wasn't."

"Where did you feel safe?" Zoe asked me.

I tried to answer, but my voice broke around the lump in my throat. I held my hand up instead, helplessly waving my cloth-wrapped wrist.

Zoe nodded. Then she reached behind her desk. A large blue bundle emerged, the same blue as my bracelet and my father's shirt and the nightgown I ran away in.

My knapsack, neatly stuffed, with the tent canvas wrapped in the folds of the sleeping bag. I reached for it, something I didn't even know I was missing, and when my fingers touched the fabric, I pulled it close and cradled it like a baby. I buried my face in the rough cotton and remembered every night it had been my pillow. My eyes slid closed as tears slipped down my cheeks and sank into the cloth, bringing a deeper blue.

Zoe's voice reached me, quiet and slow. "Would you like to see your room?"

The room they put me in wasn't *my* room, it was *a* room. There were three private bedrooms on the first floor, and the one she led me to belonged to a live-in counselor who was away that week. The bed, Zoe told me, was small but very comfortable.

I didn't care about the bed. The second the door closed behind her, I stripped off my wet clothes and dug inside my pack for Cole's white T-shirt. We'd washed all our clothes under the showers, and the dank, mildewy scent of the locker room was still embedded in the fabric. I breathed it in until I could pretend he was with me again.

The smell was in the sleeping bag too. I left the bed untouched, unrolled the bag, and spread the worn flannel on the floor. It was bigger than I remembered, stretched out from the strain of holding two instead of one. There was a straight-backed chair against one wall, and I positioned it a few feet from the bed with the sleeping bag in between. It pitched the canvas over my head nicely.

Someone was singing in a room nearby, something lilting and slightly off-key. It was pretty, as good as a lullaby. I remember closing my eyes, but I don't know if I dreamed. I don't even know if I slept. It seemed like every time a shadow fell, my eyes were wide open.

# NINETEEN

---

HAVEN HOUSE HAD A LIST OF RULES GOVERNING ITS RESIDENTS THAT
would have made my father proud. No prying. No questions. Everyone
was anonymous unless they chose not to be. The name penned on
the bottom of my contract was *Avery*. They wanted me to make it
official, to write Celeste Bishop on that line, but that would have
been a lie. There were things I was willing to abandon, but my name
was not one of them.

My own programming, as it was, my ability to adapt, was probably why I did so well there. The biggest changes I made were made
for other people, and they were necessary. I can't say that I owe Zoe
and Haven my life, but I probably owe them something. Normalcy,
maybe, or the ability to pretend. I didn't walk out of there whole, but
it was where I started to shed the poisoned thoughts my parents had

pumped into me and began to assemble the fragmented memories that were left.

That alone should have made me better, but it didn't. The things my mind was too scared to remember were worse than anything it could have dreamed up.

My fear never leaves me—the thought that everything could suddenly end. I doubt the fear ever will. Especially now. I know better than ever that the worst can happen because it's happened before. It's not like a fear of the dark, not innocent and absurd. It's deeper than that; it's part of who I am, and the best I can do is pretend it isn't there. It's a tumor I choose to ignore, a throbbing tooth I hope will go away. I have no choice—it's hard to rationalize disaster when there's no one there to listen. It's the one thing about the compound that I miss.

I've read stories about people who waded onto thin ice for one reason or another—ice that cracked under their weight and sent them plummeting into dark water. All the accounts, from the people who lived, were the same: the problem with going under is that you never come up in the same spot. No one wants to fall into a hole, but once you do, you better hope that hole sticks around to let you out. Fighting only makes you weak. You can rise and fall and try again, but the ice is always there, cold and invisible. I understood that. From the very beginning, the first morning I woke up on Haven's hard, carpeted floor. I could see everything clearly, but seeing didn't help me.

"Hello? Hellooooo?"

A voice buzzed in my ear. It was a sweet, singsongy voice. Everyone sang here. I tried to open my eyes, but they felt rough and gritty. It hurt, so I didn't try again.

"Hello? Cock-a-doodle-do, girl who isn't Hazel…"

The floor under my head was itchy. The zipper of the sleeping bag scraped my bare arm. I opened my eyes.

My first thought was that I'd woken up dead and here was an angel to greet me. In the next breath, I felt a hysterical urge to cover my face. Considering how much Amelia and Zoe tried to sell me on a women's shelter, I found it mildly disturbing that the first person to bust into my room was a boy.

A beautiful boy. When I opened my eyes, his lips curved into a rosy smile that could have blotted out sunsets and falling snow and the first sip of water when you're dying of thirst. I had to blink a few times, like he was too bright to look at.

He seemed content to stare at me until I finished waking up, so I tried to be quick about it. When he took in my makeshift canvas drape, his smile rose to a grin. "I thought I was the only one who could pitch a tent around here."

His eyes were bluer than Cole's, deep enough to swallow me whole. He eased himself to the floor with fluid grace and gestured to the folds of canvas over my head. "Is this normal for you, or were you hitting the Boone's last night?" He rubbed the frayed material between his fingers. "Where's Hazelnut?"

"Where's what?"

"Where's *who*. Hazel, this is her room. I came in here looking for her, but lo, there lies a flaxen beauty asleep in her place. In a tent. On the floor." He leaned back on his elbows and studied me under a canopy of dark lashes. "Imagine my surprise."

His eyes stayed on mine. I waited for him to ask me who I was, to ask me anything. He didn't.

"Who are you?" I asked.

He laughed. "Breaking the rules already?"

"I—"

"It's okay, I'll tell you," he said. "And I won't tell *on* you." He extended his hand—the minute I touched his skin, I knew he'd never plowed a fire or dug a hole in his life. "Toby."

"I'm Avery."

"Avery," he repeated. "Avery, Avery, Avery. Unexpected. Androgynous. I like it." He lifted a strand of my hair that was as long as his arm. "Is this real?"

I blinked. My brain was three topics back. "Is my hair real?"

"The color," he said, leaning in closer. His skin was flawless. He held the lock of hair to the back of his hand. "It's so pale. I've thought about going blond, but I'm afraid it'll wash me out." He studied my hair a second longer and then shook his head. "Doesn't matter. The upkeep would be hell."

The door creaked open again. "Avery?"

Toby threw back his head. "Oh God. Zoe patrol. Watch, she's going to throw me out."

Zoe stepped through the door with a white mug in her hand. It teetered in her grip when she saw Toby. "What are you doing in here?"

"Told you," he whispered. "I'm looking for Hazel," he said, peering at Zoe upside down.

"Hazel's gone until next week, you know that."

"Well, someone was in here, shoot me for checking. Is that coffee? Can I have it?"

Zoe's eyes widened almost imperceptibly as she took in the campsite I'd set up on the floor. "There's coffee in the kitchen," she told him.

"The kitchen coffee is awful. Please don't make me drink it," he said plaintively. "That's amaretto from the Keurig, I can smell it."

"This is for Avery."

"The kitchen coffee is child abuse," he huffed.

Zoe's eyes hardened, a silent warning. "Toby..."

"He can have it," I said.

Toby beamed at me. "I liked you the minute I saw you."

Zoe shook her head and handed him the steaming cup. His fingers snatched it up as she said, "Take it and go. You know you're not supposed to be in here."

"I know no such thing," he said, getting to his feet. "I visit Hazel all the time."

"Well, Hazel isn't here. Go to breakfast. And no more breaking into rooms. You know the rules."

"I do indeed." He rolled his eyes at me, an expression that was impossibly charming. "Delighted to meet you, Avery. Please forgive the intrusion. Ta, Zoe."

"Ta," said Zoe, with her own eye roll. She turned to me with the click of the door. "Don't mind Toby. He's a handful, but we love him."

I blinked. "He lives here?"

"Yes."

"He lives in a woman's shelter?"

"Not in the women's wing, no. That's under lock and key. He has access to the main dining room and the common area, but his living space is in a separate part of the house."

"Why does he live here at all?"

"I can't tell you that. He can, if he chooses, but you're not allowed to ask him. Are you sure you don't want coffee?"

I shook my head, still staring at the door. "He seems so normal."

"He is normal. You're normal. Being here isn't a sign of some defect. It's just a place where you can be assured of your safety. That's not a bad thing, right?"

I shrugged and loosened the zipper on my bag.

"How did you sleep?"

I shrugged again, keeping my eyes down. I felt embarrassed all of a sudden—rude for not taking the bed I was given.

Zoe sat on the edge of the bed as I scrambled to my feet—even sitting, she was taller than me. I began rolling my sleeping bag into a ball.

"Why did you sleep on the floor, Avery?"

I didn't respond.

"You don't have to, you know."

"I know."

"How about some breakfast?"

"I'm not hungry."

"You still have to eat," Zoe said. "So let's get moving."

I stared at her, but it didn't do any good. Fifteen minutes later I was standing in the dining room holding a steaming plate of pancakes I didn't want. Zoe had outfitted me in a purple T-shirt and the jeans I'd been wearing the day before. She ushered me to the end of a long table.

"Do you want some juice?" The voice in my ear belonged to a little girl with a shiny white scar running down her cheek, tugging one side of her mouth into a frown. "It's pineapple."

"Sure."

She pushed a plastic cup toward me, leaving a sticky trail of yellow juice. Before I could thank her, she was already scurrying away.

"I can't fuckin' believe they found that kid," said a woman at the end of the table. She was round as a ball, sucking on a plastic stick. At first I thought she was talking about the little girl, but then she slapped the newspaper in her hand. "At Clovelite," she added. "*Clovelite*. Freaks." Tendrils of white leaked from her mouth.

"Watch the talk, please, Bev," Zoe said.

Bev placed the stick on the edge of her syrup-sticky plate and lifted a mug to her lips. "Two kids for the price of one, and they won't even let us see 'em. They probably have some kind of membership mark burned into their faces."

"The girl was from around here," said a woman wearing a stained T-shirt. "I googled her name, but there isn't much on her."

"'Course not," Bev snorted. "She was poor. Rich kid goes missing and you hear all about it. Poor kid disappears and it's probably because the parents were drunk and to hell with 'em. Bet there'll be plenty on her now."

I looked down at my plate, the cold pat of butter swimming in syrup.

"And I don't care what anyone says. That fire was no accident. Those maniacs killed themselves," Bev went on. "It's like those nuts who wanted to fly on the comet."

"Heaven's Gate," another woman piped up. She had a sweet pixie face and a baby bouncing on her knee. He wore green pajamas and a gummy smile. "Jonestown, too, hundreds of them—they poisoned their own kids."

"See?" Bev said, taking up her stick and poking the paper. "Proves my point."

"Poisoning your children?" asked the woman with the baby.

"No, they killed themselves. They lit the place up so no one would find out they'd been stealing kids."

"Smart," came a dry voice from behind me. "Lord knows the long arm of the law smacks the hardest when you're dead."

"Shut up, Toby," Bev said.

"Enough," Zoe said. "Dishes back to the kitchen."

Without a word, everyone except for Zoe and I got up and carried the remains of their breakfast into the kitchen. "Are you okay?" Zoe whispered.

I pushed my plate away.

"Come on," Zoe said, getting to her feet. "I want to talk to you."

She brought me into a big, airy room with yellow walls and a bright-blue ceiling. There were clouds smudged in white on the plaster sky. Zoe led me to a window pouring sunlight in the corner. The window stuck out like a bench, with big blue and white cushions. I sat at the very edge. I felt filthy.

"Those people are saying things that aren't true." I hadn't meant to speak, but once I did, I couldn't stop, even though the words barely had room to squeeze through my swollen throat. "No one was trying…" I lowered my head, staring at the still-tender skin on my palms. "They didn't want to die."

"Of course not."

I held up my hand. I had more to say, essays' worth of arguments carefully outlining why my presence in Haven was so wrong, but now the words wouldn't come. I clamped my lips between my teeth to keep them from shaking. "I want to leave," I managed.

"Honey, you can't."

Two angry tears streaked down my cheeks. "You can't make me stay."

"I know that, but I…" Zoe's voice trailed off, her eyes caught on something over my shoulder.

"What?" I turned when she didn't answer. A white van was rolling down the street, a huge number four painted on the side. A minute later it was joined by a two and a seven.

"Get out of the window," Zoe said, tugging at the curtains. "Ronnie!"

"Yeah?"

"Can you have a cruiser sent here, please? I need everything on lockdown. Don't let anyone in or out." She turned back to me and shook her head. "Twelve hours," she said, mostly to herself. "Not bad."

# TWENTY

IT WAS A SMALL LEAK, AS THEY GO, BUT THAT'S THE THING ABOUT leaks—even a little bit of water can do a lot of damage if it gets the wrong thing wet. There were three pictures. They were posted on Reddit first before trickling down the usual channels, and within an hour, the photos of Cole and I were trending on every newsfeed in the country.

The clearest picture showed the two of us in the hallway of the hospital, wads of cotton taped to the crooks of our elbows. Whoever took the picture had been almost directly in front of us. Cole was squinting slightly, but his expression was relatively blank. I had hard lines of worry carved into my forehead. There was a nurse behind us. Cole looked younger than I remembered.

The second picture showed us in profile, standing in the lobby of the police station. I couldn't place it in the timeline, but once I saw the last picture, I didn't care.

The fact it had even been included frightened me more than anything. It wasn't clear, it wasn't sharp, and it wasn't from the police station or the hospital—it had been taken *before* all that, before we'd even been picked up. The picture was colorless; it showed me sitting on the curb my face made of gray shadows, my feet wrapped in denim. Cole was in front of me, midstep, his pack slung over his shoulder. He had one hand out toward me. We weren't in the middle of the picture; we were off to the right and slightly blurry, like the camera had been smeared over us.

But when the news vans rolled up to Haven, we didn't know any of that yet.

"Toby," Zoe called, marching me through the foyer. Her fingers were digging into my arm. I didn't even remember her grabbing me.

"It's not that hard to under*stand*," Toby was saying. We followed his voice to the kitchen, where he was perched on the edge of the counter next to the sink, speaking matter-of-factly to a red-faced girl seething in front of him. "It's just like the smell of the dishwasher. I hate the smell of the dishwasher, and I hate you."

"Zoe!" the girl shrieked, spotting us in the doorway. "Do you hear him?"

"Yes, I'll talk to him later," Zoe told her. "Toby, I need to talk to you."

He smiled. "Already?"

"Now."

Toby slid off the counter and followed us back to the foyer. Ronnie was on the phone.

"We're on lockdown," Zoe said quietly. "Can you get on the intercom and ask everyone to come to the common room?"

Toby's expression didn't change, but he paled beneath the smirk. "Yeah," he said, glancing at me. "I'll take Avery—"

"No," Zoe said. "I'll take her. Just call everyone down here, tell them there's nothing to worry about."

Toby hesitated, the uncertainty in his eyes edging toward fear. "Really?"

Zoe gripped his shoulders and pointed him toward the door. There was comfort in the gesture. "Really. Go. Put something trashy on TV."

The same reassurance didn't extend to me. Toby's heels had barely scraped the floor when Zoe dragged me down the dark hallway to Hazel's room. "Stay here," she instructed me. She yanked on a cord and wooden slats covered the window, painting lines of light on the floor. "There's nothing to worry about. I just don't want the press to know you're here. I bet they're making the rounds at every shelter in the city. Just sit tight."

Ronnie's voice echoed down the hall. "Zoe!"

"Coming! Don't worry," she said to me. "Everything will be fine."

By the time I drew my next breath, the door was closed, and I was left in stark, empty silence.

Time passed slowly, the minutes stretching like taffy. My sleeping bag looked like an invitation, but I knew if I got in, I'd never get back up. I let myself fall backward on the bed, draping the tent canvas over me.

With the shades drawn, the room was dark but not dark enough to hide the shadows. I stared at the floor for a long time, watching the strips of light that fell through the slats. I tried to count the yellow lines, but I got a different number every time. The canvas on my chest was heavy, and it smelled like smoke. It brought memories of waking to the clean air of early morning—fresh breezes that carried the heady remains of the night away.

"Focus," I mumbled. It would do no good to get lost. "Focus."

There was no breeze. The smokiness just sat there with nothing to break it up, and the smell invaded my sinuses until my head ached.

Someone had returned the straight-backed chair to the corner. There was a darkness seated there that my eyes couldn't penetrate. I blinked, but the shape didn't morph, and the shadow didn't shrink. I lifted my head, and the movement made my vision swim. It made the darkness more solid.

"Mother?"

The shape didn't respond. Still, I was scared to look at the light, afraid I would see strips of yellow cutting over her gray face. I squeezed my eyes shut.

Behind my eyelids the room grew busy. I saw Cole dart in and out while my father paced by my feet, a bright-yellow crown around his head. Hannah stood next to the door with a pencil in her hand. I didn't speak to those shapes because they were not hiding in the shadows. I could see them. I was afraid they might talk back.

It was impossible to tell how long I lay there, but when the door creaked open for real, my eyes were leaden, and my mouth was dry. I was afraid to get up. I was afraid I'd see Jane's empty eyes staring at me from the floor.

A head poked through the door. I heard a voice I barely recognized as my own. I was still wedded to my dream.

"Cole?"

The shape slid wordlessly inside. The silence felt measured—like a test. It dared me to say his name again as the form marched toward me, one hand held aloft. As it got closer, I saw there was a light attached to that hand—it was pointed the wrong way, but it showed me what I needed to see. Blue eyes made bluer by the glow, darting madly from my face to the screen and back again.

"Toby?"

He lowered the phone.

"Celeste?"


"I'm sure you want to talk about it."

"No, I really don't."

"You should. It would be healthier for you to get it out. Should I call you Celeste?"

"No. There's nothing to tell."

"Nothing to *tell*, listen to her!" Toby exclaimed in a whisper on the edge of a shriek. "All right, forget the psychobabble. I'm breaking major rules by calling this meeting, but you came out of *Clovelite*, sweetie. Don't tell me there's nothing to tell."

We were both under the canvas. Toby had invited himself to join me when I confirmed that while I was now Avery, I used to be Celeste. The effect that admission had on him convinced me not to tell anyone else, ever.

Too bad it wasn't up to me anymore.

"There's not," I insisted. "You know what happened. It's been on television. You probably know more than I do."

"Television lies," Toby said. He was looking at me like I was a diamond he'd dug up in the yard, something with a million shimmering facets. "First rule of mainstream society: everything you see on TV is bullshit." His eyes danced, lit with curiosity. "I want to know what it was like inside. I can't ask. Just tell me something."

My face burned from my last memory of what it was like inside. "They brought me here from the police station. Cole—I don't even know where Cole is, they took him—"

"If you're talking about America's sacred son, Noah Reid Pierce, he's in Canaan," Toby said, leaning back on one elbow. "Washington."

His eyes stayed on mine as the name washed over me, burning my stomach before it filled with ice.

"How do you know that?"

Toby held up his phone; the screen winked at me. "Awful little things, aren't they? Also this." He reached into his pocket and flicked a small square of yellow paper into my lap. "You'll learn, if you stay, to always walk behind Amelia. Amelia," he went on, hugging his knees, "drops everything. Not that, I stole that from your folder, but in general she's usually good for leaving a few bucks on the floor."

I stared at the words in the dim light. They were written in a wide, childlike scrawl: *Brian and Katherine Pierce, 214 Lees Court, Canaan, Washington.*

"Come on." Toby said, poking me in the leg. "Tell me."

My mouth was dry. I could barely pry it open enough to speak. "Cole and I lived on the compound, and it burned down," I said quietly, tucking the paper into my palm. "So we ran away."

"You're right, I did know that. I want to know *how* it burned down. How come you were the only ones who got out? Everyone's saying it was a suicide pact. Were you trying to kill yourselves?"

"No. We spent most of our time learning how *not* to kill ourselves." My headache returned, pounding the base of my skull, and a black hand passed over my eyes, pausing only briefly. In there I saw—I *felt*—the baby in my arms, saw his bloody little face on my chest, my father's hands, and Cole slipping into my room. My tongue felt thick and furry, and it blurred my words. "I don't…I don't remember."

"You don't remember?"

"No." My head snapped up, my eyes hot as ball bearings. "Now you."

"Now me what?"

"Tell me something."

"About me?"

"Yeah."

Toby blinked, but to his credit, he recovered quickly. "I've been here for almost a year."

"Yeah, but *why?*" I pressed, mimicking his tone.

He leveled his gaze on mine, proud, it seemed, to have a good answer. "I was arrested for prostitution," he said coolly.

"What's that?"

"Sex," he said after a moment. "For money."

Already naive of so much, I felt his response bring heat to my cheeks. It also turned my stomach. He looked like a baby. "You got paid for that?"

"For sex, people will do anything. Trust me. I got caught by an undercover cop in a gas station bathroom. If you ask me, he was into it. Back to you. If it wasn't suicide, how did the place go up?"

"I don't know." I tried to start from the beginning, but I couldn't find it. The memories were slippery, too slick to grab. "I was asleep. I was talking to Cole, and I fell asleep." The sleep was the most vivid

part. I remembered my father and my mother and the baby, the crackling that roused me, and waking in the dark. After that everything sort
of ran together.

"When I woke up, I could hear everything burning. I ran to the
door but…" A gnawing pain in my stomach joined the ache in my
head. There was traction to only one thought, and I would have
preferred it slip away.

*They blocked me in.*

They blocked me in. It was a fact I'd never processed. Amaris or
Seth or all of them had trapped me in that room. I'd screamed, ripped
my hands to shreds clawing at the door. But they didn't hear me. I
never stopped to wonder why.

*Were you trying to kill yourselves?*

Toby didn't notice—he was hung up on logistics. "So Cole is
Noah?" he asked.

"No, Cole is Cole," I said, sounding angrier than I wanted to.

"Did they change your names, or did you?"

My anger lifted me up, away from the black and the flames.
"They?"

"The…I don't know, you tell me. Your leaders? Your…church
elders? I don't know what you called them."

"Our parents."

He blinked. "Really?"

"Who named you?"

"My mother. She named me Tobias, and for that she deserves to be in prison."

"Where is she?"

"I just told you. In jail."

"Why?"

"Because, as it turns out, it's illegal to livestream your underage kid screwing random men you brought home. Profitable, but illegal," he added. "She had me in a bunch of pedo rings by the time I was thirteen, and let me tell you, those people pay to keep things hush-hush. Six figures for her, and if I was a good boy, she'd give me a little blue pill—"

*Take the pills, Avery.*

"—to take the edge off. Big shakes, baby. You go."

I couldn't. I was shaking all over. "What did—"

"You heard me. Need any definitions?"

"No," I said. "I'm sorry, I just—I didn't know."

"Now you do. Little tip from me to you: Don't let people feel sorry for you. It feels good at first, but when those pity party invites start going out, you'll be the only one who shows up. Don't feel sorry for me. I don't. So, the people who took you, you legit thought they were your parents?"

He was like a whirlwind; every time he spoke, he spun me around to look at something new. His words didn't trigger a thought but something else. A sensation, thick and heavy, flowed over me, and when it did, I could smell the bonfires, smoky and sweet. I bit down on my knuckle to keep from gagging. "Yes," I managed. "You go."

"Ask me."

"Why are you here?"

"In a women's shelter? Mostly because I'm a bit skittish around men after all that. Which, being gay, is unfortunate." He fiddled with the frayed edge of the canvas. "I was in another group home, but that didn't go so well. And there aren't many foster parents willing to take in someone my age. Zoe was. Ideal, it's not, but I'll be eighteen in a few months." His eyes darted to mine. "I've been beaten up so many times, I can't worry about pride. I'm lucky I got caught.

"The guys who were interested, a lot of them had wives and families," he said. "Usually it was something quick in the back seat, but afterward a lot of them would get pissed, and they took it out on me. I probably would've ended up getting killed. I was sixteen when my mom was arrested. I ran away before I could be taken away, and my first thought was to keep up the gravy train. It was all I knew how to do. But I got picked up a couple of weeks later." Toby faltered for the first time, dropping his eyes.

"When I was twelve, my mom walked in on me with one of my friends one day after school—we had our pants down, but it was hardly anything, just hands. Kissing was scarier. I was terrified, but she seemed glad. Like that tipped her the way she'd been leaning. I was already ruined, so why not, you know?"

I did.

"I lived outside," I said quietly before he asked. I felt like he'd earned it. "This was my tent."

"Just you?"

"Yeah."

"Was there electricity, or were you in full Amish mode?"

"No. We had electricity," I said, trying and failing to keep the fatigue out of my voice.

"Were you more with God or Satan? I'm just trying to understand…"

"Neither," I said, my voice growing dimmer, duller. "Putting your faith in a higher power is a sign of weakness."

Toby's palm landed on his forehead with an audible smack. "This is so bizarre."

I shrugged. Something in the gesture must have triggered sympathy, because Toby leaned closer and touched my hand. I yanked it away.

He stared at my red palm, feeling, I knew, the thick cracks of skin as it left his. His eyes asked without asking. "You kind of…you seem a little skittish too."

I couldn't look at him.

It was late, nearly dusk. The sun had lowered, painting the room with bright, golden strokes.

"Please don't tell anyone about me," I said. My voice didn't even convince me, but I was too tired to beg.

"I won't breathe a word," he said, his eyes wide and sincere. "You gave me your coffee."

Toby's phone was on the bed between us. It made me uncomfortable in a way I couldn't articulate. "Could you tell it was me right away? In those pictures?"

"Oh, not right away," he said. "No one else did."

"Yet."

"Yet," he agreed. "At first I was like, okay, those are the Clovelite kids. They're pretty cute for cult members, but whatever. I'd seen the story, but I wasn't craving it like those biddies at the table this morning. But then I looked..." He looked at me, and he was beautiful, blue eyes wide and wondering. "And I said, 'Oh my God. The coffee girl.'" Toby smiled ruefully and tugged on a strand of my hair. "I can always spot a bottle job. I could tell this morning you were legit." He tapped the phone. "And so was she."

His fingers slid over the screen, and one of the pictures flashed on, the black and white *before* picture, the one no one should have known to take. "Can I see that?" I asked.

Toby handed me the phone. It was heavier than I expected. It looked strange in my hand. "Go like this," he said, pressing two fingers to the screen and sliding them apart. "That makes it bigger."

I moved my own fingers over the picture slowly, haltingly, until only Cole and I were visible. It was an apple in his hand—it must have been for me. Cole hated apples. I couldn't place the day.

Toby was either really perceptive or reading my mind. "When was that?"

"Early," I said, squinting. "I don't know why anyone would have wanted to take it. Nobody knew us."

The uncertainty that crossed his face earlier crept in again, weaker, but still there. His next words weakened me more. "Maybe you guys weren't the only ones who got out."

# PART THREE

# TWENTY-ONE

---

EIGHT WEEKS LATER, I STOOD ALONE ON THE CORNER OF MAIN STREET and DeKalb, waiting for the light to flash green. It wasn't late, but it was hot, punishingly so, and because of that, most of the neighborhood found reasons to stay home. Farther ahead, I could see a few small clusters of people braving the heat for the sake of ice cream, but the rest of the street was deserted. I was focused on their shapes swimming in the deepening twilight when I felt a shadow stir the air next to me. I whipped my head to the side, but by the time my eyes focused, it had already changed. The shadow turned into a man in a baseball cap who stopped and stood deliberately close, close enough for his shoulder to touch mine. I stepped forward and off the curb.

He stepped down, too, blowing the stink of beer into my face. "Hey, doll."

My right hand rotated my keys until the longest one stuck out like a spike in my fist. It was too soon to run. I stared straight ahead.

Humanity wasn't dying. It was already dead. The outside people—not all of them, but most—were more programmed than I was. I could still feel, still sense there was more to the world than myself. But these people existed in a bubble, shadowy figures in their own little haven where they could do what they wanted and say what they pleased with no thought to what it might do to someone else.

And being out, without Cole, I felt worse than vulnerable—I felt traced. Far from enjoying my supposed freedom, I lacked relief or safety or a respite from the evil that shaped us in that circle of trees. It followed me. When the fire burned, the smoke rose until it morphed into a cloud that lived at the very edge of my vision, something noxious and hooded. Under that hood was all of it: my family, the buildings, and the scuffed wooden floor…everything that had happened. It was like the darkest parts of my memory had broken free and turned solid. I could find nothing specific to fear in that darkness, and that was the worst part—there could be anything in there.

It was so vivid, the shadow, that I could feel it brush against my cheek moments before I was captured by sleep. It lurked around corners, and sometimes it clouded a stranger's face into someone I didn't want to see. More than once I had to close my eyes and tell myself I couldn't be seeing Jane or Seth or my father. It was an entity that was strong enough to follow me, and it knew what scared me.

I could barely see inside my own head, and I didn't want to. I was happy to leave what was lost behind. But it wouldn't leave me behind. The shadow was always there, whispering that I wasn't safe and never would be, taunting me. I saw it everywhere.

"How about a smile?" the man said, his voice pushing through the hot air like molasses.

One blow to the face would do it. If my aim was good, I could take out an eye. A quick uppercut might earn him a lobotomy or at least a torn nostril. Even a wild thrash, if it was hard enough, could send the metal key punching through his cheek.

"Pretty girl…don't be selfish…"

*You've been selfish.*

His finger grazed the skin of my arm. His nail was long enough to scratch. I smelled…

*meat*

…sweat rolling off him, and I took a step away. My fingers tightened on the key. My voice was low. "Don't touch me."

"Aw, don't be like that," he drawled. "I'm not doing nothing. I was just hopin' to see you smile."

My head turned, pulled by an invisible string. I could see my father's face, bubbling and bleeding under this man's. *"Avery."*

The light burned red—I didn't even wait for a break in traffic. I burst into the street, pounding the asphalt with hard, stomping steps. A white truck slammed on its brakes and left six inches of melted tire in the road. I crossed in front of it without slowing. There were honking horns, and in the distance, I heard the man on the curb, not my father at all, yelling now.

"Crazy bitch!"

The passing headlights hurt my eyes, but I didn't stop. My heart slammed against my ribs, hard enough to break, but I knew it could take a beating. A glance behind me showed no sign of the man, and as the gap between us widened, I got lost in the people holding sweating plastic cups and melting ice cream cones.

The air felt sinister, the way only summer air can, heavy with the threat of any and everything that could be hurled from the sky. We'd had a tornado scare two days earlier. The storm hit just west of us and petered out after taking down a handful of power lines along Route 35. Later, I'd sat on the porch in the eerie light and watched a little girl named Jessica play on the swings in the yard. She'd arrived late the night before with dirty clothes and a bruised mother, but she seemed cheerful, buoyant, kicking her feet against the bubbling green sky.

Watching her was as good a distraction as any. I needed the distraction. It had been two months since I'd been in the same room as Cole and five and a half weeks since the press conference issuing a national plea to find my family. Nothing had changed.

Nothing that mattered, anyway.

The press conference made the Reddit leak look like a lone flyer on a telephone pole, and once it aired, Cole and I were back in the news every night. They didn't show my face or his, but they didn't have to. The entire world suddenly knew way too much about me and not enough at the same time.

The police were inundated with dead-end leads: people who said they were my parents, psychics who wanted to find my parents, people who wanted to adopt me or house me or write the story of my life. I got calls from six different psychiatrists who offered to pay me for interviews. Charity groups started fundraisers in my name and wanted to film me getting the checks.

"Mail call," Ronnie said every day, bringing stacks of letters addressed to Celeste Bishop, never to me. For the longest time, I didn't open them—I stuffed them in the bottom of my blue bag until it crackled and bulged. Then I got one letter with handwriting so bad, I could barely read it, a plain, white envelope addressed to *Noah's Sister Celeste*, postmarked Olympia, Washington.

I tore into that letter even though I knew Cole would never call me that. When I ripped the flap open, a square of notepaper and a twenty-dollar bill floated to my lap.

*...used to live two towns over from the Pierce family...oldest son was in the search...hope you find your family...*

There was no return address.

I spent the next hour opening all the envelopes. They held pages torn from books, handwritten prayers, and more money—bills that ranged from one to one hundred dollars. I stacked all the letters, folded the money into a wad, and hid everything at the bottom of my bag.

By then everyone at Haven knew who I was, but their contracts forced them to keep their mouths shut. Some people were even helpful. One woman, Roxanne, had worked in a salon before her boyfriend tried, and almost succeeded, to kill her with a tire iron. After days of watching me walk around with a hood over my head, she held a whispered conference with Toby and then ushered me into the bathroom, where she cut my hair. Short. She called it a pixie, but when she was finished, I looked like a boy, gaunt and underfed.

Toby disagreed. He told me I looked like I was ready to birth Rosemary's baby, and he promised that was a compliment.

With my hair gone, I barely recognized myself. Ronnie taught me how to apply makeup, and even a little made an alarming difference. I could walk around with less fear of being recognized, but it didn't stop the calls and the mail from coming.

But there was nothing from Cole. Not a word.

Now here was August. The ice cream crowd thinned as I crossed the town square, and my steps brought my destination into view: the massive red-and-white marquee of the Hearth Theatre jumped out from the gray stone building. It was an actual verified landmark, which basically meant no one could tear it down no matter how decrepit it got. *Vintage*, everyone called it.

I called it old.

There were red ropes set up outside the ticket window even though the lines weren't exactly wrapping around the block. A lone figure was inside, sweeping dust into circles on the floor.

"Hi, Henry," I said, slipping through the double doors.

"Avery!"

Henry was as old as the building and twice as charming. He was stooped and gray, but his eyes still knew how to dance. I was never quite sure where he fit in—sometimes he ran the box office, sometimes he tore tickets, and more than once, I spotted him in the audience with a bucket of popcorn. "How's my favorite girl?"

"Fine," I said, trying to smile. I didn't make it. The darkness was there; it was the man on the corner, all sweat and drawl and jagged fingernails. The adrenaline that had kept him back was fading now that I was safe, and tears came to my eyes as I stood in the cool air of the lobby and let myself remember. It wasn't hard to understand why my old memories had fled. Even the new ones hurt.

Henry didn't notice; he retreated to the snack bar with a wad of paper towels and a bottle of Windex. "What are you spinning tonight?" he asked, tossing me a giant box of Raisinets.

I caught it in one hand, swiping a finger under my eye. "*Spellbound.*"

"Have you seen it?"

"No."

"It's a classic."

I managed a better smile. A real one. "They all are."

For the first few weeks after arriving at Haven, I hadn't even left the house, but at some point, amid the search and the circus and the chaos of not knowing, Zoe sat me down and told me I should have a job. Just a little something to keep my bed, she'd explained, which wasn't exactly fair, because I slept on the floor every night, searching for somewhere dark enough or comfortable enough or quiet enough to keep me sleeping until morning.

"I was thinking it might be time for you to have a job," she told me that hazy morning. Toby was teaching me how to play chess on the porch while we waited for it to rain. You had to catch the quick, cool breezes that blew in ahead of the clouds—we could smell the storms before they hit. "It would be good for you."

"A job?" I repeated dubiously. "Doing what?"

"What are you good at?"

I shifted in my seat, staring at the shiny black pieces on the board and mentally tallying my skills. "I don't know."

"Everyone should have at least one thing they're really good at," Toby declared, sliding his bishop. "Like cooking or blow jobs. Something useful."

I blinked at him. "What?"

"Nothing," Zoe said, shooting Toby a filthy look. "I just think you might feel a little better if you had something to do. It would be nice for you to earn something for yourself."

She made it sound like a harvest I didn't have to share. But I did have to share it. When I got my first job at the theater, I made seven dollars and fifty cents an hour. Ten percent of that was deposited directly to Haven. Zoe worked in conjunction with three local businesses—a diner, a hotel, and the movie theater. Like Haven, all three were dirt-cheap charity places that helped poor or homeless people one way or another. Haven provided them with low-cost workers, they gave a cut of our pay back to the shelter and kept cost down for the community. Zoe called it esprit de corps.

The suggestion to work nights was mine. That was around the time the dreams started.

It wasn't one single dream, rather a more colorful version of my darkened memories. A jumbled kaleidoscope of sounds and smells and voices. Some of them were expected, but others I didn't understand. I woke up every night with a scream in my throat, bathed in sweat and the irritated groans of whoever had been forced to sleep next to me.

"For Christ's *sake*, shut her up!" was the new mantra, the one everyone screamed when the sky was inky black and my head was bursting. It was my cue to gather my things and go to the dayroom, go to the bathroom, go anywhere. Ignoring my cue meant being accidentally stepped on in the morning—arms, legs, head. I had a lot of accidents the first few weeks.

Perversely, it reminded me of the commune. I put up with more than I should and heard more than I wanted to—hushed whispers suggesting Zoe just keep me in the bathroom or the hallway if I wanted to scream all night and sleep on the floor.

But I didn't *want* to sleep on the floor. I had to if I wanted to sleep.

Zoe tried to draw me out, but it didn't do any good. I didn't want to talk about what I did remember, and I couldn't talk about what I didn't. And there was a lot that I didn't. The more she asked me, the more holes I fell into. She told me that was normal. She wanted to try something with me—regression, she called it, to try and bring those memories to a head, but I wouldn't let her. They were gone for a reason.

So I didn't mind staying up all night. Aside from letting everyone sleep, my eyes were used to the dark. Zoe didn't consider that a marketable skill, but I proved her wrong at the very first interview she sent me to. In a darkened box suspended above the velvet seats at the Hearth Theatre, after only a ten-minute explanation of how to thread the spools of film, I had the ancient projector rolling along, shining pictures on the giant white screen on the other side of the window. I started as the Hearth's projectionist the next day.

Toby waited tables at a diner down the street, and he would join me sometimes for the midnight show. My employment started with a Hitchcock run, and on my first night, I sat through *Strangers on a Train* three times in a row, captivated every time. Toby had seen all the old movies and would act out scenes with panache and grand gestures while I watched, the projector flicking cool-white light over our faces.

I loved those moments, the brief flashes of normal. I didn't get them often. Usually there was only my secret fear, the one that kept me awake at night. If I found something to smile about one day, I'd see ten men who looked like my father the next. I should have known what to do. They had prepared me for any eventuality but not this. They could still be out there. With every dark thought, I could feel myself going slack. Defenseless.

Weak.

# TWENTY-TWO

---

*AVERY*

"Avery?"

I recognized one voice but not the other. It echoed in my head, my own name repeated over and over. It was calling to me. "No," I mumbled.

"Avery, wake up."

*Avery...*

I *was* awake. It was black and horrible. There were no pictures, just a sensation. Of rising and falling and the hard ground digging into my head. I felt a hand on my wrist, and then I saw a bright flash that started small and exploded with a high-pitched, terrifying noise. I felt it, a deep, burning pain stretching all the way to my fingertips.

"Avery?"

The weight was back. Hands were pressed to my shoulders, and I could feel something nudging me, looking for a way in, and I pushed, looking for a way out. "No…"

A cool hand touched my forehead, but there were no quiet words. Just pain and pressure and that ache, that deep, deep ache splitting me in two. I tried to kick, but my feet were bound.

"No! I can't get up! Let go of me, *please!*" I screamed. "Stop!"

"Avery, stop!"

I blinked and saw Zoe, and my words cut off like a wire had been snipped. Everything disappeared as quickly as it had come, and I was left sweating, tangled in my sleeping bag with my heart throbbing against my rib cage. I moved automatically to push away hair that wasn't there anymore.

"What was it about?" Zoe pressed. "Try to remember."

I shook my head, and it hurt, like I'd been pounding it against the floor. "The…the Man," I mumbled.

"What man? What were you dreaming about?"

"I don't know…I couldn't see."

"Are you all right?"

The throbbing glow was still in my head, steady, like the pound of my headache. "Yes."

She sat back on her heels. "There's someone downstairs to see you."

I flew into a sitting position, ignoring the grating burn in my eyes. "Cole?"

Zoe looked at me for a long moment before shaking her head. "No. It's a police officer. He'd like to talk to you."

"Officer Rodolfo?"

"No, it's someone from Latham," she said. "He said it was important."

"Is it about—" I swallowed hard; my throat was on fire. "What does he want?"

"I don't know," Zoe said.

"I don't know," Officer Mason said, leaning back to stare at me. I'd told him I hadn't seen enough to help, and he didn't like that answer. He didn't believe me, which was a shame because it was true. I kept my face carefully blank.

We were in Zoe's office, the two of us and Amelia—Zoe must have called her before she woke me, because Amelia arrived about three seconds after I got downstairs. It was a good thing she was there, because I'd nearly passed out when I saw the policeman waiting in the lobby. I shocked myself by remembering the shout for Mason that shattered the air and the two figures standing a stone's throw away from where Cole and I were stretched out in the grass.

"The thing is," said Officer Mason, "we've looked at this from a lot of angles, and the more we dig up, the less it makes sense. You were there, so anything you could tell us could be helpful."

"Why now?" Amelia asked. "It's been months."

"Forensics can take months. It would be one thing if this were just a building fire, or even if we had a single clue on the victims, but at least eight people died, and we can't identify them."

My stomach rolled with acid, a sick, watery wave that sent bile up my throat. "Only eight?"

Officer Mason gave me a hard look. "Only?"

"No, I'm sorry, I meant…you can't identify anyone? None of them?"

"None. I say at least eight, because you said there were twelve of you, and that means we're still two short. We've scoured every inch of debris. The odds that the two missing got out and are just hiding somewhere are looking better and better."

I felt the blood drain from my face. My hands grew slick in my lap.

He leveled his gaze on me. "You ran out of a cult. That could be a problem."

"Officer, she—" Amelia glanced at me. "She's been fairly well harassed already. The media has been brutal. We can't locate her family. Her memory is marginal at best. Dr. Pyne has seen increasing evidence of PTSD. I don't think this is wise…"

It took me a minute to realize Dr. Pyne was Zoe. It was true, she had tried to make me talk a few times, but even when I did, it didn't do much good. I kept falling into those pockets of nothing—my memory was like eraser dust. I could sense certain things that used to be there, but I couldn't see them anymore. Zoe said I was trauma-tized, and I didn't disagree.

Officer Mason wasn't impressed. "We won't do any permanent damage." He leaned closer. He was younger than he'd looked from far away. His face was scarred with deep pockmarks that dotted his cheeks, and I stared at them in grim fascination. "Did you see anyone else get out?"

Amelia started to protest, but he held up a hand. "Just answer if you can."

I moved my eyes to my lap, smoothing my hands over my legs. "Yes."

"Who?"

"My sister. Jane."

"You saw her?"

"Yes."

"Where did she go?"

"She was dead. She fell…or jumped—she probably jumped—out of an upstairs window. She was lying in the grass."

He made a scribbled note on a chart of some kind. "You're positive she was dead?"

"Yes."

"Did you try to move her away from the fire?"

"No," I said, looking up at him through hooded eyes. "I ran."

Officer Mason stared at me for a moment. The chart he was writing on was actually a crudely constructed map of the compound;

he rotated it to face me. "Let's start from the beginning. When the fire started, where were you?"

The room was very dry. When I opened my mouth to speak, I coughed hard, but my throat didn't clear. I hacked for a while before Amelia touched my shoulder and handed me a cup of water from the cooler. "I really don't think she's up to this."

"I'm okay," I told her. "I was asleep," I said to Officer Mason.

"Where?"

"In my room."

"Which room was yours?"

"It was—um…the third room to the left of the kitchen," I said, closing my eyes to see. When I opened them, I pointed to the spot on the map. "Here."

He darkened the square with a black pen. "How did you get out?"

"My door was stuck. I went out the window."

"Do you have any ideas about where the fire could have started?"

"Officer Rodolfo said he thought it started in the kitchen," I replied.

"I want to know what you think."

"I don't know. I was in my room. But my door started to burn before I got out."

"That stuck door probably saved your life. There were no alarms. Usually the smoke knocks people out before they have a chance to even react. How did you know something was wrong?"

"I could hear people in the hallway."

"Did you call to them for help?"

"Yes, sir. They didn't hear me."

"But you could hear them. How many people did you hear in the hallway?"

It was an easy question that sent me into a brick wall of nothing—I could hear voices, but they were layered and dull. "I don't know. Maybe three."

"Where was Noah when all this was happening?"

"Cole was outside.."

"How do you know he was outside at that point?"

I paused a moment. "I don't, but he must have been. I didn't hear him inside."

"So you're saying he was outside before the fire started, right?"

"I think he was. Otherwise…" I paused. The officer was watching me closely.

"Otherwise what?"

"Nothing—he must have been. He would have tried to get me out if he knew the building was on fire."

He made a note on the map. "You two were close?"

"He's my brother."

"No, he's not, and that's not what I asked you. The two of you were the only ones to get out, and it doesn't sound like you hung around looking for the rest of your family."

He made a rabbity gesture with his fingers when he said *family*. "Yes," I said. My voice was low and strained, but I refused to cry—he would have liked that too much. "We were very close."

"He never told you why he was outside?"

"I never asked. He was unconscious when I found him."

The officer leaned back in his seat. "He was unconscious? Why?"

I shook my head slightly and squinted like it would make my mind's eye clearer. "He…um. I think he was thrown," I said, remembering my own cartwheel through the air.

"You don't sound so sure."

"I'm not. There was a lot going on. But the shock wave picked me up, so he must have been thrown too."

"Yes, but thrown from where? He couldn't have been inside when it blew. It would have killed him."

"I know," I agreed, even though it felt traitorous to do so. He was right—Cole wasn't anyplace that made any sense. "I don't know why he was outside."

"Where was Noah when you found him?"

"In the field."

"Sorry, I meant in relation to you. Was he closer or farther from the building than you were?"

"Farther. I was trying to get to my…to the woods, and it was a few minutes before I found him."

"Okay, so to me that can only mean one of two things," he said, scribbling something else on the map. "Either he was close to the building when it blew and he somehow flew past you, or he was already ahead of you, and it just knocked him out. Are you sure of your positions?"

"Yes. He was farther on than I was. And he wasn't awake."

"I have some problems with this," Officer Mason said. "The fact Noah was already outside is unusual. Did he have reason to be out in the middle of the night?"

"He could have."

"Like what?"

"We—" I glanced at Amelia. She no longer wanted me to stop. "We ran drills in the middle of the night sometimes. He could have been practicing. He could have just wanted to go for a walk. It was a nice night."

"No, it *wasn't* a nice night," Mason said. "That's why I can't see him going for a stroll. We had storms rolling through. No thunder but plenty of rain."

I sat back. I could feel the sharp stab of the cucumber leaves, the tangled bits of wire. No rain. I blinked. "It wasn't raining."

"No?"

"No," I said, looking at Amelia again. "Not at all."

"Okay," he said, with a false air of dismissal. "Must have been some other reason we had to tow one of the trucks out of the mud the next morning. We'll assume he was out for a walk at two in the morning on such a nice night. You said he would have come back for you if he saw the place on fire. Why didn't he?"

"The fire started on the inside. He might not have known what hit him."

"I'm still hung up on why he would have been outside."

"We had a barn. Animals we tended to. Cole was…"

"What?"

"He was…outside."

"Yes, we've covered that. Good place to be when the house is on fire."

"He was—"

*I'm not going to help them hurt you again. No matter what.*

I went very still. Officer Mason was watching me. So was Amelia. She touched my arm. "Avery?"

"I—I'm sorry, can you repeat that?"

"You were talking. He was what?"

*Like water. He could slide around no matter where you put him.*

"Nothing."

"Did it occur to you or Noah to look for the rest of your family?"

I swallowed. "I guess."

"You guess? That's the first thing I would have done."

"The trucks came," I said, lights flashing behind my eyes. "I was afraid."

"Just you?"

"Cole wasn't awake," I reminded him. "And when he woke up, he *was* scared, he was—"

*Not right.*

"So what were you afraid of?"

"Being caught."

"Caught doing what?"

*I did it for you.*

"No, caught like this," I said, tearful at last. "I was afraid of being taken away."

*Where was your focus?*

"So afraid that you would abandon your entire family?"

*We have to leave!*

"…you and your brother must not have liked them very much."

*Where should it have been?*

"We had no choice!"

*On the fire.*

Officer Mason leaned forward in his chair, staring at the map he'd drawn. Silently he penned a little stick person lying in the field. "Sure you did."

The tip of his pen rested on that tiny figure, the only one outside the box.

On Cole.

# TWENTY-THREE

---

"I've tried, Avery. They don't want anyone talking to him."

"No, I don't want to talk to him, I *need* to talk to him." My hands were balled into fists, I hadn't sat down since Officer Mason left. Amelia made him leave. "I just…five minutes, that's it."

"Avery—"

"They think he started the fire!"

She cocked her head. "He didn't say that."

"He was thinking it."

"Is that what you think?"

"No! Why would he do that?" I ground the heels of my hands against my eyes and yanked out bits and pieces of that night. Cole's hair was wet because I poured the bucket on him. Mine was wet because I was sweating. He was confused because he was upset…

He was crying. He never cried. Jane jumped, and everyone else burned.

Amelia's hand touched my shoulder; I shook her off. "No…"

"What are you thinking?"

"Nothing. I can't…I can't even see anymore."

"You mean you can't remember?"

*I'm not going to help them hurt you again.*

I took a step back until I hit the wall. "There is no way he would have set the place on fire with all of us inside, that doesn't make sense."

"You both admitted you were abused by the people who took you," Amelia said. "Might he have done it to protect you?"

*Yes.*

"No! While I was inside? That makes a lot of sense."

"Maybe it was an accident? Something that scared him so badly, he ran? You can talk about it, Avery."

"There's nothing to talk about. I told you I don't know."

"You're safe here."

"No, I'm not. I wasn't safe there, and I'm not safe here. No one wants me here, I can't do anything, I can't…" I buried my head in my hands, and my voice came out in a moan. "I don't know who's dead and who's alive or if they're coming back for me."

"Avery—"

"*What?*" I shrieked, snapping my head up. "What? Avery this, Avery that, Avery, Avery, Avery—*what?* What am I supposed to do?"

"Sit down," Amelia said. "You want to talk to Cole, I want to talk to you. Sit."

I didn't sit. My back was glued to the wall.

"You're allowed to be upset," Amelia said.

I slid down until I hit the floor, pressing my hand to my forehead. I hid my face, but my voice came out worse. "I don't want to be out here," I whispered. "I don't want to. I want to go back to the way we were before—not with my parents, but just away from all this. And he promised," I moaned. "He promised to come back."

Amelia gathered her skirt and crouched down next to me. "Honey, you gave him an impossible job. He can't just waltz out of his house just because he's able. He's been inundated with reporters, the same as you. He would have no means to travel that far on his own. His parents have been very careful with him, and there's no way they'd let him go."

"If he wanted to, he could."

"You think so?"

"I know so. I know *him*." I wiped my face and looked up. "You don't."

"So let's talk about it."

I let her pull me up and into a chair. Officer Mason had left a card on the desk with a number on it in case I "remembered anything useful." I flicked it across the wood with my finger.

"I don't want to talk about what happened to me," I said.

"Neither do I. I have a different question."

"What?"

She sat down next to me and leaned forward, resting her arms against her knees. "I want to know why you and Cole left when you did."

"The whole place burned—"

"No, not why, *when*. Why then and not before?"

"We had nowhere to go before."

"You had nowhere to go after. Why didn't you ask the police for help?"

"We were scared."

"I know. You were scared enough to stay."

I became fascinated with the desk blotter just to avoid her eye. "Why would we want to leave?"

"Why would you want to stay?"

The pattern was green and gold; I scraped some of the leaf off with my fingernails. Shrugged.

"There are scars all over your body."

I scraped faster, sending little flicks of gold onto the desk.

"There are whip marks on your back. Burns on your arms and legs. Your hands—"

"I know about my hands!" I spat, even as they started to shake. I took a deep breath. "We couldn't leave."

"Why not?"

"I don't know," I said. And I didn't. I felt like I used to—I must have—but nothing specific came to mind, no particular punishment that would have been worse than what happened anyway. "I told you, I had nowhere to go."

"Did you ever try?"

"No."

"Why not?"

"I don't know! I…"

"What, Avery?"

"I don't—"

"Try. Say it."

I squeezed my eyes shut. There was no darkness and no light, no pinprick stars shimmering in a velvet sky; there were trees. A circle of trees, like a—like a fence.

*Mind the perimeter and remember your partner.*

"What?"

I lifted my head—Amelia's eyes were huge. "What?" I asked her.

"You said something."

I shook my head hard, once. "I didn't say anything," I mumbled.

"It's important for you to let yourself remember, even if you don't want to. Those people did more than isolate you—something must have made you afraid to leave. Tell me what it was."

"We were…"

*Partners.*

"Say it."

"No, there's nothing to say," I said jumping to my feet. It was too dangerous to speak. I might say something I didn't want to know. "I'm tired, and I just wanted to see if I can talk to him. It's been months."

"You can't keep running away from this. Avery…"

I stopped. My fingers curled around the doorknob. "I want to move out of the yellow room," I mumbled.

"What?"

"I want a different room." The yellow room was one of three dormitory-style arrangements of folding cots. My current bed was there, but I never used it. Since I started working nights, I'd gotten into the habit of rolling my sleeping bag out on the third floor, where I couldn't bother anyone.

"That's really up to Zoe," Amelia said. She sounded surprised, but she didn't ask me why. "She'd have to see where else she can put you."

"She doesn't have to put me anywhere," I said, still speaking over my shoulder. "I don't use the bed, so she can take someone else in. I can stay upstairs, or—what about Toby? He has his own room. Maybe I could stay in there."

"I don't know if Zoe would allow that."

"Ask her," I said, twisting the knob and stepping outside. "You said you wanted to help me, so ask her."

# TWENTY-FOUR

Long after it mattered, I saw a doctor about my hands. He examined the cracked skin and suggested chemical peels and exfoliating treatments—things to promote turnover. It was important, he told me, to remove what was dead so fresh cells could emerge. Even if the nerves were destroyed beyond repair, it was still possible—even likely—that they could look normal again.

That's true of a lot of things.

A few weeks after my interview with Officer Mason Toby turned eighteen and Zoe allowed me to move out of the dormitory, and into Toby's room. It made sense. We both worked nights, shuffling back to Haven at three a.m. and sleeping until noon, hidden behind blackout drapes. He'd been campaigning to bunk with me for a while, but Zoe didn't think it was appropriate, and I didn't think it would make a difference. We were both wrong. Once I was off the main floor, there were fewer hateful glances thrown my way. Only a handful of people actually talked to me, but I didn't go out of my way to talk much either.

I *had* thought—hoped—a smaller space might settle my mind, make the nights quieter. It didn't. But Toby was inspired by my unrest. He never minded being pulled from sleep; he treated my nightmares like an ailment, something he could cure by rubbing my back and dosing me with funny stories and cold drinks. It worked, sort of. The dreams didn't dissolve, but when Toby was with me, the shadows retreated faster. They stood a little further away.

Work was the best part of my day. I liked being left alone with just the whir of the projector for company. I liked being invisible. And for a while, I started to feel better; the cord between Cole and me was still there, but it was thinner. I felt like I could move again.

That was true until one day in September, when a pipe burst an hour before my shift and sent water flooding into the lobby of the Hearth. My boss called to tell me I had the night off. His voice suggested I should be happy about it.

But there was nothing to be happy about. There was nothing to do. My internal clock wouldn't let me go to bed, so when everyone else went to their rooms, I headed for the porch with a fat paperback in my hand. There was something about the porch—it inspired all sorts of hopeful, clueless fantasies that Cole would show up while

I was sitting there unaware. I could rest without feeling heavy, even though I knew how bad it would feel when I had to walk back inside and Cole wasn't there.

But without that night, without that broken pipe and yards of sodden carpet, I wouldn't have known how bad it would feel when I walked back inside and he was.

"Avery?" Zoe was standing behind Ronnie's desk, both of her palms braced against the wood.

"Hi," I said.

"Why aren't you at work?"

There was a note of accusation in her voice. I took a step back. "A pipe burst. They had to close."

"Oh." Her face was scrunched up, like she was trying to decide something. Ronnie's eyes bounced from Zoe to me. Zoe asked, "Where are you going?"

"To read."

"Where?"

"On the porch," I said slowly. She was still looking at me funny. "Is that okay?"

"Oh, sure."

"Okay," I said, turning again.

"Where's Toby?" she blurted before I could take a step. "Did he go to work?"

"Uh-huh."

"Okay."

I walked to the front door, and the minute I got there, it flew open and nearly hit me in the face. Toby rushed in with the warm summer air.

"Avery!" he shrieked, gripping my shoulders. "Thank God, I just saw—"

"Toby!" Zoe called from the desk. "Come here."

"But did you see—"

"Don't say another word!"

"Oh, you can't be serious!" he said, pushing me down the hall. "You didn't tell her?"

"Tell me what?" I asked.

Toby and Zoe were deadlocked in a vicious stare-down. Finally Zoe shook her head and crooked her finger. "Both of you come here."

Toby bounded toward her, dragging me along. Zoe looked at me for a long time before she spoke. "I wasn't going to say anything," she began, "but I guess it should be your decision…if it's something you want to see."

"*What?*" I asked.

"*Dateline,*" Toby said in delirious glee. "Noah—Cole—he's on it tonight."

"Jesus Christ, are you serious?" Ronnie breathed.

"You mean he's going to be on TV?" I asked, my heart picking up. "When?"

"Now!" Toby said. "I seriously ran out of work. I bet they fire me."

"They're not allowed to fire you. It's in the contract," Ronnie told him.

He frowned. "Really? Even if—"

"Toby—please. Would you like to watch it, Avery?" Zoe asked. "You don't have—"

"Yes!" I said.

"It might be upsetting—"

"So come with us!" Toby said, pulling me through the frosted doors.

We went into the playroom—it was the only place that was empty. Toby dropped me into a giant beanbag and flicked the remote at the television.

I could feel my heart beating in my ears. The black screen lightened, bringing an absolutely gorgeous house nestled in a miniature forest of green trees and blue sky.

"Holy shit," Toby whispered. "Can they adopt me?"

My fingers were clawing at the cloth still tied to my wrist, yanking and pulling at the knot. When I closed my eyes, I felt Cole's fingers against my skin.

"It's been fifteen years since Noah Reid Pierce disappeared without a trace." The announcer's voice was strange, like she had something stuck in her throat. "Fifteen years marked by searches and prayers—a nation transfixed, hoping for a miracle. All for a family that refused to give up."

The scene changed to a bright and airy living room—beige couches, a fireplace lined with several photographs of two boys and a girl. The boys were identical to each other and to Cole when he was younger. Cole's baby picture was in the middle.

My eyes narrowed.

"It was just…a moment," a new voice intoned. "He was in the sandbox and then—he was gone. I never pretended it wasn't my fault, but I knew he was out there." Katherine Pierce appeared on the screen wearing a tight-lipped smile carefully designed to trap the tears in her eyes. "I think when you're a parent, you can feel it in your gut when your children are still with you. For me it wasn't a matter of if we would find him, only when."

The woman with the weird voice had stiff hair and eyes that were appropriately concerned. "What was it like for you," she asked in the same muted tone, "when Kansas authorities called to say they'd found your son?"

Kate's eyes blanked for a second and looked far away. "Like I won the biggest lottery in the world," she whispered. "I've spoken to so many parents who've lost their children, and there is nothing like the pain of not knowing. I accepted his death even though I didn't believe it, and then he…he came back to life. He's sitting next to me. There are no words to describe it."

The screen flashed back to the baby picture, and then Cole's face replaced his younger self. It was a slap I wasn't prepared for, and my breath cut off. Zoe made a small sound behind me. Toby squeezed my arm as the room tunneled and swam. I gasped, "Oh, my God."

"He looked better before," Toby murmured.

He was right. Cole looked so familiar and so *wrong* that it was hard for me to equate what I was seeing to what I knew. I had to examine him in pieces. His clothes were clean and crisp, and his hair was shorter, but the disconnect had nothing to do with those things. Anyone could be dressed up.

It was his eyes. I saved them for last because that was where I expected to see the most. He was wearing glasses. Behind them his eyes were calm, bigger than I remembered or maybe just made to look that way by the lenses. There was no panic, none of the pain and fatigue I remembered. It was Cole, but his face was all wrong. After a moment I realized why.

He was happy.

Zoe's voice came from behind me. "Avery?"

"She's crying," Toby said. When he did, I felt the hot tears spilling over my cheeks, and I pressed a hand to my mouth.

"Turn it off," Zoe said.

"No," I managed. "It's just…he's not squinting. He looks so different."

"He looks a little high to me," Toby said.

"How does it feel, Noah, being back with your family after all those years? They must have felt like strangers to you."

Cole shook his head, and I felt a rare tingling in my hands, a desperate need to reach out and grab him.

"They really…they didn't," he said. "I was just so happy to be out."

My stomach dropped.

The reporter's voice took on a tinge of curiosity. "You never left the compound before that day?"

"No."

"That's not true, Cole," I mumbled. "Dad took you out."

Toby glanced at me sideways.

"So tell me—how did you know that there was something better waiting for you?"

He gave a half shrug. "I didn't."

I blinked and shook my head.

"Not many people would've had the courage to do what you did."

*I did it for you…*

"When the fire started, I knew it was my last chance. The other kids always did whatever they were told, but I wasn't like that."

"Do you think that's why you survived?"

He didn't hesitate. "Yes."

"You're lying," I whispered.

"Tell me about the other children," the woman went on. "Did you consider them your brothers and sisters? Your family?"

He looked thoughtful. I squeezed my hands into fists tight

enough to drive my nails into my skin. I didn't feel it, of course. It didn't matter anyway. Breaking every bone in my body would have hurt less than what was in front of me.

"No," said Cole, fixing his eyes on the camera. "Because they weren't."

# TWENTY-FIVE

THE FIRST THING I SAW WHEN I STARTED SEEING AGAIN WAS THE window in the bedroom Toby and I shared. A framed portrait of a room that wasn't real at all. My face reflected in the black glass wasn't real either. I was an empty shell, trembling in the aftermath of Cole's interview.

*It wasn't an accident.*

"Can I get you anything, Avery?" Zoe's voice jerked me from the window.

"No."

She paused. "Is there anything you'd like to talk about?"

*We had it backward. We killed ourselves.*

In the glass behind the curtain, shadows danced. They were waiting for me to close my eyes. The minute I did, they would ooze inside and sit on my chest until I couldn't breathe. They would cling to my wrists and my ankles and hold my head, keep my whole body frozen in place until my mind couldn't take it anymore.

Until I wanted to scream.

"Try to get some sleep," said Zoe.

The door closed behind her. The patch of glass winked.

It took me an hour to get to the bus station.

I'd tried to sleep, but the winking glass followed me to the floor. It wasn't just my memories taunting me; now Cole's were there, too, and they were just as false, just as lying. The window turned into an eye that stared at me as I turned Cole's interview over and over in my head.

He hadn't said my name. Not once. He said *Celeste* without stutter or hesitation, as though that's how he'd always known me, a now-stranger he remembered from some other time and some other place. There were no secret signals, nothing in his eyes to reflect his promise as he sat on the couch between his mother and father and spouted things that weren't true.

But the things that were true were worse.

Flashes of red and white light danced across my legs. My blue bag was in my lap. I tried to keep my fingers steady as I worked a needle and thread through the fabric, marrying the ragged edges back together. I hadn't brought much: a change of clothes and a toothbrush; Cole's baby picture; a jagged square of canvas I'd scissored off my tent, and the yellow square with Cole's address that Toby had given me. I'd collected all the money I had and wrapped it in the torn envelope from the woman in Olympia.

I'd boarded the bus half an hour before departure and chose a seat all the way in the back. The trip was scheduled to take forty-two hours, but I knew they wouldn't feel as long as the thirty minutes we spent parked in the bus depot . When we pulled out of the station, the wheels were limber and light, flying over the pavement as Wichita faded behind.

The needle was slippery in my hand. In and out, in and out. I attached the straps and moved on to a long, straight tear that ran down the side.

It was a clean line. I'd torn a hole in myself just like it a few years earlier when I sliced my leg open on a jagged chunk of rock. Or a piece of fence wire. I'd had a million cuts, but the clean lips of that one scared me—whenever I moved, it opened, and I could see white tissue underneath. Hannah had grudgingly sewed it shut.

Up and down, up and down. The bus was bouncy but not uncomfortable. The seats were soft, padded in blue. Nearly everyone on board was looking at a phone. I could see the lights on the ceiling; a woman a few rows up had headphones attached to hers. The man behind her was asleep and drooling.

"Hey. Hey. What's it going to be?"

The needle jerked in my hand—a bubble of blood tipped my index finger. "What?"

"What are you making?" The voice was in front of me. When the light flashed again, I saw the glint of one brown eye staring at me through the crack between the seats.

"Nothing." The eye disappeared with the return of the dark, but I knew it hadn't moved. It could still see me. "I'm fixing my bag."

"Where'd you get that bag?"

"My sister made it." My stitches were aimless now; I was punching the needle through solid patches of cloth, stamping it with crimson fingerprints. Every flash of light glazed over that eye. I was wildly, irrationally terrified of seeing the face that went with it.

"Where is she?" the voice asked me. "Your sister?"

"She's dead." The seat in front of me moved with an odd little jiggle that looked like laughter. I broke the thread without knotting it.

"Are you sure?"

The answer I expected, the right one, didn't come. "No," I whispered.

The eye flashed again, and I clutched the needle tighter. It was a long needle. Long enough, I thought, to poke someone's eye out.

"Do you miss her?" the voice was asking.

A sob rose in my throat—if that eye didn't turn away, I was going to claw my own out. "Yes. I miss her."

"Really?"

"Yes. That's why I want to fix my bag."

"Are you sure that's why?" the voice asked. "Or are you—"

"I'm going to sleep now," I cut in, propping my head against the window. My eyes stayed fixed to the stream of budget motels and gas stations flying by.

"Okay," the voice said. There was movement to it, as though whoever was speaking had finally turned around. "Good night."

"Okay," I breathed. The voice didn't sound like Jane. It didn't. Jane was dead.

Colored lights wiped my reflection clean, and in the next breath, I jerked awake, my heart hammering against my ribs. My bag was in my lap, the long sewing needle neatly tucked beneath a line of tight, even stitches. The bloody fingerprints were gone. I pressed my thumb against my stuck finger, but there was no blood there either. The seat in front of me was still and silent.

Jane wasn't there. She'd never been there. Jane was dead.

I rested my head against the back of the seat and watched my own face shining in the dark window, my glassy stare fixed and unmoving.

I looked dead too.

After two days and five transfers, I arrived at Seattle's bus station early Sunday evening, the sky dark and spitting rain. The ride had been painfully long, and I was a jumpy mess the entire time. I dozed on and off until I woke to find my own eye staring at me in the window and treated the entire bus to the kind of high-pitched yelp the residents of Haven had come to expect from me.

After that I stayed awake.

The station was huge compared to the one in Wichita, filled with ticket machines, newsstands and coffee shops, and dozens and dozens of people running across the wooden floor. I let the crowd jostle me along until we passed a bathroom. I broke free and ducked into a stall. My elbows raised a tremendous racket against the narrow walls, but I managed to change into jeans and a T-shirt. At the sink, I scrubbed my hands and face with pump after pump of almond-scented soap and worked my wet fingers through what was left of my hair. The water put some pink back into my cheeks, but the dark circles hooking my eyes wouldn't rinse away.

The main lobby was vast, the walls covered with squiggly charts. I gave up trying to make sense of them and approached the information desk to ask for a real map.

"This is all I got," the man said, pushing a glossy pamphlet at me. "It'll give you the transit routes."

I studied the back—it cut off just north of Seattle. "Do you know where I could get a better one?"

He shrugged. "Google."

I thanked the man and stuffed my fist with pamphlets and schedules anyway. Then I staked out a patch of floor near the rain-soaked window and sat there for twenty minutes trying to decipher a route, even though there were no arrows to my destination. Canaan was, if Toby and *Dateline* were to be believed, tiny and right next to Canada, but it didn't show up on the bus map.

It grew darker and rainier the longer I sat, and my nerves rose with a sense of urgency I couldn't pat down. It was the same way I always felt when I was working the fire-plow: desperate, with an aching need to be done already, to have results that would help, all the time knowing I was more likely to end up tired and bloody with nothing. The lines on the pamphlets started to move the longer I traced them, scurrying away from my searching fingers. I blinked hard to clear the blur from my eyes.

A man nearby was staring down at the phone in his hand. Across from me two little kids shared a bigger screen, fighting over who got to run their fingers over it. A teenage girl was tapping away on hers a dozen steps to my left.

The urgency was replaced by a rising sense of possibility. Craftiness. Lighted screens were visible in every direction, people passing, running, sitting, sipping coffee. They were all lit up, and there I was on the floor with my board and spindle, trying to plow a flame when there were a million matches right in front of me.

"Excuse me," I said, getting to my feet. The man nearest me barely moved, but when I tapped his shoulder, he stopped dead and stared at me. "Could I possibly borrow your phone for a minute?"

He didn't answer. He kept staring at me, his gaze so steady and dead, it felt like I was trying to wrestle a bear for a stick. I pushed past him.

No bears. I mentally crossed the grown men off my list. I needed something smaller. Something I could trap, something...

I stopped. There had been a break in the crowd while I was on the floor, a mass exodus to Los Angeles or Reno or one of the other cities being blared over the loudspeaker. There was a clearing now, and I saw eyes, young eyes, that darted away as soon as I met them. A guy about my age sat at one of the tiny tables that lined the perimeter of the room. He was looking at me.

No, he *wasn't* looking at me. He was looking at his phone or at least pretending to. I could see his fingers moving madly, too fast to be productive. After a beat he looked up again. His expression wasn't threatening, but it was vaguely hungry. I glanced away, and I could feel his eyes stay on me. For no reason, I liked it. Something about the way he was looking at me made me want to give him something to look at. I felt my color rise and my cheeks burn. All this reminded me of what Toby had said about how he'd survived, doing godawful things in godawful places, but it paid, he told me. At first, I thought he only meant money, but in that moment, with that boy watching me, I understood it might have been something more. Easy for me to say when it was only eyes on me, but from what Toby described, the full product wasn't much different from what I'd grown up doing—painful, ugly things that paid off in the end.

Once you got what you wanted, it didn't seem so bad.

I rolled my shoulders, leaning forward slightly, and started to walk. Not my normal walk, it couldn't have been—not when I was so aware of how I wanted to look. I was trying to walk the way Cole did, loose and long-limbed. I remembered his walk, the way it changed almost overnight, like his voice had. His body had grown too fast, before he was ready to fit in it, and something was always stooped or halting—that was a particular grace in itself. I tried to capture the innocence that had always captured me as I made my way toward the table, taking my time. I was never a very good stalker. Some of us were; my brothers in particular could follow and shoot anything they wanted. I had to stop and aim and take my time.

I tried to tell myself this was the same thing.

"Hey." The word spilled from my lips before I'd even committed to speaking; it paralyzed me.

Being frozen, I had no follow-up. I just stood there prepared to run, because no hunter in their right mind saunters up to their prey. Had some stranger wandered up to me and said *hey*, I would have run. But, I had to remind myself, people were not like me.

Here was proof. "Hi," the boy said. His cheeks got pink when he did, and that made me feel like I was doing better than I thought. "I'm sorry…"

"For what?"

"Being creepy. I know I was staring, I just…I like your shirt."

I looked down at my shirt. Toby had given it to me as a "house-warming gift" when I moved into his room. It was black and sleeveless, with a pale-blue silhouette of a girl and an astronaut. The astronaut was offering the girl a bouquet of balloons, nine of them, each a brightly colored outline of a planet that stretched toward a glittery sky.

"Because to me," he went on, gesturing vaguely toward the ceiling, "Pluto got a raw deal. I'm always happy to see a fellow sympathizer."

I didn't have the slightest clue what that meant, but I smiled anyway. "Thanks."

He smiled back. It was a genuinely striking smile on an otherwise unremarkable face, but I was used to Toby, which had made me hard to impress. "I'm on a three-hour layover if you want to sit down," he offered, gesturing to the other chair. "Or are you on your way out?"

"Thanks," I said again, dropping down in the seat across from him. "I'm supposed to be on my way out, but I'm a little bit stuck. Where are you headed?"

"Canada—Vancouver. I'm meeting up with some friends."

"I'm almost going to Canada," I said with another smile. "I mean, I'm supposed to be almost going to Canada—sorry, I've been on the bus so long, my brain isn't working anymore." I was channeling Toby now, the way I'd seen him talk to customers at the diner, leaning in as he spoke and dropping his voice slightly. He did it to women more than men, older women mostly, and when I asked him why, he said it made for better tips.

*If you've got something pretty, use it*, he'd said.

"I'm Avery," I told the guy.

"That's a pretty name."

I smiled—it felt weird and stretched out, but he grinned back.

"I'm Jules," he said.

"Jewels?" I repeated. "Like diamonds?"

He laughed, and it was beautiful—a fatal shot straight through the heart. "Like Julian, but nobody calls me that."

"Where are you from?"

"Oklahoma."

I blinked, making my eyes wide and surprised. All I knew about Oklahoma was that it was next to Texas, and all I knew about Texas was that it wasn't near Washington. "You took the bus all that way?"

"No, I flew in. This is just the last leg. Where are you from?"

"Wyoming," I said after a pause. "I'm just going upstate a bit more, to Canaan." I sighed heavily. "If I can find it."

"Are you afraid it'll move?"

I leaned over and slapped his arm lightly, something else Toby did for tips. "No. I lost my phone and all my directions. I was trying to figure out a route, but the buses don't go that far up."

"Well, I can help you," he said, his voice so fast and so eager, I cringed a little. "I have plenty of time. We can get coffee or—"

"I hate coffee."

The smile dropped slightly. "Oh."

"But I love milkshakes."

He brightened again, and it was so sudden and plain that I almost felt guilty. "We can do that," he said. "Name your flavor."

I shrugged, tugging on the neck of my shirt. There was something, Toby had told me, highly appealing about collarbones. "You decide."


"Okay, so Canaan is way up here…way up. You're going to have to cab it the last leg."

"Will that be easy?"

"It's kinda in the boonies, so I don't know. It sucks that you lost your phone."

"Tell me about it," I said, blowing my bangs off my forehead. My voice, and my words, felt sticky—I was speaking a foreign language, and my accent was all wrong. "I can't believe I did that."

"What kind of phone was it?"

"Like—same as yours."

"Then, here," he said opening a new screen. "Just log into your account, and we can track it."

*They give you numbers. They can track every move.* My mental blueprint wrinkled a bit. "What?"

"If you have the tracking on, you can log in on my phone."

"I'm pretty sure it's sitting on top of a sink at a gas station. We hit the rest stop so early this morning…"

The sympathy on his face was wildly out of whack. He looked like I'd told him I'd left a baby there. "That's the worst. You better have it shut off in case someone grabbed it by now."

Another wrinkle. "I will. It was a nice phone. I used it all the time."

A real wrinkle appeared in his forehead, and he let out a small laugh that seemed equal parts charmed and confused. "Hopefully you have all your info backed up somewhere." He turned back to his own phone, which was the same kind Toby had but smaller and bulkier. "It looks like the farthest train you can get is Bellingham. From there I would ask about buses, because there might be something to get you closer. I can't tell you what a cab would cost."

I took a long pull of my milkshake. It was chocolate—the icy sweetness cut through the dust in my throat and the ache in my head. We'd gone to a diner directly next to the bus station. Jules ordered an omelet that came buried in cheese and a huge plate of french fries. I had a cheeseburger, rare, that was as big as my head. I had to cut it in quarters to take a bite.

"So what's in Canaan?" he asked me, his eyes darting to my face. "Boyfriend?"

I should have laughed—at least a little—but my voice came out flat and mirthless, almost dead. "My brother."

"Do you want to call him and let him know what's going on?"

"No," I said, fiddling with my napkin. "He doesn't know I'm coming. It's a surprise."

An hour later the bill was placed between two empty pie plates. It was after eight, and Jules's bus was idling at the station. He reached for the slip of paper, but I slapped his hand away and paid for us. I'd kept him busy. He'd tapped away on his phone until every detail of my trip was in place, and all I had to do was sit there and smile. I was switching from the bus to a train—the nine twenty-three would pull into Bellingham about two hours later. If I timed it right, I'd be able to catch a local bus that would put me three miles from the Canaan city line.

"Feel better?" he asked me, scribbling something on a paper napkin.

"Much. Thank you," I said, smiling. "It was very nice of you to do this."

"It was nothing. I'd hate to be stranded without my phone. This is my number," he said, pushing the napkin toward me.

I let out a small laugh. "He tells the girl with no phone."

He smiled. "Maybe I'm hoping you'll call me when you get a new one."

I lowered my head and raised my eyes to look at him. "I will."

"How long are you planning on staying?"

I shrugged, my mind drumming up the image of Cole printed on

the television screen, his face blank and happy. *Until he remembers.*
*Until he relents. Until he leaves.*

"As long as it takes."



The bus belched white fumes, and then I was alone, tired enough for
all of it to be a dream. It had that kind of feel; the air, the sidewalk
under my shoes—entire states away from my almost home, my sort-of
home. A dream where I was lost and wandering, too far away to walk
back to anything I knew. I could see outside of myself when I got off
the last bus, a spectator to the sight of my feet shuffling aimlessly
toward the tiny town that had swallowed my brother. It was one
o'clock in the morning, more than forty-eight hours since I'd jumped
out a window for the second time, and I was just about done. There
were no waiting cabs when I stepped off the bus, no random helpful
strangers. There was a curb and a glass box shining in the moonlight.

But that was all I needed.

The moon was crooked, a lazy, barely there sickle in the sky. I
pulled out my sewing needle and held it up to the tips of the crescent—
the straight angle pointed south. I turned north and started walking.

The air reminded me of when I was tented. It was thin, cold
enough to make me glad I'd brought a sweater. The sweater was
Toby's. I'd snatched it out of his closet, and the softness of the fabric
told me I'd be in trouble when I went back.

If I went back.

My steps eventually led me to a circle of grass in the middle of four intersecting streets, like an island. In the center was a playground—tall mounds of molded plastic and an obstacle course of stairs and slides. I climbed to the top and found a tiny plastic room carpeted in a dimpled rubber mat.

I curled up on the mat with my satchel under my head and examined the view, calculating the odds that someone would find me before I could slide away and disappear. I guess I thought about it for a while, because I barely blinked before the world was lit with people and cars and sunshine, everything busy and bright. I sat up in my hiding place and stretched, letting myself feel every sore muscle under the simple agony of propping my eyes open. It drowned out the head pain, the shadows and the voices and the memories clawing at the crumbling wall between who I was and who I had been.

The sorest spot was the bump on my left hip, and I reached into my pocket to free the culprit. Jules's phone still felt like a brand-new appendage, something I desperately needed but hadn't gotten around to growing until now. I'd switched it off the night before, because I knew from watching Toby that phones could die just like people, and he made it seem just as tragic. I held the phone in the palm of one hand and pressed the button to turn it on, suddenly terrified that I'd broken something, that the screen would stay dark. But it didn't. It lit with cheery brightness, and a banner on the screen informed me of twenty-six missed calls.

It had been easy, sickeningly easy, to slide the phone up and out of his pocket when Jules offered me a hug goodbye. Just as easy as it was to watch his fingers tap out his code over and over as I thought of new things for him to look up for me. It was about a minute wait each time for the screen to go dark again, and then I would ask for something and he'd have to punch out that code again. He did it quickly, but my eyes were quick too: three-seven-one-five.

I probably should have felt bad about it, but I didn't. I never felt bad for cutting branches off trees and setting them on fire. It was necessary. I needed it to survive.

Plus I could always send it back to him when I was done. Three-seven-one-five. It was Monday, and I'd watched groups of kids march past my perch with longing glances on their way to school, so I knew I had a little bit of time before I had to abandon my shelter. What I needed didn't take long to find. I wasn't completely ignorant—I had a singular purpose, and it was simple: find Cole. I could do that. Toby had taught me back when there was a lot to find. On the train the night before, I had no trouble touching the right part of the screen and typing *Noah Reid Pierce* into the right box.

I knew I had to be quick. Jules had put the fear of God into me with his talk of tracking and turning off. The usual stories showed up on my first search: the three images of Cole and me on the outside, our baby pictures. There was something about the *Dateline* interview, and it jolted me to think it had only aired three days ago. I thought about Zoe and Toby and Amelia, what they must be thinking.

Didn't matter. My fingers moved faster. I pressed the button that would bring me back to the screen with the squares. One of the squares said *Maps*. I tapped out the address and waited for the phone to tell me where to go. It was a long wait while it decided, a long time before the word *start* lit up to lead the way. But it did.

The slide to my left was blue and steep and twisting. I rode it to the ground.

Cole's house was all redbrick and dark wood, with a hundred feet of steep, winding driveway and a porch floored in blue glazed tiles. I was panting by the time I reached the end of the blacktop, and my legs shook as I climbed the porch steps.

The front door had a brass knocker. Before my mind could barge in and stop me, I picked up the knocker and slammed it down three times. Something stirred behind the skinny windows framing the door, and I heard footsteps that weren't too quick or too slow. Easy steps.

Cole opened the door.

He was smiling, but his eyes were blank, the same vapid expression he'd worn during his interview, and I could have run up and down the driveway twice in the time it took for that look to melt away. A tiny wrinkle appeared in his forehead, and his eyes widened in...

*fear*

...shock. Or panic. Something.

There was a cry from high up in the trees, a long, throaty screech—it might have been a hawk. On the commune, I used to hear the hawks at night, and sometimes I could see them, diving and clawing and snatching small prey right off the ground. They always took what they wanted.

At the sound, Cole blinked twice, quickly, his Adam's apple working up and down. My own throat felt cinched shut and would allow no comment. I held up my arm instead, brandishing the worn strip of blue cloth still tied to my wrist.

Nothing. I took a slow step forward, and Cole stepped back. For a minute I thought I'd been granted entry, but then he jumped backward, and the door flew toward my face.

"Cole!" I shrieked. My reaction was pure reflex, fast and incredibly unwise. I stuck my foot out, and the door slammed on my ankle, ricocheting off the bone with an audible crack. I cried out in pain and surprise. "What are you doing?"

"Get out," he said. His voice was lower than I remembered, deeper, or maybe it was the fear bleeding behind it. The hawk screamed again. "Get the hell out of here before I call the cops."

*"What?"* I cried. "What are you talking about—"

He shoved me, hard. I took a quick step back, but my ankle was numb. I lost my balance and fell hard on the tiles.

There was something then, only a flash, but it was something—concern, honest pain in his eyes, and it was *for* me, not because of me. "What's wrong with you?" I managed. Both of my elbows were scraped, and my voice was full of tears. "It's me."

"Noah?" A girl's voice echoed down the hall. My heart took a skipping leap into my throat. "Who is it?"

"Mailman!" he hollered back. Then he bent and grabbed the strap of my backpack, yanking me to my feet. "If my parents see you, they'll call the police. I'm doing you a favor. Get out."

"I'm not leaving until you talk to me!"

"You're leaving now."

"Why did you lie about us?"

He stopped. Stopped and froze, still holding my pack strap. His face underwent a gradual metamorphosis from anger to confusion to…something. Hurt, maybe. I had hurt him, and I wasn't sure how. I stood as straight as I could with one shoulder hoisted in the air and my ankle puffed tight inside my shoe. "I saw the interview," I went on, fighting the tremble in my lips. "You lied, Cole. About all of it."

The voice came again. "Noah?"

He shut the door. Without a word he half carried, half dragged me off the porch and down the steps like he was taking out the garbage. There was a tearing sound as my feeble stitches ripped free. My own metamorphosis had taken place while I was watching his, and I was aware that I was a lot of things—angry was high on that list, right under confused, but I was willing to put that aside and concentrate on the simple fact that he was holding me again.

We got to the end of the driveway. I expected Cole to just dump me there or maybe drive down and run me over, but he didn't. He didn't even let go.

"I'm sorry," I said finally. His eyes were blank and unseeing. "I'm sorry for just showing up like this, but I saw you on television, and I needed...I needed to see you. I miss you so much," I whispered. "You didn't come back, and when I saw that interview, it was like you barely even remembered me."

The world spun all of a sudden, literally, bringing a wave of nausea as all the air was pushed out of my lungs. I couldn't move and I couldn't breathe. I could hardly process that Cole had thrown me against the brick wall framing the entrance to the driveway.

"Cole..." I choked.

"That is not my name." His voice was singsong, like he was reciting by rote—a trick to help him remember something he kept forgetting. His hand gripped my neck just under my chin, pressing my head against the wall.

"You want to know why I never came back?" he hissed. "You don't know why I didn't come *back*?" His expression wavered, and he let out a shaky laugh. "Because it was all bullshit, that's why. I know that now. And it's *your fault* that I know that. It's your fault I'm here. *I* never wanted to leave. I was thinking about us, but you were only thinking about you, and you were too *fucking* selfish…" He broke off, stopped spewing his brand-new language as he stared at a spot over my shoulder. A bit of shine escaped his eye and ran down his cheek.

"You wanted to get away," he said. He was nodding to himself, talking to himself. "I get that. I felt guilty about what happened to you, about what Mom and Dad did, so I tried to fix it. I shouldn't have. Because here we are, right? Everything's great, everything's *fiiine*…"

He smiled again, and I felt a sharp blast of panic. He looked rabid. Driven there by someone or something, but this wasn't Cole. I had no idea who was in front of me. I wasn't even sure he did.

"What happened to you?" I whispered.

"Oh, that's the question of the year, isn't it? Have people been asking you that? Because *everybody's* been asking me, and the more I tell them, the more pills I have to take. But the pills don't stop me remembering," he said, tapping his forehead. "The doctors, my parents, they want me to remember everything, even though I told them once I start, I can't stop, and it's so *hard*.

"They don't care," he said, quieter now. "They don't care how hard it is. And there's no pill that makes it easier to explain what it's like knowing that your sister is in the next room getting fucked and beaten by a guy off the streets, and all you can do is sit there and *listen to her scream."* His voice rose with every word. He let go of me then and held his own head, taking a shaky step back.

"And that wasn't even the worst thing," he whispered. "Not even the worst…"

"Cole, please," I begged him. "You can't—"

"*They* lied. About all of it. Nothing was coming, and they made us live in that place like animals. We were always starved or freezing cold. They made us so *scared*—we were scared of each other inside and everything outside!"

"That doesn't matter now! We got away, Cole!"

He smiled, turning his bleary eyes skyward. "I'm not Cole," he whispered. "Cole was broken, so they swept him up and threw him away." He pressed a hand to his head like it hurt, like there were things inside of him banging to get out. "Be careful," he added, waving his finger at me. "Avery's broken too."

I watched him stumble over his own feet, barely catching himself before he fell.

"All those meetings," he mumbled. "All those drills, all those reasons why. My parents—these people," he clarified, gesturing toward the house. "They made me tell them all of it. Things I didn't want to say, things I didn't want to remember, things I wasn't sure were true. But they made me. Like just talking about it would make them go away." He looked at me, his eyes huge and wet. "Remember Benji?"

A sob spilled from my lips; I pressed a hand to my mouth. "Yeah, of course I do."

"He lost his shoe once. You hugged him, and then you beat him with a switch."

My throat tightened and refused to let me swallow the words. They burned my mouth; I had to say them. "I know."

"Why did you do that?"

I bit my lip to stop it shaking. "They made me."

"Because he was your partner."

"And you were mine. If I didn't punish Benji, they would have hurt you worse."

"Oh, I know." He laughed a little. "I remember. *I* remember. Did you ever think about that? They made us hurt the ones who were supposed to protect us by not leaving. We shouldn't have stayed."

"We were scared to leave."

He nodded. "Partners. You were mine. Jane too. You remember why they made you and me partners? You do, right?"

"Cole, listen to me. All that is *over*. They are *dead*."

"Are they?"

I stopped. Cole's face was blurry through my veil of tears—he didn't look real. "What?"

"Do you really think so?"

"I... Don't you?"

He shrugged. "Maybe."

"Then let's just go! We can get away again. We can start over—"

"And what, live in the woods? Find a nice, abandoned building and breed our own? I thought that was why we had to leave."

"No, I didn't mean…"

"I would have, you know?" He grinned. "Yeah, you do. You know. You know I thought about it. It used to make me sick. I thought I was sick because why would I think something like that about my own sister? But you weren't my sister," he said with a casual shrug. "That was just me being healthy as can be…which, I guess I should have figured out."

"We did the best we could."

"That doesn't make it okay."

"No, you're right. We weren't okay there, and we're not okay here. We were okay when it was just us. We were happy—"

"No," he said, shaking his head. "It's too late. Take my advice, sis, if you don't want to talk about being stuck in that tent and bred like a dog, just make something up and take the fucking pills. Because Av…" A bark of laughter sent tears running down his face. "You're okay. I don't know how, you out of *all* of us, but you are. You still don't know how bad it was."

His hand drifted to his face, his glasses. "I can see now," he said. "That's one of the first things they fixed. The doctor gave me these, and everything looked different. All that time, my whole life, I couldn't see, and I didn't even know it. I didn't know what things were supposed to look like."

Cole's head dropped like it was too heavy to hold, his neck thin and breakable. "I do now. This...what happened to us—to me—is your fault. I can't forgive you for that. I can't forgive you for *them*. I tried to save us, but you only wanted to save you, and God, I hate you for that."

His face blurred and shimmered. My head was heavy, too, but I held it up. "I love you."

"Shut up."

"No. I never said that, and I should have. We both should have."

"I don't love you!"

"I know you do," I said. "You don't have to say it."

"You don't know *anything*!" All at once I was slammed into the wall again. My head bounced off the bricks so hard, I saw stars, every constellation in the sky. Cole was sobbing, the entire length of his body pinning me down. "You don't..."

My hands were halting, but brave. They circled his waist. "Tell me."

"We never should have left," he moaned.

"We can go back," I said, gripping him tightly. "Right now. I'm asking you to come back with me."

"No," he said, pushing me away and wiping his face. "Not with you. She was right about you. I didn't believe her, but she was right."

My thoughts trembled through the pain. The back of my head felt sore and lumpy, and I was such a dizzy mess, I wasn't sure I'd heard him right. "Who?"

"Go back, Avery." His mouth twisted, as if my name were that bitter. "You got what you wanted. You don't need me anymore."

"Cole, please, who were you talking to?"

"Mom," he said easily. "And Dad. Jane, Benji...all of them. Don't tell me you haven't seen them." He tapped my forehead with his finger. "You've seen them."

"Not for real," I told him.

"Real? Nothing is real. All of this," he said, gesturing vaguely. "It's fake. It looks nice, and everyone keeps telling me I'm so lucky. Lucky, lucky me." He fixed me with a look that was almost sane. "Don't think about it, Avery. Just go. Run and forget everything. Forget Cole, and forget what he did. Do that for me."

I took a step back. "What did you do, Cole?"

He shook his head and smiled, the same slight, sunny smile that had greeted me when he opened the door. He could turn it on that fast. "I did exactly what you wanted me to do."

# TWENTY-SIX

I CALLED TOBY. THERE WAS NO GUILT OR FEAR ATTACHED TO THE gesture, even though it crossed my mind that he might be worried—I just didn't know anyone else's phone number.

He didn't know this one, and I didn't expect him to answer at all, but he did; so fast that the phone must have been stapled to his head. His voice blared in my ear, high-pitched, on the edge of hysteria. "Avery?" he shrieked, in lieu of hello.

"Toby?"

"Avery?!"

"Yes—how did—"

"Jesus *Christ!*" His voice choked and rose even higher. "Please tell me you're okay."

"I'm fine."

"Where are you?"

I squeezed my eyes shut. "Canaan," I whispered.

"What's Ca—*what*? What the fuck is *wrong* with you?"

There was more choking and sniffling, and even though I could tell he wanted to be furious, he couldn't hold the tone. He could barely speak "Are you crying?" I asked.

"Yes, I'm fucking crying! I've been scared shitless for the past three days. Zoe called the cops, we thought the fucking cult came for you, and you stole my sweater! How could you do that?"

"I'll bring back your sweater."

"Not *that*!"

"I'm sorry." I pressed a hand to my forehead. I was sitting on the curb with my leg stretched out in front of me. The pain in my head had taken a back seat once I'd started walking, and my ankle throbbed in time with my heart. After Cole left me by the wall, I'd barely made it a quarter of a mile, and I wasn't going any farther. That, really, was only partly my ankle—the rest was the look on Cole's face when I'd scrawled Haven's address on a slip of paper and forced it into his hand without even knowing if he could read it on his own. The way he'd crumpled the paper in his fist and let it fall to the gravel. "I need to come home."

"You're damn right you do, because I'm going to kill you when I—"

There was a scuffling sound and a new voice sounded in my ear. "Avery?"

"Zoe?"

"Where are you?"

"Washington. I'm sorry, Zoe."

"Don't be sorry yet. Let's just get you home. How did you get there?"

"Bus," I said, squeezing my eyes shut. I wiped my cheek with the back of my hand. "Five of them. And, um, a train. And another bus."

"Can you get back?"

"No. I hurt myself," I said quietly.

"Hurt yourself how?"

"I think I sprained my ankle. The station's too far."

There was a brief, muffled conversation in the background, and then Zoe got back on. "Toby is getting the number of a cab company. Do you have cash with you?"

"Yes."

"What about your bank card and the picture ID we had made for work?"

"I have them." I hoped I did. I'd stashed the two plastic cards in my bag and forgotten about them—both cards said *Celeste Bishop*, which had little to do with me. "How am I going to get back?"

"Have the taxi take you to the airport—I think it's Seattle–Tacoma—and call me back when you get there. I'm going to buy you a ticket, and you are going to give me your next ten paychecks." She hesitated. Her next question sounded like it came out before she was ready to ask it. "Did you see Cole?"

My eyes turned up to the sky. It had gone gray since that morning. A heavy belly of clouds sagged over my head. Nothing sang and nothing cried.

"No," I said after a moment. "I looked, but I couldn't find him."

After I returned to Haven, I spent a lot of time sitting on Toby's bed, contemplating my toes. I'd never thought much about them, but now they were the last thing I saw when I fell asleep and the first thing to greet me in the morning. They were safe—it was safe for me to linger there, to focus only on what was in front of me. For about a week after I got back, I wasn't allowed to walk around much; I had to keep my foot elevated on a wedge-shaped pillow with a groove cut out for my leg. My toes looked little and pink sticking out of the cast.

Cole used to occupy most of my thoughts, but he didn't exist anymore. Sometimes, mostly late at night when the shadows were looming and I didn't even have the option to run, I let myself think about him. The way he was before. And it was like allowing myself to drink nectar laced with poison because it tasted so good.

Cole's—or Noah's, whoever he was now—well-aimed shot with the front door had fractured my ankle in two places, according to the doctor who'd reviewed my X-ray. He'd been impressed with my splinting.

Of course he was. After I hung up with Zoe, I forgot everything that was emotionally wrong and stuck with what I knew. While I was tearing cloth and looking for branches, I fell into a giggling fit that lasted so long, it scared me—I finally had a problem I knew how to fix. I crawled around until I found two straight sticks on the ground and wedged one into each side of my shoe, tying them in place with strips of a T-shirt and the strap Cole had ripped from my bag.

The plane ride was agony; my ankle throbbed, and thank God for that. If I laid my head back and closed my eyes, I could focus on the pain and forget about Cole, forget I was trapped in a metal tube barreling across the sky. I was happy to have something concrete to cry about, a physical pain to blame my swollen eyes on when my makeshift splint and I limped off the plane and found Zoe and Amelia waiting for me.

We went straight to the hospital, where I was given a shot that made the air thicken to syrup and my mind settle in ignorant bliss. When I swam back up, a nurse was asking me what color cast I wanted. I said I didn't care.

Not caring got me a bright-orange foot I'd have to wear for six weeks. Toby drew all over it every time he sat with me, so after a few days, the color didn't really matter.

"Do you want to talk about it?" he asked me one night. An early autumn thunderstorm was raging outside, one of those wild, pattern-less squalls that throw twelve bolts of lightning for every clap of thunder and whip the rain sideways.

"About what?"

"Your northwest excursion."

I tilted my head back until it touched the wall. "No."

He'd been pretty good about not asking—even better for giving up his bed in lieu of a rollaway cot while I was in the cast. The day I got back, I slept for nearly twenty-four hours, and when I woke up, he stuck to basic questions as he helped me unpack.

"You *stole* it?" he'd gasped, pulling the purloined phone from my bag. "You stole someone's phone?"

"I had to."

"You most definitely did not have to. That is sacrilege. People carry their whole lives around in their phones."

"That's what you're upset about?"

"No, that is what I'm outraged about on this poor boy's behalf."

In the end, getting the phone back to Jules was pretty simple. Toby pressed a button, said *directions home*, and an Oklahoma address popped up. He shook his head at me as he loaded the phone, now bundled in thick plastic, into a padded envelope.

"He didn't even cut the service. You must have really done a number on him. You ought to send him a couple hundred dollars or a kidney or something."

But the phone debacle aside, Toby hadn't pressed. Now his marker skipped across my orange shin—he was running out of room. "Will you tell me if I ask?"

"I don't really feel like playing that game right now," I said, rubbing my eyes.

He capped the marker and looked at me. There was no light or levity in his eyes. "It's not a game."

I shrugged.

"Did you see him?"

I shrugged again.

"I can't hear you."

"I saw...I saw someone," I mumbled. It was no good; my throat was instantly choked with tears. "But it wasn't him."

Toby thought about his next question for a while. "Did it look like him?"

I swallowed hard. "Yeah."

"Okay." He picked up the marker again and started etching something that didn't look like anything yet, but I knew it would. Toby could draw better than I could walk when I had two working legs. "You know, Zoe is a good person to talk to," he said idly. "She helped me a lot when I first got here." He moved to the other side of the bed to attack my cast from a different angle. "I wasn't always the ray of sunshine I am now."

"Did she tell you to tell me that?"

"No, I'm just telling you that. Information to be used at your discretion."

"Can I see your phone?"

He deflated a little. "Avery…"

"What?"

"You can't keep doing this."

He was right—because there was no answer to *why*. I knew that. I wanted to know how. "Can I?"

He flipped the phone into my lap. I picked it up and started typing. *Fire. Clovelite. Cult. Suicide.*

"Not healthy, Av."

"No, Cole wasn't healthy," I said and immediately bit my tongue. Toby raised his head. I didn't, but he refused to look away. "No?"

I glanced at the door. "No," I whispered. "He was out of his mind. Screaming and crying. He was talking about the other kids in our family and how terrible we were to them." I met Toby's eye. "He said it was all my fault. Everything."

"Why was it your fault?"

"Because he wanted to stay there?" I guessed. "I don't know. It was my idea to run."

"Survivor's guilt," Toby said with a nod. I felt a curious chill at the phrase—*survivors*. We would always be survivors now; it wasn't a choice anymore. We couldn't even run from the past; it was chasing us. "I bet he's feeling bad that you guys made it out and no one else did—"

I bet he was too.

"—and it's just easier for him to blame you, that's all."

"He said his parents and the doctors were making him talk about everything and take pills."

"Knew it."

"But it wasn't good, Toby," I said, tearing my eyes from the screen. "He looked awful, and he wasn't even making sense."

"So you want to join him?" he asked poking the phone in my hand. "Because you ain't too steady these days either, sweetheart."

"I'm fine."

"No, you're not. You never sleep, you're on the damn phone more than I am—"

"Because I want to know what happened!"

"It happened! Why does it matter now?"

"Because," I said again. "Because if—because if I know, maybe I can tell him. I can explain it to him or at least understand why he..."

My voice died. The phone tumbled to my lap. Toby moved to sit next to me, and I let my head drop to his shoulder. We didn't speak. The walls were patterned with bright-white flashes that sent the shadows running. But they always came back.

I could feel his lips move against my forehead. "You gotta let him go, hon."

"I can't..."

"You have to try."

"I can't. The fire got everyone, and now Cole's gone too." I sat up and wiped my eyes. "He was the only person who ever cared about me, and I don't even know who he is anymore. *He* doesn't know who he is anymore. And I need to know why, because I can't let that happen to me. I made it out. I'm out."

*Why, though?* A dark little voice whispered the words as I rounded my shoulders and picked up the phone again. Why was I out? *How* might be a better question, *how* was I out if they locked me in? I could save the why for Cole: Why would he burn us down when I was inside…?

*This is the only safe place.*

Maybe he did do it on purpose. Maybe it really was mercy, to put us all out of our misery, and I messed that up too. Survivor's guilt.

"Avery?"

"Mercy," I mumbled.

"What?"

I blinked. The words were rolling around in my mouth, I could feel them—a few must have gotten out. "Nothing."

Toby raised a perfectly arched eyebrow and got to his feet. "I think we're done for the night. You need to go to sleep. I'm going to help Ronnie for a while, and I'm taking the phone with me. I will be checking on you. Please get some rest, and try to be coherent in the morning."

I watched him walk almost all the way to the door. Then he stopped. He stopped and he faced me, and his face was new and strange—there was anger painted there. "Actually, no," he said, vitriol bleeding through. "Because you just spewed a whole bunch of bullshit that concerns me too." Toby knelt next to me, leaning in until we were eye to eye. The lightning snapped his picture, bathing his face in white. "Guess what?" he said. "Cole doesn't get the monopoly on caring about you. He isn't even here. I am, and *I* care about you. I love the shit out of you. I don't want you to run away, I don't want you to have nightmares, and I don't want you to hide in this room anymore. I'll even take one out of three. And if that means kicking your ass a little bit, I'm going to do it." His expression softened, and he surprised me again; he leaned in and kissed me quickly on the forehead, gripping my head for a longer beat. "Free Avery. Quit using up my battery."

I gave him a watery smile as he pulled away; my response was serious too. I hoped he knew it. "I love you, Toby."

"Of course you do." He got to his feet with a sigh. "Everyone does."

# TWENTY-SEVEN

_____

_CLOVELITE CULT. FIRE. CELESTE BISHOP. NOAH REID PIERCE._

I quit looking things up on Toby's phone. I felt guilty about making him worry. I used his computer instead. Haven had three communal computers that everyone fought over all the time, but Toby had some kind of secret portable version that he'd "inherited" from a former resident. Most of the time, he kept it stashed under the bed. He'd showed me how to play cards on it once, sort of like a gateway drug, I guess. It always seemed too complicated to bother with.

But it wasn't. It was like a phone, I discovered once I started fiddling with it, only bigger. I knew the password—that had also been inherited from the computer's former owner, an homage to her ex-boyfriend that Toby never got around to changing. Toby worked at the diner five nights a week in four-hour chunks. As soon as I heard him tell Ronnie good night, I would type *Motherfucker123* into the password box and start scanning articles and news sites for anything new. Anything.

*Suicide. Arson. Kidnapped. Missing children found alive.*

I hadn't thought about it from a public perspective, but there was a degree of interest in my other brothers and sisters that surprised me. Peter, Sarah, Amaris—their names were out there. Officer Rodolfo had taken excellent notes that day in the interrogation room. He must have, because that was the only time I'd let those names pass my lips. There were theories about who the other kids were and pages and pages of photographs of children who'd been lost or stolen and never seen again. Having the advantage of knowing what to look for, I pored over those pictures, trying to find a younger version of Jane, or Seth, or Candace...any of them. I sifted through missing faces, even though it wasn't so easy to remember what they'd looked like anymore. My own image had been placed inches from my eyes, and I hadn't even recognized myself.

I hated typing the words—*Clovelite, fire, cult.* Every search felt toxic. Cole had been sickened by saying them and poisoned trying to squash them with pills. I had plenty of words that were far more relevant and would do me no good. If any of the words, searched or not, hurt me, I couldn't let it show. Plenty of people in here had to take pills—I'd seen them at breakfast swallowing handfuls of white, washing them down with coffee or orange juice. If anyone caught on to how much I was thinking about what I was thinking about, I would either have to talk or swallow. And look what that did to Cole.

I couldn't do either, I knew that, and the why and the how weren't in my head anyway. They were all of us, the whole picture: twelve burning people scattered in chunks of bone and ash. We had to be put back together to understand it, and I was the only one left.

I'd been pushing wood into dust for a long time. My hands and my head were tired. I had to see a spark soon.

A few days after the thunderstorm, I dragged my orange cast down the hall, hobbling toward Zoe's office. The crutches were hard for me; the doctor wanted me to get used to them before I went back to work. My hands felt like sheets of cracked plastic against the foam rubber—it was incredible how my palms refused to heal. Zoe, I knew, was upstairs dealing with a rooming crisis. It only took me a few minutes to find Officer Mason's business card in the pile of papers covering her desk.

"You back from your little trip, Houdini?" he sneered down the line. "You know, I don't like wasting man power on high-risk runaways."

I'd called him from the clunky phone that was next to Toby's bed and doubled as a speaker when Ronnie needed to scream something at us. The black handle was slick in my grip. "I'm sorry."

"What do you want?"

"I wanted to know if you wanted to talk to me again."

"What for?"

"Anything. I'd like to help if I can."

"Now you want to help? I thought you told me everything you knew."

"I did."

"So what have you got for me? A new story? Or maybe a different version of the old one?"

I hesitated. "I've been trying to think of something that I missed, maybe. I've been reading the news—"

"Why?"

"Because," I stammered. "Because it's—"

"You know more than they do."

"I don't."

"Who was there, them or you? Don't read stories. You're gonna call me up one day, your brain knotted up in six different conspiracy theories—don't go looking for answers from people who don't know. You know. You were there."

"I don't know," I whispered.

Now Officer Mason hesitated, and when he spoke again, his voice was marginally kinder. "I don't think you want to know. Whatever happened that night was bad enough to leave behind, and that's just what you did. I see this all the time. People blot out all kinds of bullshit. But the truth is like cancer: it's there and it might hide, but eventually it'll metastasize, and either you get it out, or it'll eat you alive."

"Did you find out anything you can tell me?"

He hesitated again. "No," he said, not sounding so sure. "But your little brother sent us a dozen steps back with the grade A shit-stirring he did in his little interview. Contradicted pretty much everything you said."

"I know."

"So, you tell me: Who do we believe?"

I wrapped the cord around my hand, poking my index finger into the long, twisting curl. "He was lying."

"Are you sure?"

"No—I mean he wasn't really lying," I corrected myself. "He was remembering wrong."

"He said the same thing about you. Not in so many words, but he did. Your story throws him under the bus. How do you know you're right and he's wrong?"

I paused. The cord was cutting off my circulation. "You know how Amelia said we were brainwashed while we were there?"

"Yeah."

"I think he still is. Not the same way, but he is. Just…" I trailed off.

Officer Mason chuckled a little. "Just a different kind of soap?"

I nodded, clutching the black phone tightly in my hand. The window was bright and orange with dusk, a steady fire of autumn leaves and early sunsets. I hated it during the day, and when the brightness left shadows behind, I hated it at night. "Yes."

I heard something in the background, a scratching sound. "Can you come and see me this week?" he asked.

My heart picked up. "Yes. I'll need a ride, though."

"Then how about I come see you? Thursday, say around noon. And we'll try and get this sorted out."

It was Monday. Thursday was a blink away. It was forever. My cast was silhouetted against the window, my orange foot blending into the sunset, melting in the fiery light. I jerked it away before I could feel it burn. "All right."

That night I had a dream. When I woke up, I remembered it. Not the whole dream, but things that were more solid than anything that had come before. It was just a flash at first, a quick shot of my father's face—he looked normal, but after the flash, he fell to the floor and melted into something horrible. He looked the way he'd felt the last time I'd seen him, deformed by my own eyes, morphed into a monster. His features ran like melting wax, pooling onto the wood, and oozing under my feet until they were glued to the floor. I stood and watched, knowing I should run.

But I didn't want to.

Another flash, and my eyes were open, staring blankly at the curtained window. My ankle was throbbing in the cast, but my heart and my throat were quiet.

Everything was quiet; there were no feet pounding the floor above my head or knocks on the walls—none of the music that usually woke me. I turned and saw Toby sound asleep on his cot. I blinked. My father's crayoned face was still mud in my mind's eye.

I found the article the next day.

It wasn't much. I wasn't even looking, and if Bev hadn't been running her mouth, I wouldn't have seen it at all.

"Did you hear me last night?" I asked Toby in the morning. He was shoveling cereal into his mouth, and I was watching. He reminded me of Cole sometimes, the way he ate breakfast so desperately, like the fast had been eight weeks instead of hours. The way they both got hungry again an hour later.

"Hear you what?" he asked. Behind him I saw Bev and Julie glance at each other over their own bowls.

"I—anything," I said after a moment. "I didn't wake you up?"

"Nope. That's the best thing about your half-baked holiday," Toby said, cramming a triangle of toast into his mouth. "You finally shut up at night."

I paused again. "Really?"

"Look at my eyes," he said, leaning closer. His eyes looked exactly the same. "Rested and refreshed. I was seriously considering kicking you out if my bags got any worse, but I didn't want to hurt your feelings."

"Why didn't you tell me?" I asked as he stood and collected his cereal bowl and coffee cup.

"Because the jinx is a thing. It happens. Mark my words: You'll start screaming again tonight." He started for the kitchen. "I have to go pick up my check. You want anything?"

"No. Yes."

"Chocolate croissant?"

"Or a checkered brownie if they have them."

"'kay. Back in an hour."

"How's your foot?" Bev asked me after Toby trotted away. Her tone was solicitous, syrupy. Julie had her head bowed and was pretending not to listen. Whether they remembered me sitting at the table my first morning there as Bev blasted me and Cole, I didn't know. But since she found out I was Celeste, Bev was always nervous and always nice.

"It's okay." I focused my gaze on a newspaper someone had left on the table, examining the soft pencil strokes on a partially completed crossword puzzle. The paper was barely five pages cover to cover; I guess nothing much happened in our county. My eyes darted to the list of clues, trying to figure out which letters belonged in the leftover boxes.

"Getting used to the crutches?"

"Uh-huh." I didn't understand crossword puzzles—I liked word searches, and the Jumble. I flipped the page over, looking for either, but there were no more puzzles. Just an article: *Danver Runaway Returns*.

"When do you get the cast off?"

"Few weeks," I said, scanning the text so I wouldn't have to talk. *After nearly a decade of mystery and fear over her whereabouts, a young Danver woman returned to her parents' home after disappearing without a word more than eight years ago. Emily Barrera was fifteen when she packed a bag and fled her bedroom in the middle of the night, and despite extensive search efforts from her family and local law enforcement...*

"It's gotta be itching you by now."

"What?" I asked, squinting at the page.

"The cast. I had a cast on my arm once, and it itched something terrible...I could never quite reach..."

*...amid speculation that she'd been lured from her home...*

"...scary when they take it off."

*Her parents, James and Susan Barrera, had noticed a disturbing change in their daughter's behavior in the weeks leading up to her disappearance...*

"And the doctors just sliced it off with a saw. A great, big power saw. You'd think..."

*"Emily had been acting up for months. We knew she'd run away. But she left her phone. This was a fifteen-year-old girl. She'd have been on that phone twenty-four seven if we'd let her. We went to her room that morning, and it was stripped. She took clothes, shoes, as much as she could carry. And she left her phone on her nightstand. That terrified us. It wasn't an accident."*

My eyes drifted to the picture. It was really two pictures set in one square, two images side by side, the same girl eight years apart. The first one looked professional; it had a fake, bland background, and the girl wore a fake, bland smile. She was pretty, though—pretty enough for it to show, despite all efforts to the contrary. The unnatural tilt of her head and shoulders should have been awkward but instead showed fine bones and delicate angles. Her dark hair hung to her shoulders.

"...you get to keep the cast, you know. It'll smell like death, just warning you, but you should keep it. Toby really made it pretty..."

I leaned closer. The girl in the first picture had wide, wondering eyes and tiny hands folded primly in her lap. Her smile was patient. She was patient. She didn't want to be there, and maybe she already knew she wasn't going to stay.

"...it's a shame he's such a pain in the ass."

*It wasn't an accident.*

The girl in the second picture was Amaris.


Somehow, I made it back to my room—I must have, because I was sitting on the bed with the newspaper in my lap when Toby returned. I could have copied Amaris's picture from memory by then. The camera had caught her midturn, pushing a strand of hair from her eyes as she walked toward what, I guessed, was her parents' house.

She had the same faraway, slightly annoyed look that I remembered from sitting next to her my entire life.

Or eight years.

"Here," Toby said, thrusting a white paper bag at me. "I got you both. Don't eat everything at once or you'll be bouncing off the walls."

I looked up at him blankly. "Where's Danver?"

"Along Route Fifteen." He shook the bag at me. "Six or seven miles east of nowhere—please take this before I eat it."

"I found my sister."

"What?"

"In the paper," I said. My voice was weirdly calm. I felt like I'd been marching toward a cliff and all I had left to do was jump. "She's in the paper."

"Your real sister?"

"Yes. No."

"What are you talking about?"

"Amaris," I said, flicking the paper at him. He caught it and studied the picture. "Danver Runaway. That's my older sister."

"From Clovelite?"

I nodded.

"This is her?"

"Yes."

He paused, and I watched his eyes scan the article. "Eight years ago you would have been, like, twelve." Toby told me, looking up.

"I know."

"So, forgive me, I'm not schooled in the ways of the cult, but did you just not notice that your *older* sister arrived fully formed? Way after you?"

"No," I said, pressing my hands to my temples. "I didn't." I tried to pull back, to remember a time when Amaris wasn't there, and I couldn't do it. There was no first memory, no black hole where she didn't exist. There were certain moments I couldn't tie her to, like the people on the couch, and my bloody pink shoes—but that had always been just Cole and me. I wasn't supposed to remember her then because she wasn't there.

Yet.

"It's her," I said, rubbing my hands over my thighs until my skin burned. "She's…that's her. She's alive. One of two, and she's alive."

"One of two what?"

"What do I do?"

"Do you have to do anything?"

"I have to talk to her! She might—" I stopped. My *last* memory of Amaris stopped me, her voice in the hall, shouting above all the others.

*Push!*

"She locked me in," I breathed.

"Locked you in where?"

My eyes got hot and itchy. I remembered the heavy thud against the door, the barking orders. I knuckled the burning pain away. "In my room when the fire started. No, *Hannah's* room. I didn't have a room."

"Avery…"

"She locked me in," I repeated. I saw Toby then, and there was pain carved in his face. I felt nothing for myself. "She did it. I want to talk to her."

Toby looked at me coolly for half a dozen heartbeats. He folded the paper and dropped it on the nightstand.

"So let's go talk to her."

# TWENTY-EIGHT

DANVER'S ONLY ROAD WAS A LONG SNAKE OF A STREET LINED WITH doll-sized houses. Amaris's was on the far end. Cracked wooden siding. Small and white.

"Right here," I told Toby. "Stop."

My forehead nearly kissed the windshield when his foot met the brake. "Do you want me to come with you?"

I shook my head before I was sure. "No. But watch me, okay?"

Until that moment, the hardest part had been convincing Van Driver to loan us his van, assuring him Toby could drive just fine. Which he couldn't. With Toby behind the wheel, the van bucked and sped and screeched. He floored the gas and slammed on the brakes, jerking us forward with every stop.

"This thing handles terribly," he kept saying.

But I barely noticed. The blame had shifted, lost its grip on Cole. If I thought too much, it might swing back to me. I couldn't be afraid. I couldn't confront her with anything less than the chaos that had been consuming me since the day we ran—the nightmares, my fury over losing Cole—all of that had to be encapsulated, ground up, packed tightly into a tiny little pill. Something small enough to carry and heavy enough to throw.

"What are you going to say?"

"I don't know."

I *didn't* know, and I didn't move. I was frozen, idling at the curb. "Are you sure you don't want me to come?" Toby asked.

"Yes."

"Stay outside," said Toby. *He* sounded scared. "I want to be able to see you."

My hands were shaking as I pushed open the door. The rubber tip of the crutch caught on the curb, and I stumbled, nearly losing my balance. I couldn't lose my balance.

"She's not going to let me in."

There was no winding driveway to Amaris's front door, no wide steps, and no blue-tiled front porch. The house was plain painted clapboard, and when I touched one of the boards, some of the white came off on my hand. There were fake spider webs taped to the window, with a fat plastic spider stuck in the middle. Someone had placed a hollowed-out pumpkin with a crude carved face on a stand next to the door. One side of the pumpkin's face had rotted and collapsed.

I knocked on the door.

Silence. The blue curtain in the front window swished to the side and back again. The door opened a crack and a small, solemn face peered up at me. She was slight and pretty, like Amaris. "Hi."

"Hi." My voice cracked, and I cleared my throat. "I'm looking for Am—Emily."

"She's not here."

"Oh." That tiny face had bled me some. I couldn't rain fury on a little girl. "Do you know where she is?"

"She's at the doctor."

"Oh," I said again.

"Soren? Who's here?" The door opened wider, and a soft-faced woman appeared behind the little girl. "Can I help you?"

"She's looking for Em," Soren said.

The woman's eyes sharpened. "What do you want with her?"

I took a step back. Dead grass scratched at my ankle. "I'm a friend of hers."

"She's not here."

"Okay," I said, stumbling as I turned.

Her voice hit me like a whip. "Hang on!"

I jumped, but when I looked back, some of the malice was gone. "You want to leave a message for her?"

"No—it's nothing. I'm sorry to bother you."

I swung my way across the patchy brown lawn, even though it was looking more and more like a great place to lie down. There was a sick, rolling feeling in my chest. Toby was mouthing something at me, making a shooing gesture. I shook my head.

Another car pulled up to the curb behind Toby's and stopped directly in front of me. The door opened.

It was Amaris...and Emily. Out here Amaris didn't exist, but just like Cole, I could still see her. Only she fit better than Cole and I ever would. Amaris hadn't been reborn to something unknown; she'd slipped into her old skin as easily as changing clothes. It hung a bit differently—one of her cheeks was shriveled and burned, as though the fire had slapped her across the face. Her eye on that side was white, sightless. But her first fifteen years were shining stronger than the past eight. I felt a rush of something cold and terrible, because I didn't know this person.

And she was looking at me like I was a ghost.

"Avery?"

My teeth clenched. I could barely get the word out. "Em?"

Her unburned cheek paled and some of the shock went with it. "What do you want?"

"What do I *want*?" I choked.

"Leave me alone, Avery, just go. I can't—"

"Where have you been?"

Her eyes—her eye—widened. A blotch of pink splashed across the smooth side of her face.

"Who else got out?" I spit, louder with every word. "Where are they?"

She took a step sideways, but even smaller than her, I was bigger. She was afraid. She was afraid like Cole was afraid—here, too, my presence was a weapon.

"I have nothing to say to you," she mumbled.

"Tell me who else got out."

"No one got out," she said bluntly. "You know that. Not even us." Her fingers feathered over her cheek.

"Why did you lock me in?"

The first real strength bloomed on her face. "I had to. I had to get the other kids out."

"By trying to kill me?"

She jerked back like I'd thrown something. Like I'd hit her. "I answered your question. I want you to leave."

"Have you seen the news, Amaris? Have you been paying real close attention to what happened to us?"

"That wasn't my fault."

"You could have helped us!"

"I helped you by staying away."

"I mean before. Because you knew, didn't you?" I whispered. "You knew who we were."

"I didn't—"

"Maybe not by name, but you knew who we weren't. Right?" I pressed. "You knew we weren't supposed to be there, because you weren't supposed to be there either."

She cast a panicked look toward the house. The woman and the little girl were framed in the front window, their faces blank and featureless through the glass. "I can't talk about this, Avery."

"Why not? What could be so bad? You let me get raped, and you locked me in that room. What else did you do?"

Her face glowed red, a vein in her neck throbbing like something trying to escape. "I didn't do anything. Get the hell out of here."

"Tell me what happened!"

"It happened! It's done! If you don't leave, I'll call the police—"

"I already did." She froze midstep at my words, her back stiffening. "I've been talking to the investigating officer," I said slowly. "He wants to know what happened too. He knows that Cole got out and that I got out, but he doesn't know that you got out, does he? No one even knows you were there, and I don't think you want them to. Right?"

She turned to face me again. "You can't prove it."

"That's a nasty burn you've got there."

Her hand drifted to her wasted cheek. "Avery—"

"If he finds out you were there, he's going to want to talk to you. I'll tell him you were with us. I'll tell him you locked me in that room. Everything."

"You're lying. You would never—"

"I would do it," I said slowly, "in a heartbeat. I have nothing left to lose. Do you?"

She lifted her head and studied me. Something was different. I couldn't read her anymore.

"Tomorrow," she said finally. Her eyes bounced to Toby in the van. "There's a Starbucks about eight miles from here, past Derby on Route Fifteen. Do you know where it is?"

"I'll find it."

"Noon." Her lip trembled. "Don't bring anyone. I won't either."

Toby was vibrating in his seat when I got in the car. "What happened?"

My eyes followed Amaris as she walked toward the front door. Her steps were slow and meandering, her feet clumsy, like they were carrying her against her will to a place she didn't want to go. The door swung open, and the little girl was there again. Amaris shuffled past, ruffling her hair absently with one hand.

The door slammed. I shook my head.

"I don't know yet."

# TWENTY-NINE

FOR BEING PRETTY CLOSE TO NOWHERE, STARBUCKS WASN'T EMPTY
at noon in the middle of the week. Machines bubbled and hissed
on top of a soft murmur of voices. Menus hung on the wall, huge
blackboards with seemingly hundreds of drinks chalked in white. I
didn't like coffee, so I tried to choose something else, but I couldn't
focus—the letters swam until they looked like some alien language.
At the counter I bought a bottle of water and faced the room. Entire
tables were claimed by computers and their people, wide eyes
searching for more to see as they tapped away on one screen and
stared at another.

There was an empty table in the back of the room, next to a
pyramid-shaped fireplace cut into the stone wall. The fire was throwing plenty of heat, but I was shivering. I hadn't brought anyone with

me—not even Toby, even though he'd begged, pleading entitlement first and my safety second.

"What if she walks in and shoots you in the face?" he'd whispered the night before. His voice was a splash in the darkness.

"Then all my troubles will be over."

Now it was five after twelve. No Amaris. I sipped my water.

Twelve ten. Twelve fifteen.

At eighteen minutes past, the door opened. Amaris stepped in swathed in a sheer orange and red scarf. She walked to the counter and placed an order for something I couldn't hear. Cup in hand, she turned to scan the room. I waved.

Her steps slowed as she got closer, but she kept walking. She slid into the chair across from me with a glance over her shoulder at the fire. "Nice," she mumbled.

The ice cubes in her cup shivered and danced, and her fingers smudged the black letters spelling *Emily* on the side. "I didn't think you were going to come," I said.

"I wasn't. But I thought about it, and there are things I want to say. One thing in particular."

"So say it."

She fiddled with a sugar packet. The buzz of people and machines seemed to relax her. She breathed with it, made buoyant by the noise. "Didn't you have things to ask me first?"

I drew a breath. The fire crackled at her back, lighting up the twists of red skin on her cheek. "Where did you come from?" I asked finally.

Amaris nodded, smiling a little as if I'd gotten a hard question right. "From here—outside. I was chosen, just like you."

"Not like me."

She conceded with another nod and took a sip from her straw. "You're right. Mom and Dad chose you. I chose myself."

"What does that mean?"

The glow from the fire wrapped around our table, me waiting to listen, and Amaris deciding what to say. Despite my confusion, sitting there with her, I felt chosen again. When it was just me, it was easy to feign normal, but with Cole and Amaris...even unrelated, we matched. Our differences were deeply carved, and together, it showed. We'd done things, shared things that made us irreversibly altered, irrevocably marked. No one could deny we had been chosen for something.

But now I had to listen, because her story was not mine.

"I hated my parents," Amaris said, staring at the table. "My real parents. I hated that we didn't have money like my friends' families did. I hated that everything I had was cheap or secondhand. It seemed like everyone else had everything that was good—everything I wanted.

"I wanted too much," she breathed, falling to a whisper. She blinked, her milky eye blank and sightless. "Do you remember when I came to the commune?"

"No," I said. "You were always there."

"No, I wasn't. I was fifteen years old the first time I walked through those doors. There was no formal induction, none of that shit. They treated me like I *was* always there. They gave me a room and the chair next to you, and the next day I started training with everyone. You were maybe twelve, Cole had to be nine or ten—"

"Yeah, but how?" I cut in. "They didn't take outsiders."

"Right." She stared past me. "They took kids."

She went on a moment later, "I worked when I was fifteen. As a bagger at a grocery store. I hated it, but there were things I looked forward to. Like this one man who used to come in with his son. They would buy cartfuls of stuff, practically every can in the store, all kinds of things. But it was good for me, because one of my jobs was to help them carry everything to the car, and they always tipped me ten dollars. They came in a lot."

"Dad?"

"And Seth. They always parked far away, and while we walked to the car, Dad would tell me stories," she said slowly. "Incredible stories that were so beautiful and so scary. He was smart. He knew exactly what to say to make me listen. He made everything sound possible; he made me think it was all my idea and that I was special at the same time. I remember one day I was upset. I was crying because I cracked my phone screen—my phone was the only good thing I had, and it wasn't even that good. I could barely breathe, I was so upset. He took the phone away and told me it had poisoned me. That there was no need to get upset over things, because pretty soon there would be no things. And that sounded good to me."

"Having nothing?"

"Having everything. He told me I could have everything that was important and that only certain people could understand that. He told me it was his job to find the ones who were chosen and make them his sons and daughters, keep them safe until the end." She spread her fingers wide on the table. "It was everything to be told that I was special. To hear that I was more than everyone else, especially when I felt like so much less."

An ache began to bloom in my head, a dull throb that rippled on and off in waves. "You came on purpose?"

She nodded. "It was a mistake. After a few weeks, I saw what that life had done to you, to all of you, and none of you had any idea. I tried to leave. I was going to tell. I swore I was going to get all of you out of there. Dad caught me. I thought he was going to kill me, but he didn't. He just brought me back." She took a deep pull from her straw. "The next day we got our partners."

The throb was spreading through my temples, agitated, it seemed, by the beat of my heart. "But if you were only there a few weeks, we were nothing to you."

"Who was my partner?"

"Benji."

"Right. Benji was a baby. He wasn't even two years old. I knew what they were capable of. All of you were so programmed. They told you to do something and you just did it—I saw you whip each other, burn each other…the first week I was there, I watched Cole stick the tip of a knife into your leg because Dad told him to, and he cried more than you did. You think I was going to run away and let all of you beat Benji to death because of me? So I stayed. And I started to believe what they told us—I had to. If I believed that it would all end, I had something to pray for, something to look forward to. We would be free.

"But then…" She pulled a quick, whistling breath. "Then the baby died. And Mom told me I was going to have a new job. She told me that I was the oldest, so I was going to get to have the babies." Something flashed in her eyes, and when they flashed on me, I drew back. "It was supposed to be my job," she said quietly. "I wanted it to be. It was going to make me special again."

"Is that why—"

"But it wasn't true. It was a lie. They picked you," she spat like I hadn't spoken. "After they told us you weren't even good enough to live inside, that you were a mistake. You weren't special, you were weak, and you…" She took another breath and met my eyes, blinking in the warm air.

"They did it on purpose," she said in a more tempered tone. "Just like giving you Hannah's room and making the little kids take your chores. So we wouldn't fight them when they brought that man in. They wanted us to hate you, Avery. They needed us to.

"But I guess in the end, I got what I wanted. I got out. So did you." She lifted her cup toward me. "Cheers."

I couldn't focus. She was putting too many things on the table. I couldn't look at them with so much pain in my head. It made me sick to my stomach, the pain, but I asked the worst question anyway. "Tell me what happened that night."

Amaris laughed. "You're asking me?"

"I know what I know and what Cole knows. I want to know what you know."

"I don't think Cole knows much of anything. How did you get him to do it?"

I blinked—the air was thick. It was coating my eyes and making everything blur. "Do what?"

"You sent him outside—in the middle of the night in the rain. What did you say to him?"

"I didn't say anything to him…"

*I did it for you. I waited for you. You said go to the tent. You said that's our place.*

I shook my head again, pressed my fingers to my temple. The pain was coming in waves. It would almost disappear, but then it surged, breaking things up that were supposed to stay whole, things that wanted to break free, and I couldn't…

"I asked him, but he wouldn't tell me," Amaris said.

Her face swam in front of me until both halves matched and she looked burned all over. "Why did you call him and not me?" I asked. "Why—"

"I wanted to make sure he was all right."

"He wasn't all right."

"I know," she said. Her face looked normal again, the smooth side bathed in an orange glow. "What happened to you guys?"

"We—we got arrested—"

"Before that."

"We camped…hid in the woods."

"For three months? No wonder he was such a wreck. Did you sleep with him?"

"No!"

"Really?" she asked. "I'd have put money on it. I'd have put money on it way before the place burned. Three months," she said, shaking her head. "Poor Cole."

"He's my brother."

"No, he's not. How'd you get him out?"

"I don't know what you mean, he—how did you get out?"

"The front window." The levity died, dissolving into blank narration. "The walls were burning. Peter was already dead, and so was Candace. The smoke knocked Sarah out, I couldn't get to her in time. It spread too fast. The front wall collapsed on top of Hannah, but I almost got Seth and Benji...almost," she said, touching her cheek absently. "Maybe I could have. But I knew if I didn't, I'd have to watch...I'd see them burn..." Her hand fell away. "So I ran."

"What about Mom and Dad?"

Amaris blinked. A tear slid down the twisted road map on her cheek, and her tone filled with wonder. "How can you ask me that?"

"How could you lock me in that room?"

"I had to," she breathed, her voice choked. "When you walked back in there, I thought you wanted to die anyway. I was afraid you'd stop us from getting out. I didn't...I mean I know it was bad for you, but all of us?"

*When you walked back in there.*

Back.

I stared past her. The fire was at her back. Cole's voice was in my ear.

The pain in my head moved lower.

*"Avery, you—I know this is bad but—you're okay. Right?"*

*"Sure. I'll get cleaned up, I'll have a little chocolate, I'll be absolutely fine."*

*"I didn't mean—"*

*"Go to bed, Cole."*

*"No, I—I'm worried about you..."*

"I don't blame you for them," Amaris said in a rush. "Mom and

Dad. It was awful what they did. God, when he brought you back out, you looked so…"

"You knew. All of you."

"There was nothing we could do."

"You could have tried." The vise around my head squashed my voice to nothing. "Cole was the only one, who…"

*"I'm not going to help them hurt you again. No matter what."*

"What?"

My breath came fast and hard. "Who did something."

"What did he do?"

I raised my eyes to hers. "The fire. He started the fire."

"What?"

"He did," I said. "It was him. I saw the soot on his fingers. That was the only part of him that—"

"No, Avery." Her voice was frightened and far away. She may have been watching me, but my head hurt so bad, I couldn't see. "No…"

"He did it to help me," I whispered. "He was coming to get me when—"

"No," Amaris repeated quietly. "He didn't. He didn't have to. That was Mom and Dad's mistake. They thought you were weak, and they were wrong. You never needed anyone's help."

"I—"

"They taught you how to take care of yourself. And you did."

Over Amaris's shoulder, the flames danced. They waved at me, my ally from the start. Her face was suddenly firm and whole—young and terrified, framed in the kitchen doorway at the compound. It lit up before my eyes, and I blinked myself back to our little table by the fire. My own voice sounded, and it was filled with wonder. I spoke and released the pain, giving birth, finally, to the seed that had been planted so long ago. I said the words and delivered my burden because it wasn't Cole or my family that had me so scared, it was that—the thing that had been following me the whole time.

"I started the fire."

# THIRTY

———————

I LIT THE CANDLE NEXT TO MY BED AND GOT TO MY FEET—SLOWLY, because it hurt. Every step was like a stab to my belly, but I'd stopped bleeding. Even so, there was a fullness there, a wormy ball of squirming pain begging to grow. The hallway to Cole's room was dark and narrow. I could see my parents' feet in the kitchen as I passed.

My own feet were bare. I stepped lightly. My fingers were wrapped tightly around a jar of orange juice. I carried the candle in the other hand; it showed me one step at a time.

Cole sat up when I opened the door. His room was very warm. It flowed, the warmth, thick and heavy like it was being pushed out by a beating heart. I closed the door, sealing us in the chamber.

"Avery?"

"Shh…" I walked to his bed and sat down. "Mom and Dad will hear you."

"They'll see you if you don't put that out." Cole reached for the candle and vanished the flame between his fingers. "What's wrong?"

"I can't sleep."

"I knew you wouldn't be able to. Do you want me to come sit with you?"

"I'm not staying in that room. They might come back for me."

"You can sleep in here," he offered.

"I don't want to. I want to sleep in my tent."

His eyes scrunched up. "Why?"

"It's safe there."

"It's raining. You're all beat up. Don't sleep outside."

"That's why I want to," I whispered. Tears made clean tracks over my cheeks and cut off my voice. "I can't sleep in here…I'm so scared. Everything hurts. I just want to be in my tent…"

He fumbled for my cheek, smudging the wetness across my skin. "It's okay. Don't cry."

"Will you come with me? Sleep in the tent with me?"

"If you want me to."

"Yes. But we can't go at the same time," I said. "Mom and Dad might see us."

"Wait until they go to bed."

"I can't wait, Cole, I'm so afraid they'll come back for me. You go first, go out the back, and wait for me in the tent."

He frowned. "If they see me—"

"They won't. You're the best at sneaking around. You can do it."

"Okay." He fumbled for his boots. "Is your sleeping bag in the tent?"

"Yes."

"I'll try and get a fire going." He shook his head. "It's going to be freezing. You really want to sleep out there?"

"I have to."

He started to protest, but my hands found his face in the darkness. I leaned in close. "Please. The tent is our place," I whispered, my swollen lips brushing against his with every word spoken in a voice that wasn't mine. "It's safe there. Wait for me."

We sat there breathing in and out, the same air. His hand closed over mine. "Okay."

"I'll bring the chocolate. We can share it."

"No, that's yours."

"Then here," I said, offering him the jar. "Orange juice. I don't want it to go bad."

"So drink it."

"I can't," I said. "My mouth is all cut up, it'll hurt."

He hesitated for a second, and then his fingers closed over the jar. He drank deeply.

There wasn't much in there. Just enough to hide the pill I'd ground as fine as walnut dust. Mother told me to take only half if I couldn't sleep, but I gave Cole the whole thing. He made a face as he lowered the glass.

"I think it already went bad," he said with a shudder.

"It's fresh. Mom just gave it to me."

"It's awful."

"It's good for you. Finish it."

He drained the jar and stuck out his tongue. "Ugh…I'm telling Mom to get rid of those oranges."

"I'll tell her. Hurry up."

———————

"Avery?"

Amaris's voice brought me back to the table. It hurt, being ripped from Cole again, but the pain in my head was gone.

"I gave him the pill," I said, squinting—the room was too bright. "The sle—the sleeping pill. The one Mom left me." A group of kids banged noisily into the shop, pushing one another and laughing. The machinery behind me hissed and spit.

Amaris's face didn't change.

"And then I sent him to the tent. It knocked him out before he got there. That's why…" I pressed the heels of my hands into my eyes. "That's why he was so…"

"Avery…"

"Wait, no—I was having a dream—something about the baby… and then I woke up, and it was all happening, and I saw Jane…" I wanted to stop, but it was the abscess all over again, the poison was pouring out, and the pain leaving me was wonderful. "Then I found Cole, and I thought he hit his head." I looked up. "No, *Dad* hit his head," I said with sudden clarity. I could feel the fire-plow in my hands, splintered but solid. The meaty thud as it connected. "I hit him in the kitchen."

"Yes."

"I hit Dad on the head." My voice was warming, speeding, lighting… "And Mom. But Dad first. Then I sent Cole out. Once he was gone, I covered them with alcohol from the cupboard, and I started the fire with…"

"Your fire-plow."

I looked up. Amaris's face was a sick yellow on one side, swollen red on the other. "You saw me."

"Too late," she said. I flexed my hands. They looked a lot like the skin on her face, but I didn't remember burning them. "I was too late. I was in my room when I smelled the smoke—when I got to the kitchen, they were on the floor. Their clothes were lit, their skin looked like it was melting…"

"Where was I?"

"You were watching them," she said. Her face told me it was their feet she still saw splayed out on the floor. "You were watching them burn. The whole kitchen was on fire, and you were just standing in the middle of it. I started screaming, and you looked at me. Your hands were all bloody. I could *smell* their skin burning. Then you walked past me and went into your room. You lay down on the bed, and I closed the door and shoved the cabinet in front of it. By the time I woke everyone else, the walls were starting to fall."

My mind felt shaky—loose. Like a piece of glass that had cracked but didn't shatter, chunks of broken ice floating on water. Loose. But still together.

"I thought you were dead," she said quietly. "After. Once the fire was out, I stayed in the woods for a long time. I looked for Cole, but after a while, I figured he was dead too. And then I saw you both. On TV."

"Where were you?"

"I hitchhiked as far as I could. And I met—" She shook her head like she was trying to dislodge a memory. "I couldn't go home, not right away. It was too risky. I let someone pick me up, and I stayed with him for a while, but it—it wasn't good. I had nowhere else to go, and I missed..." She cleared her throat. "I missed me, I guess. I felt like a ghost. Then I saw you on TV, but it wasn't you. It was Noah and Celeste. All of a sudden, everything was so much worse. They released those pictures, and I thought, if she finds me..."

I thought of the shadows that had been stalking me—blank,

faceless shapes. All that time Amaris had her own shadows that looked just like me. I wondered which was worse. "I wouldn't hurt you."

"You tried to kill me, Avery."

It sounded so odd point-blank, so arguable. Even though I could see it now and all that smoke wasn't a dream, I felt no responsibility. Maybe it was Celeste coming to life, switching me to autopilot so she could finally escape. Officer Mason said I didn't want to know what happened. He was only half-right. It was horrible to know, and wonderful. It was the most painful bliss. My mind lightened with every word, every atrocious image, because if they were true, then the shadows, the fear, were only smoke; they'd only been there to hide things, and I didn't need them anymore. I didn't have to be afraid. The end came, and I was still standing.

"You look happy," Amaris said in response to my silence.

"I'm not, but I'm…relieved. I know that sounds bad."

"No," she said, swiping at a spot on the table with her paper napkin. "It doesn't. I'll talk to the police," she said, sounding bossy, big-sisterly again. "I'll tell them it has to stay out of the press for my—our—safety. And they can't tell my parents where I was, not ever. It was Mom and Dad," she said firmly, holding my eye. "Murder suicide. They locked us all in and started the fire. You, me, and Cole ran, got it? We were afraid of being blamed. That's it."

"They won't believe that. Not after talking to me."

"After talking to me, they will," she said. "You always had it the worst, even I know that. And now you get to stay you, exactly who you are. I'll go back to who I used to be. But Cole…he's the one I feel bad for. He doesn't even get to keep his name. So we need to do this for him." She looked at me, almost fondly, I thought. "I kind of thought you would understand that. But you were never any good at seeing what was in front of you."

"You said…you said you had something you wanted to say to me," I said, running my hands over my face. My eyes were swimming, and I wanted so desperately to smile. "Were you going to say you were sorry?"

"No," said Amaris, pushing her chair back. She got to her feet, fumbling the empty cup in her hands. "I was going to thank you."

# EPILOGUE

---

Zoe suggested I write it all down.

Not to share, just for me. What I remembered, she said. And how I remembered it. That was the hard part—the how. Despite the blackness that took over that night, there were moments that followed that I'd like to keep whole. Beautiful moments that would not have been possible if the blackness had covered my hands instead of filling my head.

I didn't lose the shadows that followed me out of the compound. They changed, but they didn't leave me, and I doubt they ever will. In the days following my talk with Amaris, my fear diminished, and I gained seven tiny ghosts—ghosts that were never fully formed or realized when they were whole, and for that I am sorry. We were all poisoned, but the worst part was we were poisoned against each other.

I don't forgive my actions. And it is not a penance to keep my brothers and sisters close to me—I want to. The ten of us, forever chosen. Every day I look for signs—signs of hope—that they know more peace now than they did under our parents' hands. I've learned the signs are there if I look.

We all died that day. Cole and I too. We died and came back to life, first as survivors, then scavengers, and then as brand-new people with no history and new names. Strangers. We are still strangers now. I don't know Noah. I don't know if he chose to remember me when he let Cole slip away. I see him, sometimes—on the news, or the occasional talk show, and most recently on the cover of a book—his own memoir where he describes horrible things with simple words. It's all true, his story. It's different from what I chose to keep, but that doesn't mean it never happened. It's a terribly sad thing for me—thinking about what he has to remember.

But I haven't tried to find him again. It's pointless to go searching for someone who doesn't exist. Sometimes I think—I can't help it—that the day might come when he wants to look for me. Just like the end of the world, I could wait forever for that to happen, but training has given me the ability to wait. You wait, and eventually something will happen. If it's good, you'll be happy; if it's bad, you wait some more. In the end it's all you can do.

Going back to Haven after I left Amaris made me itchy. Suddenly my life was money burning a hole in my pocket, and I had already wasted too much. I went back to work, and four weeks later, with the help of an outreach program Zoe recommended, I moved into my own apartment. Three hundred dollars a month to be waived for the first three months I lived there. Toby and I scoured secondhand stores and consignment shops for furniture that almost matched, and I splurged over a hundred dollars to have my cloth bracelet and the square of tent canvas I'd carried from Kansas to Washington matted and framed.

The dreams still poke at me from time to time. They can still wake me up, but I don't scream anymore. Giving birth to the truth did more than clear my head; it freed me from being frightened. The images roll in my mind like they're threaded through my projector, but I'm not tied to them anymore. I can always choose to look away.

Amaris and I talk on occasion. Mostly for insurance, I think, even though we know the truth is a real thing that could topple us both. What we did knowingly was done in ignorance, and what we did without thinking was done in desperation. She understands that and so do I. We had so few chances. I can't risk this one.

The writing helped. Zoe was right, and so was Toby—she is a good person to talk to. I hope I was able to preserve some of what saved me in case it tries to slip away again. I don't want to detail the moratorium of my childhood or catalog every scar and burn and bruise. If I'm going to hold my past in my hands, I'd rather keep the best parts of Cole, the way Amelia and Zoe helped me to stand, and

the explosion that was Toby. It is impossible to do that and elimi-
nate everything that was ugly, but it makes it a little easier for me to
remember that everything doesn't have to be ugly.

My story is mine. I have no desire to self-destruct or destroy
my life beyond what was destroyed for me. I will carry Seth and
Hannah, Jane, Peter, Sarah, Candace, and Benjamin, Amaris, Cole,
and me—Avery. I will carry them all through a life we were turned
against, and for them I will try to focus, endure, and thrive throughout everything it is, good and bad.

These words are not my confession. They are my triumph.

# READING GROUP GUIDE

1.  Despite the father stating he did not trust the outside, the family
    is still clearly reliant on the outside for their survival. In what
    ways is this evident, and what do you think it says about their
    family and the cult?

2.  How does the father ensure the children do not leave the
    compound and remain complicit? In what ways are these means
    effective? In what ways do they fail?

3.  How did the skills Avery and Cole acquired while living in the
    cult help them once they got out?

4.  Why do you think Avery and Cole continued reciting some of
    the mantras their father had told them even after they were away
    from the cult?

5.  After Avery and Cole flee from the compound and are discovered,
    everyone around them says how lucky they are to have "escaped."
    Discuss why Avery and Cole might not have felt that way.

6.  Do you think the way Amelia and Officer Rodolfo told Avery and Cole they had been kidnapped in the scene where Noah was reunited with his birth parents was the right way to handle the situation? How could they have handled it differently?

7.  Avery and Cole had such a close bond while on the compound, but that is erased after they are separated. How did Cole reuniting with his biological family affect their relationship?

8.  Why do you think Cole lied during his *Dateline* interview about the cult?

9.  In what ways does Toby help Avery acclimate to life outside the cult?

10. Avery's memory from the night of the fire is foggy. For example, the police officer told her it had been raining that night, but she was adamant it had not. Why do you think Avery's recollection of the night was so distorted?

11. Why do you think Cole pushed Avery away after she went to visit him in Washington?

12. After Avery travels to Washington to see Cole, why do you think she lied to Zoe and told her she hadn't seen him?

13. Avery was twelve when Amaris appeared at the compound. Why do you think Avery thought Amaris had always been there?

14. Throughout the book, we're led to believe Cole started the fire. Were you surprised to learn the truth?

15. What do you think comes next for Avery? Is she able to move past the trauma of her upbringing and lead a "normal" life?

# A CONVERSATION
# WITH THE AUTHOR

**What inspired you to write *After We Were Stolen*?**

This book was a case of a butterfly flapping its wings and causing a tsunami. One day, a friend of mine sent me a link to a writing contest, and the prompt was to "intrigue us in seventy-five words or less." I had already been playing with the idea of writing a novel about a doomsday cult—a very persistent character kept whispering to me that everyone in her cult had died, but she managed to survive. Unfortunately, she wasn't giving me much more information than that, so I decided to try and work with her a bit and see if she'd at least give me seventy-five words. I fiddled with my entry for a few weeks (I wish I were kidding... It took me weeks!), and that's how Avery was born. I ended up losing the contest, but afterward I couldn't stop thinking about Avery and what her life might look like after being in a cult for so long. She intrigued me; she's probably the strongest main character I've ever worked with. Fortunately, that contest opened the floodgates. The more I talked with her, the more her story came to light, and in the end, those seventy-five words turned into nearly eighty thousand.

**Cults are a fascinating topic for a lot of people. Why do you think that is?**

I think there is an "otherness" to cults that is very seductive. Here are communities of people with such strong beliefs that they cut themselves off to dedicate their lives to their mission or their leader, and it's so interesting to wonder what it might be like to be in that headspace. That's one of the reasons I included Amaris in this book not as someone who was taken but as someone who was lured. I wanted to show the charisma that cults and cult leaders project when they prey on new members and how very easy it can be to be pulled into a cycle of damaging beliefs.

**After We Were Stolen is ultimately a story of resilience and the strength of the human spirit. In what ways does this mirror your own life?**

I knew from the beginning that Avery's biggest ally was going to be her brother, Cole. I have a younger sister and an older brother, so I understand that when you grow up with someone, they tend to know you in a way no one else can. I was just finishing the first draft of the book when my own brother unexpectedly passed away. And all of a sudden, everything just stopped. I'd never lost someone that close to me before, and there are no words for what it felt like. Afterward, I simply didn't want to think about this book anymore, so I put it down for a long time. I wasn't sure I'd ever be able to pick it back up. But my brother was a huge advocate for my writing, and he was a writer himself, a brilliant one. One of the things I continue to love about his

writing is how raw it is; he was always candid and very honest. I knew
that if I could manage to draw strength from what he poured into his
own work, I'd be able to finish and create something he would be
proud of me for. I very much hope that I did.

**Do you see parts of yourself in any of your characters? What
is the process you go through from that first idea for a character to bringing them to life on the page?**

There's definitely a little bit of me in all my characters—maybe
in the way they speak or in their likes and dislikes—but they always
possess attributes I aspire to have. I'm not nearly as smart or as strong
or as courageous as the people I write about. And I don't believe that
I come up with characters on my own; it feels more like they come
to me. Sometimes they'll be fully formed and ready to tell their story,
but sometimes, like with Avery, I'll only get a taste and I have to push
for more. When that happens, I have to spend a lot of time in my
own head trying to coax the story from them and decide the best
way to write it. I spent a long time talking with Avery before her story
fully emerged. Getting to know my characters is one of my favorite
parts of the writing process, and I'm always grateful to hear from
someone new. I think the most interesting characters are the ones
I *don't* expect; there's always someone who lurks very quietly in the
shadows and then explodes onto the scene and has a huge impact on
the story. Toby is a great example of that.

**After We Were Stolen deals with a lot of heavy topics. What are some tips you have for writers to not get dragged down while writing about sad things?**

I think the most important thing to remember is that everything we go through is the means to an end. Our experiences shape us, for better or worse, and grief and pain are unavoidable parts of everyone's life. You have to balance darkness with hope and trust your characters to guide you through their journey. I never throw tragedy at them because it makes for a more interesting plot; I try to really think about how each experience will color their character, their arc, and their resolution. When you leave room for hope, it makes the difficult parts somewhat easier to bear.

**What was your path to becoming a writer? Did you always know you wanted to write novels?**

Oh, always—the trouble was, for a long time, I wasn't brave enough to do it. Writing fiction felt too personal to me. It's funny, because for years I kept a semipopular blog with a couple hundred readers, and I held absolutely nothing back. When my daughter was born, I wrote about her birth in graphic detail, but when it came to revealing the characters who lived in my head? Nope, couldn't do it. It felt like I was walking around naked. In the first draft of my first novel, I didn't even refer to my characters by name, just their initials—that's how scared I was to put my ideas down on paper. However, the upside to this was that I accrued a tremendous amount of material, so when I did finally start writing, it was like a torrential downpour. I would write until two in the morning and then get up at five to start again. It was an addiction. I wrote my first novel in nine months flat, and it was two hundred and sixty-five thousand words long. (Avoid that, if possible—the editing will be hell!)

**What is your writing process like in terms of your routine (i.e., when and where you write)? Do you develop an outline for a book first, or do you let the story take you where it needs to go?**

I write every day, and I wish I could say that I sit in a pretty office with a nice view, because the truth is really boring: I almost always write lying in bed. I think best at night, so on average, I'm in my nest by nine o'clock, and I'll write for three or four hours straight— sometimes longer if I'm on a roll. On the weekends I usually switch things up—I write all day Saturdays and Sundays and try to be social at night. I rarely outline things in detail, because I never know what kind of stunts my characters are going to pull, so I leave lots of room for detours. I heard a great line once: "When I write I feel like God. Unfortunately, all of my characters are atheists." That sums me up perfectly.

**What are some of the books you've read that have influenced your writing?**

I'm dating myself with this story, but when I was a freshman at the University of Hartford, Wally Lamb came to read to a small group of us from his then-unpublished manuscript *I Know This Much Is True*. I had devoured *She's Come Undone*, so it was extremely exciting for me, and after the reading, he chatted with us about books and writing. I loved how he threw the most incredible trauma at his characters and somehow always ended on a happy (or at least hopeful) note. As a young person, I was highly influenced by writers like John Irving, *A Prayer for Owen Meany* in particular, and I read *A Thousand Acres* by Jane Smiley and *White Oleander* by Janet Fitch until they fell apart. I've always loved stories about ordinary people who are flawed and damaged, which I think is pretty evident in my own work.

**Do books have a designated place in your home? What's on your TBR (to-be-read) pile these days?**

My house is *covered* in books, but the most impressive library is in my daughter's room. She's fifteen and the most avid reader I know. She has shelves from floor to ceiling, all organized by genre and author—walking into her room is like walking into Barnes & Noble. (If B&N also had clothes all over the floor!) As for my TBR list, probably whatever she recommends! We have our own mother/daughter book club that meets every night just before bed, and she has great taste. Right now I'm reading (and loving) *The Seven Husbands of Evelyn Hugo* by Taylor Jenkins Reid on her recommendation. She also gave me *The Southern Book Club's Guide to Slaying Vampires* by Grady Hendrix a few months ago, and now I can't wait to get my hands on *The Final Girl Support Group*. We also read a tremendous amount of YA. She's particularly interested in titles with LGBTQ+ themes, and I'm always amazed by how much wonderful young adult material is out there. When I was her age, YA books were very different, and I love how edgy and smart the readership has become.

# ACKNOWLEDGMENTS

I can't say writing this book was the most fun I've ever had, but it was definitely an interesting experience. I sat through a lot of highly disturbing documentaries, tested out Avery's fire-plow in the backyard, and forced myself to be extremely cruel to characters I loved. Fortunately, my incredible support system was with me every step of the way to help me clean what was messy, polish what was dull, and take out a few things that were *really* inappropriate. (Don't ask!) There are so many people I need to take out for a drink at the very least, and I'd like to start by thanking them here.

Thank you to my wonderful agent, Melissa Sarver-White, for being my advocate, tirelessly, on this entire journey and for doing so much to help bring this story to life. You had a big job, and you did it beautifully—I am forever grateful. The entire team at Folio is so wonderful that I continue to marvel at the fact that I'm in such good company.

A massive hug to my editor, Erin McClary. This book could not have landed in better hands. Reading a story countless times can be exhausting, even when it's your own, but your enthusiasm and passion for the book made me fall in love with it all over again. Working with you has been an absolute joy. Thank you for helping me remove the barnacles and make this novel what it was meant to be. (And I really do apologize for the sheer number of ellipses and em dashes you had to deal with!)

To the entire team at Sourcebooks: you do such beautiful work. The care and creativity that went into this book are absolutely second to none, and I am so proud to work with you. Special thanks to Jessica Thelander for ensuring an impeccable final result and Nicole Hower for the stunning cover art.

To my incredibly thoughtful friend Kelly Schnorrbusch—good Lord, Kelly, I owe you one. You get *two* drinks and all caps: THANK YOU for taking the time to send me that writing contest on Facebook. I'm even more grateful that I lost, because winning wouldn't have filled me with the righteous indignation I needed to turn my seventy-five-word entry into an entire book. I can say, without hyperbole, that your post on my wall absolutely changed my life.

To the brilliant minds in my writing group, Elaine Tweedus, Shannon Quinn-Schneck, Susan Brown-Peitz, and Steven Palivoda. Thank you for your incredible encouragement and unending patience as I kept rereading the same chapters to you *just one more time*. It is an honor not only to be surrounded by such incredibly talented people but to get to hear your stories before anyone else does. Our meetings are always the best part of my week.

To my early readers, Angela Pryor and Julia Fiskin. You are two of the loveliest and most inspiring women I've ever met, and your kind words and encouragement meant the world to me.

To Lisa Tortorello-Gilligan, thank you for talking me through so much self-doubt and making sure I never gave up hope or lost my way. You are an endless source of strength, and I thank you for always helping me see what's really important.

To my husband, Brandon Powell. Thank you for not minding when I decided to publish under my maiden name and for being there for me, always. (Even when I kick you out of your own bed so I can write, which I know happens a lot.) I would be nowhere without you. You are a handsome, handsome man.

To my daughter, Tess Powell. I could only dream about being as cool as you are when I was fifteen. You are so weird, and I love you so much for it. No one can rock a wig and a pair of shoulder pads like you do. Your impeccable taste in books has opened up so many new worlds for me, and I love our Before Bed Book Club more than I can say. (Even if we do fight about Aristotle and Dante.) I'm really sorry for sending Cole away; I know he was your favorite.

To my mother, Deborah Beyfuss, and my sister, Amanda Gaynor. You are the first I come to with every bump and bruise that life hands out, and I thank you for always being there for me. Good news is always a million times better when I get to share it with you. Amanda—I'm sorry that my very first published piece was an essay about how ugly you were when you were a newborn. What can I say? I was way too salty for a seven-year-old. You're very pretty now.

To the other writers in my family, my father, Paul Beyfuss, and my brother, Daniel Beyfuss. We lost you both too soon, and we miss you terribly. Knowing you're together gives me strength. You will inspire me for the rest of my life. Thank you.

Finally, thank you to every single person who took the time to read this book. I hope you enjoyed the journey. I am so grateful.

# ABOUT THE AUTHOR

© Robert Hopkins Photography

Brooke Beyfuss is a freelance writer who lives in Woodbridge Township, New Jersey, with her husband, daughter, and far, far too many pets. She graduated from Rutgers University with a BA in psychology and comparative literature, despite failing pre-calculus three times in a row. As a freelance writer, her audiences have run the gamut from holistic healers to adult entertainers. *After We Were Stolen* is her first novel. You can learn more by visiting brookebeyfuss.com or following her on Instagram @brookebeyfuss.